strike a
pose

strike a pose

A Falling into Fame Novel: Book Two

by

Ginna Moran

ISBN 978-1-942073-94-9 (soft cover)
ISBN 978-1-942073-95-6 (ebooks)

This is a work of fiction. All of the characters, organizations, and events portrayed in this novel are either products of the author's imagination or are used fictitiously.

Cover design by Silver Starlight Designs
Cover images copyright Depositphotos

For Inquiries Contact:
Sunny Palms Press
9663 Santa Monica Blvd Suite 1158
Beverly Hills, CA 90210, USA
www.sunnypalmspress.com
www.GinnaMoran.com

chapter 1

Nice Crashing into You

BRIGHT LIGHTS FLASH in my eyes, blinding me, and I'm pretty sure in the next ten seconds I'll be dead.

Violet screams and slams her brakes hard, sending us to a halt with a dozen horns sounding out around us. She blares her own horn, dropping F-bombs like they'll somehow blow up the exotic car of the jerk who decided to drive on our side of the road to go around the other jerk, who broke down in the middle of the street on the opposite side of Wilshire Boulevard in rush hour traffic on a Friday night.

I release a breath, leaning my head against the seat, and then laugh when she continues to lay on her horn, flipping off whoever dares look our way.

"Who does he think he is?" Violet yells, her voice louder than the sound of her horn and the rock music blasting from the stereo of her monsoon gray, metallic Audi 8 she got for her birthday last year. She told me the color name at least a dozen times so I wouldn't just call it gray. Only Violet.

I lean forward to glare at the driver of the hideous yellow Lamborghini still partially blocking our lane. Violet eases forward, getting close to the front corner bumper of his car, causing the man to wave his hands at her.

"I think that's Dean Elroy," I say, raising my phone to record a video as Violet gets within an inch of the actor's precious car before she maneuvers around him and accelerates the two car lengths he forced between her and the out-of-state minivan in front of us.

"Are you kidding me!" Violet yells, jerking into the right lane. The driver of the minivan sticks a camera fancy enough to make a paparazzo jealous right out the window to snap a picture of the interesting building up ahead on our left. It looks like someone cut a wavy design through the metallic outer walls of the building to display the bright red innards of the building. "Get it together! People have places to be."

And by places, Violet means the museum that sits to our right with hundreds of antique glowing lampposts that turn on at sunset. I've seen them in front of the Los Angeles County Museum of Art and walked through the rows more than a dozen times over the last few months, but they still haven't lost their appeal. I'm obsessed with the lights because they remind me of the beloved city I gaze at from my hillside house every night. People say the stars in the sky are beautiful, but they can't even compare to the lights that have dazzled me since I was a little girl.

I roll down my window the moment the lampposts turn on, ignoring Violet as she honks her horn again even though the long line of cars in front of us isn't going anywhere. Live music swirls through the air from a stage set up in the covered area just past the lamppost art piece.

We lurch a few feet forward and stop at the yellow light. People already block the intersection as it is, so Violet just blows out a frustrated breath, sending her aqua tresses flying around her face all while watching the light change red.

"We're going to be exceptionally late," she says, turning in the seat. "I knew we should've left earlier. Why don't you get out here and meet me in front of the escalator? I don't want Julie getting mad at you."

Knowing we needed to leave earlier didn't stop her from changing dresses three times twenty minutes past the time we had agreed to leave.

I unbuckle my seatbelt. "Next time we take the limo with my parents."

"But what if it's boring? I need an easy escape," Violet says, inching forward.

"Not like you can get anywhere anyway," I say, laughing. Traffic crawls forward again, and I swing open my door when she eases to another stop barely past the lampposts. Swiping my clutch purse from the floor, I exit the car and stand in the street for a moment. "Now be careful. Some drivers are crazy."

She laughs. "I know!"

"I'm talking about you." I shut the door and rush from the street as a few cars behind Violet blare their horns at me. She flips them off from her seat before lurching forward again in the direction of valet parking set up especially for this evening.

Tonight has been on the calendar for months. Mom's the CEO and on the board of directors for Shine So Bright, a nonprofit organization that focuses on giving communities back the arts in education, and the gala celebrates being ahead in donations for the year. Most of the time, I'd ask to bail on something like this. Standing around and smiling at strangers while trying to hide the fact that I'm stuffing my face with dozens of hors d'oeuvres doesn't qualify as a fun Friday night.

But the fact that the guest list had both Violet and me drooling is the sole reason I shimmied into a five-hundred dollar dress I borrowed from my mom at the last minute since I hadn't agreed to come until this morning, strapped on heels I can barely walk in, and let Violet put fake eyelashes on me while we ate leftover cold pizza from Valentino's Italian Restaurant on North Beverly Drive. I still plan to eat as many treats as possible. Violet already had her eye on the dessert menu Mom left with the rest of the paperwork the event organizer faxed over.

A few tourists snap photos with their cell phones in front of the hundreds of lampposts, and I weave in and out of the aisles. Despite the rumble of city traffic and the group of smokers loitering on the sidewalk, I watch the soft glow of the lights turn the atmosphere magical as the night gets darker.

Lights shine on palm trees, some planted against a tall, pearlescent building and others across the way in the sculpture garden. I come here a few times a week, and no matter how often I see the place, I can't help the thrill I get from being around so many different people.

As I stare up at the lights, I walk right into a solid body. A warm hand grabs onto my arm, trying to steady me, but my tall heels make me teeter, and instead of finding my balance, I fall right into the guy. He breaks my fall on the ground, me on top of him, my dress halfway up my thighs while a few people laugh.

If it weren't for the lampposts, I could hide the fact that my face burns with embarrassment. I'm so shocked from the fall that I don't even move right away until the guy under me shifts and props up on his elbows.

I expect him to yell at me before pushing me off, but all he does is laugh and ask, "Are you okay?"

"Uh, God. I'm sorry." I scramble off his lap, but when one of my heels slips off I flounder again, leaving me wanting to cry in the middle of this magical, urban wonderland. I give up and lean back on the base of the nearest lamppost, adjusting my dress so I'm not flashing the world.

The guy holds out my clutch to me, and I finally force myself to look up. I wish I hadn't. It just couldn't have been some gray-haired grandpa to cushion my fall. It had to be a boy with a face made for the movies and the body of an athlete. He's probably one or the other or both. His smile lights up his eyes, which shine blue in the lamplight. Without missing a beat, he bends down and picks up my shoe before handing that to me, too. I slip it back on and wish he'd just politely say goodbye and turn away.

I'm pretty set on running back toward the street the moment he stops smiling at me. I'll call for a ride if I can't find Violet quickly enough. Either way, it's quite clear I should be nowhere near the gala no matter who's on the guest list or what they're serving.

To my dismay, the boy holds out his hand to me. "Urban Light is an extraordinary piece, but you should see the rest of the place. Come on, let me help you."

I take his warm hand and manage to safely stand up. His fingers lace around my elbow for a moment, like he's certain I'll have another embarrassing losing fight with the ground, but when I straighten my back and compose myself, he lets go.

I glance around to see how many people are watching, but if anyone saw us fall, they've thankfully moved on to better things.

"Sorry again about crashing into you," I say, running my fingers down the airy fabric of my black dress. "I can never walk by without admiring Chris Burden's masterpiece when I come here."

The boy smiles, sliding his hands into the pockets of his tuxedo jacket. "So, you come here often?"

I smirk when he frowns, obviously embarrassed by his unintentional pickup line. "Yeah, I love this place. I'm here for the

Shine So Bright gala tonight, though."

"Me, too. I'm Cole Vettel." He holds out his hand, and I take it.

"Sage Meadows."

He holds my hand a little longer than necessary, but I don't try to pull away. A smile crosses my lips, and we both just stare at each other because I have no idea what to say to the boy I knocked off his feet. I don't have to worry about conversation though. A familiar voice calls out my name a few times, and I force myself to turn away from Cole toward the escalator where I was supposed to meet Violet.

She glares at me with her hands on her hips before waving at me.

I press my lips together. "It was nice crashing into you, Cole," I say, pulling myself away. "I'll see you later?"

He chuckles as he nods. "Definitely. See you around."

Forcing myself to meander away, I concentrate on not letting my shoes best me again. The live band chats near the stage in between songs, and I wave at a few of the security guards I recognize hovering under the covered grand entrance.

Violet grins at me, her perfect red lips pouting ever so slightly. "I was about to tell you that you should've stayed in the car because I totally just saw Elijah Rousseau at the valet drop off, but it looks like you didn't miss much. Who was that guy? He's hot."

I crinkle my nose, stopping myself from looking in Cole's direction even though I'm pretty sure I can feel the weight of his stare on my back. "Some guy I collided with, knocking us both to the ground."

"You didn't!" she squeals, laughing.

I shiver at the embarrassing memory. "I wish I hadn't."

"At least it was an unforgettable first impression, huh? He's still looking at you."

Linking my arm through Violet's, I drag her away so she'll stop gawking, and we head in the direction of a small crowd of people. Round tables with floor-length tablecloths are scattered around the pavilion. Floral arrangements in the middle of the tables burst with bright yellows, oranges, and reds. Servers in black uniforms dash around, carrying trays of tiny hors d'oeuvres like Caprese bites, strawberry bruschetta, and shrimp cocktails. Violet snags us each a mini quiche and a glass of sparkling water. We would've gone for the champagne had I not spotted Dad watching us. Standing next to Mom, he raises a hand and motions us over.

"I hope they don't want us to follow them around the whole night," Violet mutters, plopping the entire quiche in her mouth.

I bump my shoulder against hers. "Mom already told me because we decided to come at the last minute we have to sit at one of the reject tables." The reject tables, which will seat all the guests who didn't R.S.V.P. or did so late, aren't as bad as they sound. They're usually far enough away from my parents that I don't have to worry about pretending to be the perfect daughter in front of all her colleagues and employees. She can pretend she doesn't know me at all, though she'd never.

"Thank God." Violet straightens her shoulders and smiles when we approach my parents. "Isaac, Julie. This looks amazing. I'm so happy you were cool to let me crash your party at the last minute."

Mom pulls herself from her conversation with Dr. McCormack to beam a smile at both of us. "You two girls look lovely."

"Like two stars on the red carpet," Dad says, slinging an arm around each of our shoulders. "Did you have any trouble getting here?"

"No," Violet and I say in unison even though it took nearly an hour to drive ten miles.

"That's great." Dad pulls two plastic covered cards from his tuxedo jacket and hands them to us. "These will get you into the priority exhibits before the others. I want you two to enjoy yourselves."

"Thanks!" I fake excitement, because really, I've seen everything I've wanted to here since my dad has a few pieces on display in the Broad Contemporary Art Museum building. "You're the best. Violet will love your newest piece."

He turns to Violet. "Sage hasn't brought you here yet?"

She pouts her bottom lip for a second earning an eye roll from me. "She's been so busy lately." Yeah, says the girl who has rejected my offer to bring her here seventeen times until she saw that Domingo Rodriguez, Matthew Harris, and Elijah Rousseau were expected attendees.

"Then we better get going," I say, pulling her away from my parents. "Because I'm about to get a lot busier in my future."

She tips her head back and laughs as I drag her away. We don't make it to the BCAM, though. Violet spots a few celebrities she's been dreaming about forever and leads the way to the check-in table where a woman helps people find their seating cards.

"What are you doing?" I whisper.

Violet leans against the table while the woman helps an older couple find their place cards. "Finding a better seat."

I grab her arm. "You can't do that."

She holds up a card. "I just did. Diana McGee won't mind that she's not sitting with—"

"Can I help you?" the woman from behind the table asks. I recognize her but can't remember her name. She always helps out with the events here.

"Violet Jenson and Sage Meadows," I say.

The woman's eyes light up as she looks over the VIP tables in search of my name. "Oh, Ms. Meadows, this is so strange."

"We're in the reject seats," Violet says, getting a funny look from the woman.

The woman forces a smile, discovering our names handwritten on cards for the extra tables. Neither has the fancy stickers like the majority, but I don't care about a card or where we'll be sitting. It's better than sharing a table with my parents or the board of directors.

Violet grins, turning her back on the woman when she goes to help someone else. She wags her eyebrows at me while she peels the sticker off poor Diana's card and sticks it right over her name.

Pulling a pen from her clutch, she handwrites her name next to the number seven. "Lucky number," she says.

I sigh. "You're ditching me?"

"You're at table seven, Mr. Rodriguez," the woman at the table says from behind us.

Violet and I stare at each other with wide eyes at Domingo Rodriguez, who is not only hot but also caring, smart, friendly—at least on his social media. He actually does good with his fame. Which is why he is here.

Violet steps in Domingo's direction. "See, lucky number seven," she whispers to me.

I grab her arm. "Hey, wait."

Smiling an unapologetic smile over her shoulder, she says, "Grab another card. It's easy."

But I'm not as brave as Violet, and the lady at the table doesn't stop staring at us. I've lost my window, and Violet is totally bailing on me.

"Sorry, Sage," she whispers. "Just come sit with me. I doubt anyone will care."

I'm too annoyed that she pulled a signature Violet move to respond to her. Instead, I roll my eyes and shrug. "Maybe later. Let me see who the rejects are."

"Suit yourself."

Violet waves over her shoulder, heading in the direction that Domingo, who is surprisingly alone, heads. I secretly hope his date is just late or that she's already at the table. It would serve Violet right to have to endure something like that.

Straightening my shoulders, I saunter through the pavilion toward the tables farthest from the small stage. People talk in clusters, some sitting, some standing, some taking group selfies. Everyone is dressed in their best, and a photographer weaves through the crowds taking pictures for publicity.

When I reach table fifteen, I sigh. It's empty, and there's no way in hell I'm sitting alone. I'm going to kill Violet for this. I consider just bailing on dinner to head into one of the galleries to hide.

"You don't seem like the reject table type," a warm voice says from behind me.

Slowly spinning, I turn to face Cole. Strands of his brown hair hang on his forehead, breaking away from the product he used to style it, and his blue eyes look more gray in the soft lighting. He's so much hotter now that I'm not rushing to save myself from embarrassment. Maybe Violet was wrong about her table being lucky, because I'm pretty sure the luck has fallen into my favor.

Cole smiles at me, his slightly crooked teeth making him look extra adorable. His tuxedo jacket hangs on his arm, and the twinkle lights strung overhead cast a yellow glow on his white shirt.

I shift my clutch in my hands. "And I thought I was the

only one who called the unassigned tables that."

He chuckles, hanging his jacket on the back of the chair. "They really mean business about those R.S.V.P. dates, don't they?" Cole pulls out the chair next to his jacket, and it takes me a second to realize that he's offering it to me.

I hesitate. "Imagine the chaos that would ensue without a perfectly planned seating arrangement. We might actually get to enjoy ourselves by choosing who we want to sit by." When the words come out of my mouth, Cole's smile falters, and I inwardly cringe. I meant it as a joke, and not how it came out. "I mean, that's why I'm a last minute R.S.V.P. I know exactly where I'd have been assigned otherwise, and I'd have died of boredom."

Cole laughs. "I can sit across the table if you prefer. I wouldn't want to be knocked over again anyway."

My blush deepens, but I force myself to smile. "Oh, my God. Just sit down." With a long breath, I blow a few strands of my rose-gold hair from my face. I saw the golden pink color on Penelope Plesson in a magazine and just had to copy her.

Cole plops down next to me and bumps my shoulder with his. "I'm just teasing, Parsley."

If he wasn't so dang cute, I'd get up and walk away. People always think they're so hilarious calling me by the name of some other herb or spice. I decide to let it slide because I did crash into him. "Careful, these chairs are a little rickety. I'd hate if you fell out of one."

Cole tilts his head back and releases a loud laugh. A woman

smiles as she takes her seat across from us before two other guys join us. Diana introduces herself, and it takes everything in me to hold a straight face, knowing that she's been forced upon the reject table by Violet. At least Diana doesn't seem to mind. She lively talks to the older man next to her a moment after he sits down.

"Hey, Sagie," a feminine voice says from behind me. I tip my head to look up behind me instead of shifting in my seat. Summer, a friend I met through volunteering here, greets me in her all black uniform. Her dark hair is pulled into a high pony-tail, and she holds a champagne bottle and a few empty flutes on a tray. "Ms. Meyer just stepped out for a minute. Now's your chance to get a glass if you want one."

I nod and wave my hand out for her to hand one to me. It'll probably be the only one I get tonight, and I can't resist. Mom always told me only for special occasions at home, and only a few sips, but the LACMA is like home away from home and all half a glass will do is make me feel like I fit in with all the people at my table.

"Don't serve Violet," I say. "She's driving and in trouble for abandoning me."

"What about your boyfriend?" she asks.

"He's not my—"

"No, thank you," Cole says, cutting me off. Uh-oh. Hope-fully he doesn't think I'm some party girl, because I'm not one...all the time.

"Suit yourself." Summer offers me the glass and makes her

way around the table and pours champagne for the rest of the people at our now full table. Cole and I are clearly the youngest, but it's still better than having to sit with my parents.

I baby my flute through dinner, now nervous to drink anything. With the way Cole holds my stare as he talks about a few of the art pieces he's interested in seeing, Dad's included, I can't help the nerves bunching in my stomach. The last boy I dated didn't even know what the LACMA was.

Making small talk with Cole, I pick at my salmon before Mom takes the stage to thank everyone. The moment she exits the platform, cool hands grip my shoulders and shake me.

Violet stands next to me, a frown plastered across her face. "God, you have to switch with me. Table seven is definitely not lucky."

I hide my smile with my napkin. "Too bad."

"Ugh. Then let's go walk around," she asks.

I glance at Cole watching me in my peripheral vision. "Actually, Cole invited me to join him. It's his first time here, and I thought I'd give him the ultimate tour. You understand, right?"

Violet glares between us. "I deserve this, huh?"

I hum in agreement before I stand and turn to Cole. Holding my hand out to him, I say, "You ready?"

Surprise lights his face, but he doesn't miss a beat and takes my hand. "Definitely."

chapter 2

Another Level

"YOUR FRIEND CAN join us, you know," Cole says, guiding me toward the BCAM building. "I don't mind."

I crinkle my nose. "I'm going to let her suffer for a bit. She switched seating cards and then ditched me all because she saw Domingo Rodriguez."

"The actor?"

I nod. "I guess he didn't live up to her expectations."

"I've met him a couple of times. He seems like a nice guy."

Turning my head, I study Cole in my peripheral vision to see if I'm missing something, like maybe he's someone famous that I might not have paid attention to, but he's still unfamiliar, and there is no way I'm going to flat out ask him. "Violet has ridiculously high expectations."

He raises his eyebrows while catching me gazing at him. I

lift and drop my shoulder and gently link my fingers around his arm to pull him where I want to lead. His muscles twitch under my fingers with his movement, and I slide my hand a bit higher. Not because I need to, but because I can. I can't stop myself. He's getting hotter by the second.

A security guard hits a button to open the automatic door, and cool air encompasses us, cooling me off. We're greeted by a massive sculpture that takes up the entire first room. Another security guard circles it, making sure no one touches the rust-colored piece that people can weave in and out of. I don't recognize either of the security guards but wave anyway.

"This is amazing," Cole says, stopping for a moment to peer through a passageway between the curves.

I've seen the sculpture a couple dozen times, and my eyes never lit up like Cole's do in this moment. I consider asking what he sees, what he feels, because those are the things Dad asks me. Dad loves hearing my interpretation even if I sometimes tell him I don't get it and don't feel anything.

Cole obviously sees something I don't, and I'm afraid he'll realize I'm here for the fun and not because art is my life like a lot of people at the gala—it's my parents' world. Not mine. *You're such a phony. Who is he to impress anyway? You just met the guy.*

My nagging thought gets to me, and I blurt, "It's not my favorite."

He nods. "You're not into sculptures. That's cool."

"Or most of the pieces here." Might as well be up front

about myself. What do I have to lose? This will probably be the only time I'll ever see Cole. One, I have no idea of his connection to Shine So Bright—he doesn't fit in with the old people crowd, and I'm nearly positive he's not some famous celebrity. I know of everyone who is anyone in this city. Tabloids are my weakness, but only because I think they're outrageous. And Cole Vettel isn't in the spotlight. Two, he's not the first cute—hot—guy I've met at one of Mom's functions.

"But you like the lights out front," he says, motioning for me to walk with him into the next room, a much smaller one, featuring several metal, glass, and wood structures that are cooler than the room-hogging sculpture, but still nothing impressive to me. They remind me of something from a craftsman's garage.

"I *love* the lights out front," I say, standing in place while Cole checks out each piece with a smile on his face. "They're so magical."

"And this isn't?" He waves his hand at a towering structure that twinkles under the light fixtures high overhead.

"I'm sure it is to someone." His remark gets under my skin. I know he doesn't mean to intentionally make me feel like I don't have an imagination or lack a vision, but I sure feel it as I stare at the piece looking less and less enchanting the longer I study it.

My gaze focuses on the polished concrete floor, and I sense Cole staring me down, probably questioning why he's even agreed to follow me around the museum. His jaw will probably drop the moment he realizes that I volunteer here, and that I like it. I'm just not swept away on an emotional journey expressed through someone else's art all the time.

A gentle touch to my hand draws my attention up to Cole's intense eyes. With the way the light hits his face, they're shadowed in darkness and don't show the flecks of gold the lampposts allowed me to see. "Come on, there's more to see. Maybe we can find something you like."

Instead of following him, I cross my arms. "We won't find anything that way, but you can go on if you want."

His brows scrunch together. "Did I say something wrong?"

I shrug. "No, it's just I know this place."

"Then show me something you do like."

Tilting my head, I tuck some of my rose-gold hair behind my ear. "But you didn't get to see everything."

He smirks. "I've seen it before, too."

"But I thought it was your first time here?"

He laughs, the sound of his voice bouncing off the cold walls of the quiet room. It's not until this moment I realize we're all alone. Most people are probably still in the pavilion or looking at the newly released movie effects exhibit.

"*You* said it was my first time here," he says.

Heat burns up my collarbone and neck. He's right. That's what I told Violet. Now I wonder what other things I've randomly made up about him in my head. Hopefully nothing. He probably thinks I'm so weird.

I palm my forehead. "Sorry about that."

His smile is enough to shake my nerves away. "So, will you show me your favorite piece?"

I nod. "Sure, I'd like that."

"Your favorite exhibit has a mile long line," Cole says. "You must have really good taste."

A smile erupts on my face, because Dad's exhibit always does no matter what. You have to buy tickets in advance because only a limited number of people can look at it at a time. It's not only my favorite because it's my dad's and he worked hard on it for over a year, but I feel like I'm a piece of it. Dad's creations have meaning to me.

I stick my hand into my clutch and pull out the two passes Dad gave me. While doing so, I notice a few text messages from Violet asking where I am. Then I see a picture text she sent of her posing with a few people I don't recognize. I put my cell away because she seems to be having a good time. If she weren't, she'd let the whole universe know.

I hold the passes against my purse and take Cole's hand with my free one, pulling him past the end of the line and toward the front. I ignore the few people grumbling about the wait, about us just skipping to the front, and a few musing that they hope it's worth it. I consider stopping to tell them that it is worth it, but Old Man Felix waves at me from his place near the entrance.

"Basil! What are you doing having fun while I'm stuck here manning the door?" Felix is one of the few who I actually let get away with calling me by something that isn't my name, but only because he reminds me of my gramps.

I wave the VIP passes at him. "Want to take my turn? I'll keep the masses at bay while you show my new friend Cole around. You'd probably be a better tour guide than me."

Felix chuckles. "Ain't no one want me as a tour guide, Rosemary. We'd never make it out of this building before the night was over. Plus, you know this place as good as me. And this piece? You know it probably better than—"

The exhibit door swings open as a couple steps out, cutting Felix off. Always the hard worker, Felix jumps into action, all present thoughts abandoned, and ushers us into the room.

"They encourage me to put a time limit on you all, but take your time, Cilantro, all right?" Felix pats me on the shoulder before stepping back and closing the door without waiting for my answer.

Cole stares at me for a second without peering around the room. "You got sentenced to the reject table, but you're a VIP. Who are you, Sage Meadows?"

I smirk with a shrug. Instead of answering, I stroll farther into the room and spin around, my pink-tinted hair fanning out with the movement. "I'm no one, really, but I do know people."

He crosses the room to my side. "Because you work here?"

"I'm not a regular. You see—" I pause and wave my hand at the video-screen covered walls. "My dad is the artist responsible for We Are All One Life."

You'd think I told him I was a princess or something with the way surprise crosses his face, and he looks at me like a doe-eyed boy. "Seriously? Your dad is Isaac M.?" Dad uses just his last initial to help maintain our privacy.

"You like my dad's work?"

"Like it? It's a million times better than seeing it online," he says, spinning around the room.

Every inch of the place—the walls, floor, and ceiling—display one giant setting. At the moment, it's as if we're standing on a beach with lapping waves and bright sunshine. Nature sounds come through hidden speakers and small scent boxes spritz the air with the tropical fragrances. But that's not the cool part of the exhibit. The images were digitally created using other images and if the screens are touched, a light projects them on a special clear glass screen situated in the middle of the room. In a cutout, seamlessly fit into the expanse of screens, lies a small booth where you can take pictures that will insert themselves into the art piece, so it's constantly changing. I always knew Dad was awesome, and I'm excited that so many people see that, too.

Cole steps forward and touches the wall. An image of an unfamiliar family squeezed into the photo booth pops up on the glass partition in the center of the room. "So, you know the secret stills he programmed in here? People online talk about which ones are stationary. Some say he included never-before-seen pictures of famous people and events he acquired."

His excitement washes over me—it's almost as intoxicating

as the glass of champagne I drank with dinner. I want to wrap myself in his brimming emotions to know what it feels like seeing something so amazing the first time. "Yeah, I know of some. Want me to show you?"

"Please."

I grin as I stroll along the perimeter. The beach image shifts before us, leaving us on a dark hillside overlooking Los Angeles. It was inspired by the view from my house and is one of the ten night cityscapes Dad designed. There are over a hundred settings all together made up of millions of pictures from my parents' travels over the years and others from people who submitted them. People love to be included, and while it'd be impossible for most to see them all, they're all there on the screen. All a speck to make the bigger picture—like life—is what Dad says.

Focusing on one section of the touch screen, I run my finger over the moon hanging in the sky. A few dozen pictures shuffle over the projection glass until I find the one I'm looking for. My smiling face pops up on the screen, a picture of me from two Christmases ago when I stayed at Uncle Kenneth's cabin in Big Bear. Snow covers my gray beanie and puffy jacket, and also the tall, sugar pine trees behind me. The glittering, colorless setting makes a perfect part of the pale moon.

"That's you," Cole says. "Amazing."

I tip my head back. "Sorry it's not some crazy conspiracy image."

"It's still cool."

"Want to take one, too?"

He grabs my hand and pulls me toward the semi-hidden photo booth. If there weren't a million signs outside the exhibit, most people wouldn't know that it hides waiting to snap new pictures to include in the piece, inserted by the program Dad designed.

The setting changes again before we reach the booth—to the middle of a burned forest, an image Dad took a few years ago after a wildfire—and Cole looks around once, something indecipherable shining in his eyes. I roll a moveable panel back to show the simple photo booth with an ever changing colorful backlight. I slide onto the seat first, my shoulder grazing the cool wall, and then Cole sits down next to me, the side of his body pressing into mine. His arm reaches around my back, his fingers gently touching my side, and we smile at each other.

A camera flashes, triggered by sensors, and I giggle at the image of us captured forever among the masses of portraits now part of Dad's piece.

"Talk about candid," Cole says with a smile.

I tip my head toward his, letting my hair fall over my cheek. "If we wait a few seconds, it'll take another. It's set up to snap a picture every twenty seconds as long as the sensors sense us."

Cole shakes his head. "No, it's okay. Let's check it out."

I want to protest, but Cole slides from the photo booth before I can open my mouth and offers his hand out for me to take. Our photo glows on the projection glass in the center of the room, and I pull out my phone and take a picture of our picture, because I want to save that little moment of the boy I've known for a few hours smiling at me like nothing else matters in the world. He's gazing at me like he gazes at all the art he seems to enjoy.

The setting changes again, shimmering into a lively city sidewalk scene, and our candid photo disappears, fitting somewhere among the millions of pixels. I'm glad I captured it on my phone, because I doubt we'll ever be able to see it again.

"Text me it?" Cole asks.

Nodding, I hand him my phone so he can enter his number. He taps the screen a few times, sending the picture to himself, and then he smiles at my phone.

"Violet ditched you because you didn't respond to her," he says, handing my phone back with the text message notification on the screen.

I press my lips together for a second. It means I'll have to find Mom and make sure she doesn't leave without me or text a car service.

Without looking at Cole, I respond to Violet.

Me: I guess I deserved that. Sorry.

Violet: My fault. All good, though. Meet me?

Me: Where?

Violet: Beverly Hills. I'll send a map link.

Me: You took the car.

Violet: Crap. I'll split the cost of a car.

Me: I'll think about it. Still with Cole.

Violet: Bring him.

I hold my phone for a second before I turn my gaze up to Cole. The door to the exit opens, and I spot Felix hovering. We've been in here twice the normal amount of time and others are probably getting annoyed.

I smile apologetically at the next group of people ready to go in. My phone buzzes again in my hand.

Violet: Tell me you're coming.

I sigh.

"What's wrong? Did I get you in trouble with your friend?" Cole asks when we exit the glass door and head back out toward the pavilion. Music hums in the air, but no one dances. Most still stand around and talk while others take advantage of the museum.

"She wants me to meet her," I say.

"That's cool if you want to go. I know you work here and all." He smiles as he says the words but disappointment lines his eyes. "I'll survive by myself. I had planned the night that way anyway. You were my lucky surprise, though."

I blush and consider just telling Violet no. I almost do. But then I say, "I don't know if I want to show up alone. Violet's probably already made friends with everyone."

"But you want to go," he says.

I shrug. "Want to come with me?" My heart races when he doesn't respond right away. I'm almost disheartened by the fact that he might actually pick the museum. It's not like I'm anything special to him. We just met. But being rejected sucks. "We can always come back some other time if you think you're going to miss out on some masterpieces."

That makes him smile. "I'd like that a lot."

I let out a small breath. "Me too."

The headlights of Cole's Porsche Panamera cut across the ivy-covered wall and tall hedges of a mansion just north of Sunset Boulevard on North Crescent Drive. Tall pines line the street, almost as tall as the ever-present palm trees of the area.

A small call box rests outside a black metal gate that separates the property from the rest of the world, the kind of magnificent fortress the famous need especially with the way the double decker tour buses love to weave in and out of Beverly Hills for the tourists who want to catch a glimpse of a celebrity.

Cole hits the button on the call box, and I notice a camera blinking from the wall. When it buzzes, he says, "We were invited by Violet."

The gate hums as it opens, and Cole navigates his car down a long cement driveway that curves around a sleek, modern mansion—gleaming white walls and sparkling windows, a flat roof, tiled entrance, stone drive leading to a huge garage. I kind of hate the place. Just from the outside, it feels cold and empty.

"Nice place," Cole says, parking behind a silver Mercedes. Violet's Audi is parked three cars over in front of the blue frosted glass garage door.

"I wonder who lives here," I say, hesitating to open my door.

I don't get the chance to, though. Violet taps her nail on

the window before she pulls on the handle until Cole unlocks the door for her. She flails her hand in front of my face, waving at Cole, and nearly sends me crashing to the ground when she tries to pull me from the seat.

"Took you long enough," she says, laughing. She turns to Cole. "Thanks for bringing my partner in crime."

He walks around the hood of his car to join us. "I couldn't resist when Sage promised to go out with me if I came."

Violet narrows her eyes. "You made her bargain with you?" She's totally joking, but Cole misses it because he frowns.

I touch his arm. "He didn't make me do anything. It was an incentive, though. I had no idea what you were dragging me into."

"Fun, of course," Violet says. "Now, come on. You'll never guess who I met."

Pulling me away from Cole, Violet drags me toward the front entrance of the mansion. Big white tiles lead past a sparkling, step-like fountain with rainbow lights that cast a colorful glow around us. A set of polished wood and metal doors contrasts the white walls, and two square light fixtures light up the covered entrance.

Violet opens the door without knocking, and we're greeted with the sound of acoustic music humming through the air. The interior is as stark white and cold as the exterior. Light wooden floors covered in white rugs lead us to a living room with white couches on dark legs, a glass coffee table with nothing on it, and a few contemporary canvases painted in pastel and nude shades hang on the white walls.

Floor to ceiling windows give a view of a well-manicured backyard blooming with vibrant greens I'm sure pop with color in the sun. White tiles surround a glowing pool and twinkling lights are strung from a few palm trees. I spot the backs of a few people hovering around a fire pit, and a couple of people also lie on plush, gray upholstered lounge chairs. The backyard is my favorite place of this hideaway mansion so far.

A girl strumming a guitar looks up and smiles when we enter the backyard. Her dark hair rests on her shoulder in a loose braid, and she's wearing a short jumper, revealing her long, muscular legs. After playing a few more chords, she stops and sets her guitar on her lounge chair.

"Well, if it isn't Cole Vettel," she says, rising from her seat. "How on earth did I miss you at the gala?"

Cole slides past me and hugs the familiar girl with dark hair, vivid green eyes, and a smile bright enough to overtake her face. Violet had sent me a picture with some strangers. Ariel Marin is far from being a stranger. She's one of the hottest solo acts in the music industry. She's incredibly talented and has a group of friends I'd kill to know. I can't even believe I'm here.

Cole pulls away and shifts his attention to me. "My dad forgot to tell me about it, and I heard about it from my mom this morning when she asked if I was going. I decided to show up last minute and ended up sitting next to Sage at one of the reject tables." He looks around. "I didn't know you moved to Beverly Hills."

"Yeah, decided to sell my apartment downtown to move here with my cousin." Ariel turns her attention to me and offers her hand. "And it's so nice to meet you, Sage. Violet told me your mom is the head of Shine So Bright. Julie is an amazing woman. Without her help, I'd have never gotten to where I am today."

I lick my lips, suddenly nervous. "I'm sure that's not true. You are so talented." *Calm down. She's just another person.* Who am I kidding? She might be a person, but she's extraordinary.

She bobs her head, showing off her perfect smile. "You're too sweet. Why don't you all make yourselves at home?"

All I can do is nod, because I'm pretty sure I'm star-struck. Violet links her fingers to my arm and drags me away to introduce me to a few other people. Their names go in and out my ears, because Ariel starts playing her guitar again, and all I want to do is listen.

Violet plops down next to a cute guy with his hair tied into a bun. His T-shirt fits snuggly over his muscular chest, and with the way she looks at him, I'm pretty sure I've lost her for the rest of the night.

"Let's sit by the pool," Cole says, eyeing me as I watch Ariel.

"I can't believe you know Ariel Marin," I say, strolling next to him to the pool. I slide out of my heels and dip my feet into the warm water while he takes a seat on a chair behind me. The legs squeak across the non-slip tiles, and Cole positions the chair closer so I can look up at him.

"My dad co-wrote a few songs with her," Cole says. "You kind of get to know a lot of people when you're the son of Beau Bradford."

My eyes widen. Beau Bradford is iconic. He's had more than a dozen gold and platinum albums over his career, works with the top of the top in the music and film industries, is one of the leading benefactors for Shine So Bright, and—I'm starting to freak out. I knew Beau had a son, but Cole said his last name was Vettel. There was no way to make the connection. If he has an online presence, I have either looked right past it or haven't found it. Beau isn't exactly on the top of my music playlist, but I know his stuff from my parents.

I gape at him for a moment without saying anything. It's not like he's exactly a celebrity, but he's famous by association. I've met my fair share of famous people, and it's always been casual, a quick hello, sometimes a picture. This is different. Being the daughter of a semi-famous, low-key artist is one thing. People don't know I exist. But Cole? He's on another level, though Violet would whole-heartedly disagree.

"You okay, Sage?" Cole asks, getting up from the chair to sit next to me on the ground. He crosses his legs so they don't end up in the pool.

Shaking the thoughts from my mind, I say, "Yeah, sorry. You just surprised me. I had no idea who you were."

He stares at the rippling pool. "You say that like you're no one. Come on, your dad is Isaac M."

I laugh. "Totally the same thing. Is that why you go by

Vettel?"

The smile he gives me sends my heart racing, and he reaches out and rests his hand on my knee. "Sort of. It's my mom's last name. I'd rather be in her shadow than my father's since I want to stand on my own as a musician, and most people don't know my mom."

Makes perfect sense. "She a singer, too?"

He shakes his head. "Artist."

I try to place her name. I bet Dad knows of her. I don't mention it though. "So, that's where you get your love of art from," I say.

"In a way. I'm more into photography," he says. "What about you?"

What about me? I feel like I'm definitely no one now that I know more about Cole. "Does being on the other side of the camera count?"

"You model?"

"If you count Violet as a photographer," I say. My nerves get the best of me the longer I talk to Cole. It was easier when I didn't know who he was, and only saw him as the guy I ran into who happened to like art. I don't even know what to say now. I'm not exactly someone creative or talented.

"Is that something you'd want to do?" he asks.

I shrug. "I've never really considered it. Doesn't really matter. I doubt my parents would go for it. They want me to stay away from the spotlight."

"Uh-oh," Cole says. "They're going to hate me."

I smirk at him. "And you'll never get to finish the official Sage Meadows LACMA tour."

He leans into me, twining his fingers with mine. "I guess I'll definitely have to win them over then."

Grinning, I tilt my head back and look at the twinkling lights strung from the palms. "Guess so, because you wouldn't want to miss it."

chapter 3

Fame by Association

MY CELL PHONE chimes from my nightstand, pulling me from sleep. Violet's back rests on my side, and she softly breathes next to me. I rub the sleep from my eyes and cringe when one of my false eyelashes sticks to the side of my index finger. I regret not taking the few minutes to take off my makeup last night.

We stayed out until almost four in the morning and would've crashed at Ariel's house if it weren't for the fact that there was no way I was going to wake up to a bunch of strangers looking as awful as I feel. Plus, only Violet's allowed to see me in my hellish morning glory after a night like that. It couldn't have been more magical unless a fairy godmother had shown up to grant us all wishes.

My phone chimes again, and I reach over and unplug it.

Yawning, I glance over a picture of Cole that I programmed in last night. His blue eyes smile though he only smirks.

Cole: You awake?

Me: Barely. Had fun last night btw. :)

Cole: I'm glad you asked me to go with you.

Me: Wasn't sure I could pull you away haha.

Cole: You still owe me. ;)

Me: Oh, really?

Cole: And you left your purse in my car.

I glance at the dress and heels on the floor and don't see any sign of my purse. My phone was glued to my hand, so it doesn't surprise me.

Me: Okay, but only because I need my purse. And no art today.

Cole: Haha. I think I can manage. Pick you up in an hour?

Me: Make it two.

Cole: See you then. :)

I grin as I thrust myself back onto my pillow, elbowing Violet in the process. She swears a few times, flipping over, and then glares at me. Her turquoise hair hangs in her face, and she has a pillow indent on her cheek, but other than that, her makeup looks exactly as it did. I bet she wouldn't have minded staying at Ariel's since she had claimed a permanent spot next to Andrew A.K.A. Mr. Man Bun.

Andrew turned out to be Ariel's cousin and how Violet managed to snag an invite to hang out at the house they share when Ariel's in town and not at one of her many other homes across the globe. Apparently they were sitting at table six when Violet got fed up listening to Domingo go on and on about himself without letting anyone else get a word in. After I abandoned her, she took her chair, moved it next to Andrew's, and told him that she hoped he was a cooler seatmate, and if he wasn't, she would move him herself to table seven. He thought she was hilarious, and that's how she changed her luck.

"What time is it?" Violet asks, groaning while stretching her arms over her head.

"Just past one," I say.

"Tell me last night was real." She leans up on her elbows and feels around the bed for her phone that hides under her leg.

I can't stop from smiling. "It was totally real."

She clicks through her phone. "And amazing. Look at all these pictures."

She swipes through a few dozen candid pictures, smiling wider as she looks at them. When she comes to a picture of her and Andrew, her legs over his with their faces pressed together, she pauses.

"I'm in love," she says.

I laugh. "Like you were with Domingo for a hot second yesterday?"

"This is real," she says, sighing again. "Unless he doesn't call me. Then he can f—"

"Cole texted me," I say, cutting her off. "We're meeting in a bit."

She smacks my shoulder. "And you didn't wake me up? I should have dibs for today."

I smirk. "Okay, I'll text him." Violet's full of crap, and we both know it, but it's one of the games we play with each other. It's not the first time either of us has ditched one another for a guy, obviously after the way she first ditched me last night, but it's our way to make sure it's really okay. Our friendship comes first, and if she really didn't want me to go, I'd reschedule.

She shakes her head, pelting me with flying strands. "No-o-o-o, I'll survive. You should go out and have a totally lame time instead of an awesome one with me."

"When you put it like that," I say.

Her phone buzzes in her hand, and she squeals. "Sorry, Sage. You lost your chance."

"Andrew?"

She wags her eyebrows. "God, I'm lucky."

I laugh. "No way. He's the lucky one."

Summer Conway: Sad I missed this! You look hot!

Tandy Becks: You and Vi are the luckiest.

Carlos Garcia: I don't see what's so great.

Violet Jensen: Lost your chance, Carlos. Shouldn't have left to go to Europe. :*

Sage Meadows: Thanks to everyone but Carlos. ;)

Carlos Garcia: We'll see when I get back.

Sage Meadows: Already going on sort of date #2.

Violet Jensen: We're planning a double wedding in

the fall.

Smiling, I close my laptop before I start obsessing over all my friends' reactions about mine and Violet's magical night last night on Friendconn. I consider deleting Violet's joke, but I'd never hear the end of it. Instead, I run my fingers over my hair one more time, and then head downstairs to meet my parents in the kitchen.

"I thought you were just hanging out with a friend you met," Dad comments, taking in my dress, curled pinkish blond tresses, and strappy sandals.

"I swear, Dad. Please, be cool, okay?" I say, crossing the room to sit on a barstool at the bar near the floor to ceiling window with a view of downtown Los Angeles. "He's a really nice guy."

Dad cracks his knuckles, earning a grin from me. "We'll see about that. You said you met him last night?"

I nod. "At the reject table."

"Sage, how many times have I told you not to call them that?" Mom asks, coming into the kitchen. She strolls to where my dad stands, eating a sandwich, and kisses him on the cheek. "I really hope you didn't say that in front of our donors."

I suck in my bottom lip to stop smiling. "Definitely not." Cole was actually the one to say it to me.

"What's this boy's name again?" Mom asks, sliding her phone from her pocket to check on it. I thought Violet was bad with her phone, but Mom is ten times worse.

"Cole Vettel. You might know his mom, Sandra." I look at

Dad. "He's also Beau Bradford's son." This information gets both my parents' attention. I wish I had left it at his name. They'd have found out eventually, because I'm sure Mom would've made some phone calls to find out since someone at Shine So Bright would know of him. If I wouldn't have passed my classes with straight A's before the start of summer, I'm sure they'd both be looking at me a lot harder. It's easy to get away with things when you're mostly good.

"Oh, Sage. I'm not so sure this is a good idea," Mom says, but I can tell Dad's thinking it, too. They've always mentioned how much they wanted me to stay out of the whole celebrity scene even if Mom works with dozens of them. I was just hoping that Cole wouldn't count. I didn't even know who he was.

Anger straightens my shoulders. "Seriously? You don't even know him."

"We just don't want you to get involved in that kind of life," Dad says, speaking up.

I place my hands on my hips. "What kind of life? His dad is the famous one, not him."

"But fame by association is still fame," Mom adds. "You're young. You still have a year of school left. You have your life ahead of you." *Ugh. Not this again.*

I shake my head, turning away. Sucking in a deep breath, I refrain from yelling and instead say, "I'm not marrying him. It's just a date. Please, he's going to be here any sec—"

The doorbell rings, cutting off my words and anything else my parents are about to say. Rushing from the kitchen, I zoom through the house and up the marble stairs to the foyer. Cole stands on our front porch, the door of our enclosed patio open behind him, begging me to run through it.

He greets me with a smile. "Sorry I'm late."

I hadn't noticed he was. "It's fine. Let's—"

"Sage," Dad says from behind me. "Aren't you going to introduce me to your friend?"

Wasn't planning on it after that lame conversation. I sigh, turning. "Cole, this is my dad, Isaac. He doesn't like to be called Mr. Meadows. Dad, meet Cole."

Dad climbs the stairs to my dismay. I was hoping to get away with a quick wave before I dragged poor, unsuspecting Cole away. My parents' lecture would wait for later. They might try to talk me out of going out with Cole again, but right now, neither would do something to embarrass me now that he's actually in front of us.

"It's an honor, sir. I'm a huge fan of your work. Seeing We Are All One Life in person made my day—meeting your daughter, too. She was nice enough to show me a few of the permanent stills." Cole looks at Dad like I looked at Ariel last night. I'm not sure I've ever met one of Dad's fans. Sure, people appreciate and admire his work, but Cole would definitely fall into the fan category.

Dad's eyes soften. "Well, thank you. If you want to hang out here for a bit, I could show you what went into—"

"Dad," I say, cutting him off. I have a gut-feeling that Cole might actually agree and change our date together to one with my parents, and there's no way I'm allowing that to happen. Not tonight. Not when I just met him.

Cole glances between us for a second. "Actually, sir. I've made some reservations for this evening, but I'd love to take you up on your offer some other time."

Another soft look from my dad. Maybe I won't have to plead with him about letting me hang out with Cole. "Sure thing, Cole. But I do have to ask—"

"Dad," I warn again.

He scratches the back of his neck, ignoring me. "Please, bring Sage home by midnight."

I release a breath. "Don't worry, Dad. We'll stay out of trouble." Or at least keep our trouble under wraps.

Cole shakes Dad's hand. "It was nice meeting you."

I kiss Dad's cheek before lacing my hand with Cole's and pulling him away. His car is parked in our driveway in front of the garage, and he opens my door for me. My clutch sits on the floor, and I scoop it up and stick it inside the shoulder bag I brought. Goosebumps prickle up my bare legs from the cool leather despite the balmy temperature. I almost wish I wore pants, but I had no idea what we were doing so I went with the ivory sundress Violet picked out for me.

Cole slides behind the wheel and starts the engine. The car vibrates under me, cold AC blasting through the vents, and music hums from the stereo before he turns it down.

"I almost thought you were going to choose to hang out with my dad," I say, clicking on my seatbelt as Cole reverses from my driveway.

"The deal was no art," he says, smiling at the view of the small one-lane road that'll take us from my street of hillside houses to North Fairfax Avenue.

"Right," I say. "So, what's the plan? I had no idea what to wear. I hope this is okay." I ramble when I'm nervous, and now that we're headed toward West Hollywood, I'm starting to get nervous.

He eyes me in his peripheral vision. "You're perfect. Beautiful."

My cheeks tint crimson, and I laugh nervously. "Thanks. I don't know why I'm so nervous."

He releases a laugh. "Glad I'm not the only one. I thought maybe I had scared you off when I mentioned my dad last night."

I shift in my seat and touch his knee. "I'm not going to lie. It is a little intimidating. I'm not really anything special, and you probably know a ton of interesting people."

"And who says you're not interesting? The fact that I could barely find out anything about you makes you a mystery to me. I want to get to know more about you beside who your parents are."

I smile. He did the exact same thing I did by scouring the internet. I'm almost embarrassed how much I found out from browsing his social media. For one, we're both going to be in the same grade, but he is homeschooled unlike me. I attend Sunset Prep, a private school with a heavy focus on the arts.

"I'd like that, too," I say.

Twenty minutes later, Cole pulls into the valet at one of my favorite restaurants. Estrella Bonita is a popular Mexican food place owned by famous chef Carlita Garcia. You can't walk in without a reservation, and it sometimes takes weeks to get on the list depending on the time of year, that is, unless you know someone. Like Cole.

A few camera flashes pop, startling me when I step from the car, and Cole strolls up to my side and takes my hand. He pulls me away from the few paparazzi hanging around, waiting to snap a coveted picture of someone worthy of the tabloids.

A woman in a beautiful, brightly-colored dress opens the door for us, and we head to a small podium off to the side of the small entrance that leads to an intimate dining area. Candles glow from the centers of covered tables with dark wood chairs. Twinkle lights hang across the mural-painted ceiling that looks like a night sky. Scenic paintings hang on burnt orange walls, and stained-glass sconces cast colorful light around the room. Soft Mariachi music hums from hidden speakers, though a live band will eventually come out and play an occasional song for individual tables.

A host pulls out a chair for me, and I sit across the table from Cole. I don't even have to look at the menu to know what I'm going to order.

Cole looks up from his menu. "Have you been here before?"

I nod. "I love the food here. It's been a while since it's hard to get a reservation."

"Cole!" A feminine voice exclaims from behind me. It takes all my willpower to stop myself from turning in my chair or frowning. "How's your dad? On the road again?"

Cole stands up and shakes the hand of a familiar woman. "Yeah, his summer tour doesn't end for another month."

"You know you're always welcome at my place if you get lonely." Janine Harding stands a few inches shorter than Cole even wearing her tall stilettos. The singer looks prettier in person, and I want to pull out my phone and snap a picture for Violet, but I keep my bag safely tucked away on the floor. God, but I want to.

"Thanks, but I'm cool. My aunt is staying until he gets back. Plus, I'm not home much anyway," Cole says, shifting his eyes to mine.

Janine does the same. "I don't know you," she says. "New in town?"

I force myself to smile. "No, lived here all my life. I met Cole at a gala for Shine So Bright."

"Oh, of course. An art girl. I just assumed you were in the industry. Everyone always is even when they're not, if you know what I mean." She tips her head back and laughs. I don't really know what she means, but I politely laugh.

"My dad's the artist," I say. "I'm no one."

"Not for long if you're hanging out with this kid," Janine says, nudging Cole with her hand.

His face reddens. It's the first time I've seen him blush.

"You're going to scare her away."

Janine laughs again. "I'm teasing. Anyway, you two have fun." She kisses Cole on the cheek and waves to me before strutting off to her table in a private section of the dining room.

Cole sits back down. "Sorry about that."

I shrug. "It's fine. She seems nicer than the media portrays her."

My comment gets a laugh from him. "Some of that stuff is true."

I lean forward. "Really?"

He brings his index finger to his mouth. "Shhh. I'd never hear the end of it if she heard me say it."

"I bet you have so many cool stories," I say, wishing he'd tell me about everyone he knows. Even though I occasionally get to rub elbows with the elite of Hollywood because of Mom, I've never actually had more than polite small talk at charity events and whatnot. Most of my knowledge comes from the internet like everyone else.

"I do, but I want to hear one of yours first." Cole reaches across the table and takes my hand. "Who are you, Sage Meadows?"

I laugh. "It's a mystery, really."

chapter 4

"OH, MY GOD. Have you seen these?" Violet says, spinning my laptop on her lap to face me. Her turquoise hair sits on the top of her head in a messy bun, and she's wearing a floral-print jumper and strappy sandals.

I stare at the computer screen, my mouth agape. "I hope my parents don't see these."

It's been three days since my date with Cole, and I thought I hit up every tabloid site I could think of to see if I made any headlines. I didn't, and I still don't, but the back of me ended up on some gossip blog that covers celebrity kids, like they're somehow just as important as their parents.

"They called me a model," I say with a laugh. "Don't even mention my name."

"It's because you're tall." Violet leans forward to study the pictures of Cole and I entering and leaving Estrella Bonita. Both times, I'm turned away from the camera. "And hot."

"The world will be so disappointed if they ever discover the truth," I say.

"This could be your big break."

"Or the end of the universe, like my parents seem to think."

"Julie and Isaac are so weird. It's not even a big deal," Violet says.

I close my laptop, putting it into sleep mode. "Right? Who cares if I show up on some gossip blog? People can look me up online any time."

"And now they might want to," Violet says, grinning. "When are you going to see Cole again anyway? Andrew went out of town, so I need to crash your dates."

"I don't know. I'm supposed to text him tonight," I say. I really wanted to hang out with Cole last night, but Dad swore he needed my help as a test subject because Mom was working late. I think he knew I wanted to go out since I was volunteering at the museum the day before, but he won't flat out tell me. If I have Violet, it'll be easier. I can go out with her all I want.

"Text him now. I'm bored. Tell him he's obligated to get to know me, and that we should go dancing or something." Violet snatches my cell phone from the spot next to me. "Or I can do it."

"Dancing? You don't dance. Where would we go anyway?" I ask. Most of the places that include dancing are eighteen and over.

"He'll figure it out if he wants to impress you," she says.

I laugh. "I don't need to be impressed."

"Well, I do."

"What's it like being Beau Bradford's son?" Violet asks from the backseat. She stretches her seatbelt and leans closer.

Cole keeps his eyes trained on the road. "Cool, I guess."

"That's it? Just cool? Come on, Cole, give me something to work with." Leave it to Violet to speak her mind.

I like that she's interrogating Cole though. So far, I know that the internet was right about him being homeschooled, though he stopped touring with his Dad two years ago. Either his aunt or uncle comes to stay for a week or two at a time to check up on him, but he also has a live-in housekeeper, who used to be his nanny as a kid, that watches out for him. And as for his mom, he sees her monthly and every holiday, either going to New York to visit or she visits here, staying in a condo she owns in Beverly Hills.

Cole taps his fingers on the steering wheel. "It's pretty normal to me. I don't know. What's it like being you, Violet?"

She laughs, tipping her head forward so her hair brushes over my arm. "Normal people don't get their picture taken for the tabloids."

"I did," I say, laughing.

She rolls her eyes. "You're not normal. You're a model, remember?"

Cole glances at me. "A model? I thought—"

Violet bursts out laughing. "According to the tabloids. Apparently, it's hard for people to grasp that you would hang out with boring, normal Sage."

"Hey!" I say, swiveling in my seat.

She raises her hands. "You're not boring to me."

"Me either," Cole says, reaching over to rest his hand on my knee for a second before he pulls into a parking lot on Vine Street.

Dark clouds block out any signs of stars in the night sky, though the white haze of the moon glows brightly, giving the atmosphere an eerie feel. A few strands of lights along with the orange glow of streetlamps cast light through the crowded parking lot.

Touching our arms, Cole guides us toward the street where Hollywood stars in pink and gold decorate the cracking and potholed black sidewalk. When a lot of people think of Hollywood, they think glitz and glam, but underneath the idea of ritzy lifestyles and fame lies a world that remains hidden behind glittery sunglasses. Trash litters the gutters of the sidewalk, and a police car zips down the street with its lights flashing and sirens on.

In the alcove of a white and gray painted building with bars on the windows rests a homeless man waiting for a handout. As I look around the crowded sidewalk and busy street, I kind of wish Cole would've denied Violet her request that I sent him half-jokingly and opted to take us to a movie instead.

But the trash and broken sidewalks don't faze Violet. Her brown eyes shine copper in the streetlight, and she's all smiles when we share a look. A long line waits at the entrance of a blue-painted building a block away. An awning covers the sidewalk where tarp-covered fences block off a patio section around the door. Two bouncers wait, checking IDs.

"What club is this?" I ask as Cole strolls us past the waiting crowd.

"Tonight, it's Glitter-Bomb," he says.

"What about tomorrow?" Violet asks.

"The Pink Demon. Twenty-one and over, though."

Violet bumps into Cole, making him bump into me. "Tomorrow sounds cooler."

"You wanted to go out tonight," I say, smirking. "So Glitter-Bomb it is."

A few camera flashes light up the night from a black building a block down, and I watch as paparazzi swarm the sidewalk, taking pictures of someone as they leave what I'm guessing is another club. The line is twice as long as the one we just walked past.

Cole lowers his head, and I'm pretty sure he's doing his best to hide his face so no one notices him. If I had a jacket, I'd drape it over his head, because the last thing I need is to end up online where my parents could stumble across it and discover that Violet and I are definitely not shopping at the mall in Century City before going to the movies there. Saying we were going to the midnight showing of the latest Elijah Rousseau movie would give us until at least two or three before they start questioning our whereabouts. If only they knew that Violet's car is parked in Cole's garage.

"Hey, Cole." A big guy just two or three inches taller than me waves his hand from his post at the temporary fence making it easier for him to check IDs. "How's it goin'?"

Cole shakes the guy's hand. "Good, Will. My dad misses you on tour."

"Pam didn't want me to hit the road this year," the guy says. "Maybe next tour. You guys coming here or going to Lush? Looks a little hectic down there."

Another few camera flashes light up the night.

"What's the music like here?" Violet asks, speaking up.

The bouncer smiles. "Come in and find out."

He waves his hand near the door, and a woman in a tight dress, tall stilettos, and glittering jewelry saunters from inside. She welcomes us with a warm smile, slightly swaying to the pulsing music humming through the open door.

"Ivy will show you to a table. No alcohol, though. I don't want your dad to kill me," the bouncer, Will, says.

Cole grins, shaking the guy's hand. "Thanks, man. See you around."

"Stop by on your way out."

Will smiles at both me and Violet as we pass by him. Violet follows closely behind Ivy, and Cole links his fingers with mine. Music drifts around and the strobe lights pulse to the beat. Glitter-Bomb is surprisingly packed for a weeknight. People dance together in the open space. A stage with giant projection screens plays videos along with the DJ's beats. Fog drifts through the air, making the room look even more magical with the rainbow lights. Along the back, a bench extends the whole wall up until a door with a sign for the bathrooms.

A dozen VIP booths nestle against the wall adjacent to the bench, and all but two are full of people. I almost don't make it to the table Ivy guides us to because I'm hypnotized by the atmosphere and find myself stopping to dance. If it weren't for Cole holding my hand, I'd lose myself within the sea of dancing bodies. Dancing is the one thing Violet and I don't have in common. She despises dances, though she loves being around people. That's why her suggestion surprised me.

Ivy stops in front of the farthest booth with a short table in front of it. It's to set drinks on and not much else. Cole says something to her that I can't hear over the music and slips her some cash. Violet eases down onto the seat, which is basically like a small black couch, and crosses her legs at the knees before peering around.

She grins at me from across the small table. Cole slides in first, and I get comfortable next to him, leaning into him when he drapes his arm over my shoulders. Violet tugs out her cell phone from her wrist purse and holds it up to snap a picture of us.

Ivy brings a tray of glasses of ice with lemon wedges and a tall bottle of sparkling water that she pours for us. She leaves us with a smile, and Cole clinks his glass with mine. From the grimace Violet gives, I'm pretty sure she wishes it was something else.

A moment later, she stands. "I'll be right back!" she yells over the music.

I nod and wave her away. Cole leans into me, his warm breath tickling my ear. "What do you think?"

I tilt my head toward him so he can see my smile. "It's awesome."

"Cole!" A masculine voice shouts from the table behind us.

Cole shifts in his seat, and I peer over my shoulder. A group of people, some who I think might work in the music industry, smile our way. A hot older guy with shaved black hair, a neatly trimmed beard, and a septum piercing gets up to move to the seat right behind us. He shakes Cole's hand before offering his hand to me.

"Roman," the guy nearly shouts. Roman Blake doesn't have to introduce himself to me because I recognize him. He's a rising R&B star with a new single that has already melted the hearts of millions. I downloaded it to my phone the moment I heard it.

"Sage," I say.

He smiles at me for a moment, holding my hand long enough that I pull it away. "Have we met before?"

I'd remember meeting Roman, but I don't say so. Instead, I say, "I'm not sure. Maybe."

"Aren't you the new face of Tilly Pop?" a woman asks from next to him.

I shake my head. "Maybe I just look like someone else."

"She's a mystery, really," Cole says, squeezing my arm a little with a smile.

The seat bounces next to me as Violet slides in to sandwich me between her and Cole. She sets a glass down with what suspiciously looks like cranberry juice that I know probably isn't by itself on the table in front of us.

Twisting her torso, she brushes her curly turquoise hair over her shoulder. "You're Roman Blake," Violet says. She offers her hand with a smile. "I'm Violet. Are you friends with Cole?"

"Are you?" Roman asks with a laugh.

Violet shrugs. "Don't know yet. He's supposed to impress me."

"Is it working?" Cole asks from next to me, talking over the music.

"Maybe if you can keep Sage smiling the entire night, which entails you asking her to dance. Can't you tell she's dying to get on the dance floor?" Violet asks.

Ugh. If Violet is one thing, it's not subtle. "That's not necessary," I say to Cole. Turning to Violet, I add, "And you don't even like to dance, Violet."

"You're right, but I came to socialize, and I think Roman won't mind if I hang out with him and his friends for a few songs. Right, Roman?" Violet asks, batting her eyelashes.

Roman's mouth drops open for a second before he composes himself and barks a laugh loud enough that it draws the attention of people nearby. He motions for her to come sit by him, and she ditches me for strangers. Typical. But I definitely don't mind.

Sliding from the couch, I lean over and give her an air kiss. Cole's already on his feet and hooks his fingers on my hips to let me lead the short distance to the dance floor. Roman's whole table is laughing when I look over, and I'm pretty sure Violet's about to take the celebrity scene by storm.

Cole dances behind me, staying in sync with my movements for a bit before he spins me around to face him. The colorful lights reflect in his blue eyes, and we dance with our fingers linked together.

Sweat beads down my temples, the heat of the club wrapping around me in an intoxicating warmth. Cole's eyes never waver from mine, sending butterflies through me. It's been a while since I've had so much fun dancing. The last time was at Junior Prom, and it wasn't nearly as exciting as this. My date was a horrible dancer, so I spent most of the night everywhere but the dance floor.

Cole pulls me closer after another song, locking his fingers around my lower back, and tilts his head forward. "Want to get some air for a bit?" he asks.

I nod, pressing my lips to his ear. "I'd like that."

After checking on Violet, who tells us she's fine, Cole leads the way out the front door where a little patio is set up with a few cocktail tables. A few smokers hang out near the street, and even away from the music, the excitement still lingers within me.

"Having fun?" Cole asks, leaning his elbows on the table next to me.

"A lot," I say. "But there's one thing. You're not only hot and interesting, but you're popular and a good dancer. Is there anything you're not? Are you even real, Cole Vettel?"

He bumps his shoulder with mine. "Sadly, I'm not a good cook."

I fake a shocked expression. "Oh, no. How awful. And I thought you could do it all."

"What about you? What can't you do?"

"The list of things I can do is shorter." I tap my finger to my chin. "Well, for one, I can cook."

He chuckles. "And dance. I could dance with you all night. What about singing?"

I smirk. "You'll never hear me sing."

"Not even in the shower?" he asks.

I tilt my head back and release a loud laugh. "Are you suggesting we take a shower together on our second date?"

His face reddens, realizing the way his question sounded. He opens and closes his mouth a few times, embarrassment leaving him speechless.

I giggle. Full on giggle in a way I wish I didn't. He looks so cute all flustered, and it doesn't help that now all I can imagine is taking a shower with him though we haven't even had our first kiss. My heart races at the thought now projected into my mind.

"Well, it is kind of hot in there," he manages to say, a grin now parting his lips. "I could cool off."

I slide my hand over his shoulder, turning him to the table to face me. "I don't shower with guys before our first kiss," I say, a playfulness in my voice that makes him grow serious though his eyes continue to smile. "Now, come on. You said you could dance with me all night."

chapter 5

Violet: Last night rocked.

Me: I know!

Violet: Fame, here I come.

Me: Fame better watch out.

Violet: Plans today?

Me: :(Volunteering at LACMA.

Violet: Call me after?

Me: Duh. TTYL. ;)

Stretching my arms over my head, I snuggle deeper into my cozy bed. Violet dropped me off at home just after three. Both of my parents were asleep when I got home, so I didn't have to fake my way through an interrogation. They're cool most of the time as long as I let them know I'm okay.

Holding my phone, I gaze through a few pictures I took at

Glitter-Bomb. Violet managed to get strangers to buy her drinks all night, but I refrained from taking more than a sip because Cole doesn't drink. He says he'd never hear the end of it if his dad were to ever find out.

I stop on a picture of me and Cole sitting together at Roman's table with a few go-go dancers dancing on the dividers between tables behind us. Even though I'm sparkling with sweat and Cole's hair rests flat on his head, it's a cute picture of us. I'd post it online if I didn't think my parents would blow up, which they would. Fun like going to Glitter-Bomb definitely has to stay under the radar. The less they know, the better, and the more fun I get to have. What they don't know won't hurt them.

A knock sounds on my door, pulling me from my thoughts. Mom opens the door without waiting for a response and peeks her head in. She raises an eyebrow still seeing me in bed even though it's already past three. I'd have slept longer had Violet not texted me. Unlike her, I'm fine sleeping the day away. Violet's the busy one. She survives on mere hours of sleep more often than not, because it's impossible for her to even rest and relax a minute, unless it's doing something fun. Like last night.

"Shouldn't you be getting ready? I thought Ms. Meyer wanted you there early for the opening of the Celeste Montgomery exhibit," Mom says, leaning her shoulder against the doorframe.

I shoot upright. "Oh, crap! I forgot about that." My head's

been swimming with thoughts of when I get to see Cole next that I completely forgot that I promised Ms. Meyer I'd help out earlier than usual. "Can you give me a ride?"

Mom nods. "Of course, sweetie. Just let me know when you're ready."

I hop out of bed and look down at my rumpled dress. I was too tired to even take my clothes off, let alone my makeup last night. Shimmying out of the dress, I leave it on the floor next to the heels I took off the moment I slid back into Cole's car.

After a short shower where I tie my hair up because I won't have time to dry it, I run a makeup removing cloth over my face and then apply mascara and a brown matte gloss. I'm as good as I'm going to get. It'd be easy enough to call Ms. Meyer and tell her I'll be late so I can take my time, but I know how important today is.

What would usually take ten minutes without traffic takes us thirty since it's rush hour, and Mom drops me off in the underground parking garage where I can take an elevator up to the ground level near the building I need to go to. I rush through the busy structure and hop on a glass elevator with a few strangers. As it rises, I take in the chaotic atmosphere. The museum buzzes with life, and it's easy to lose myself among the chaos.

My cell phone chimes, and I dig through my purse to grab it. Cole's picture blinks on the screen, and I smile to myself as I read over his text message.

Cole: What're you doing?

I quickly text him back.

Me: Nothing. You?

Jogging and texting is one of my specialties. Dad has art. Mom has business. I'm a big multi-tasker.

Cole: Want to hang out?

More than anything. I frown, wishing I could just ditch tonight. Mom would flip out, though. Volunteering looks great on college applications. She pulled strings to get me to work with Ms. Meyer under her event coordination instead of some other position. I usually show up for special events, new exhibits, or to work in the interactive area for kids that allows them to paint and draw their own masterpieces.

Me: Can't tonight. Tomorrow?

Cole: Thought you were doing nothing? ;)

Me: Nothing important. But I have to go. Talk later?

Cole: Sure thing. :)

Me: ;)

Putting my phone away, I fly into the Art of the Americas building where there's currently an exhibit featuring special effects from Hollywood's best, but tonight is the opening for the coveted Celeste Montgomery hall, which features pieces from some of the biggest movies in the last two decades. People will be swarming. Celeste is supposed to be here, too. I wish I was coming as a guest and not a volunteer, though. I'm here to serve instead of have fun.

"Hey, Lavender. You're late," Old Man Felix says, standing in the entrance to the Monster Madness exhibit.

I glance at my watch. "By a minute."

He laughs. "It's all good. Mrs. Montgomery just arrived. She's talkin' to Ms. Meyer right now."

Nodding my head, I stroll past Felix and head through a room set up like the inside of a spaceship, all glowing buttons and monitors. Even an image of the earth from space glows from a window-like screen. This is the second time I've been in this exhibit, and it's just as cool as Dad's.

"Sage!" a feminine voice calls from just outside the roped off Celeste Montgomery hall. Summer stands in front of a table with a few dozen brochures featuring the highlights of the exhibit. She's wearing the same black blazer and slacks I am, except she looks like she spent at least an hour getting ready with her loose, dark curls, perfect cat-eye makeup that makes her honey brown eyes pop, and shimmery nude lipstick that makes her lips slightly pout. I envy how pretty she looks and could kick myself for sleeping in so late. "Thank God you're here. It's supposed to be a madhouse."

I slink around the table and shift a few brochures across the tablecloth. "You should see the line already."

She crinkles her nose. "This should be fun."

"At least we don't have to hover and watch the crowd."

"Right? You'd think we were the bad guys for telling someone not to use their camera flash."

"Don't remind me." I laugh, knowing how often people swear under their breaths like we can't hear them, or they pretend they don't see the ton of signs around telling them not to use their flashes. It's painstaking having to just nod and smile, even though you know they just blatantly ignored the rules. They know it, too.

Ms. Meyer flutters from the exhibit, her fashion scarf blowing behind her, and she stops for a moment to say, "Thank you for coming, Sage. The Shine So Bright gala was lovely the other night, wasn't it?"

I agree with a nod of my head.

"You two get ready," she continues without letting me respond vocally. "Summer, I want you to check the tickets. Sage, please pass out the brochures."

"Sounds good," Summer and I say in unison.

Ms. Meyer strides away, already in event mode. We probably won't see her again until we close the door for the night. Once the opening rush gets through, the night will be pretty boring. I might even get to check out the exhibit myself.

Within five minutes of Ms. Meyer leaving, a crowd starts shuffling in, skipping the rest of the huge building to hit up Celeste's pieces first. I smile and greet each person, handing them a brochure, and basically get ignored half the time. Whatever.

"And you said you weren't doing anything important," a familiar voice says from in front of me.

Drawing my eyes away from one of the brochures, I glance up at Cole. Warmth crosses my face, flowing down my neck. I could kick myself a dozen more times for sleeping the day away, because I'm pretty sure I look like hell. Strands of my rose-gold hair hang from my limp ponytail into my face, and I still feel exhausted.

I smile, perking up the best I can while he just stands there and smiles at me. I'm taking too long to answer. "Because people would have no idea what's going on without these brochures," I finally say.

I wave one of the brochures in front of me before Cole takes it from my hands to unfold and look at it. His blue eyes light up his entire face though his mouth doesn't smile. He folds it back up and tucks it in his jacket pocket.

"Does that mean you might be able to sneak away when the crowd dies down?" he asks.

"She can go now," Summer says from her spot. She turns to me. "I'll cover for you if Ms. Meyer comes by. Not like she can fire you or anything."

I glance through the thinning crowd. "I won't be long."

Summer arches her brows, smirking, and I stroll around the table and stop at Cole's side. His eyes trail from my blazer to the ugly non-slip loafers Mom insisted I wear when I started volunteering, and I die a little bit inside. Going from sexy dresses to a dorky uniform isn't how I imagined I'd ever look for Cole.

His gaze flicks back to my face, and I swear he's staring at my lips. And now I'm staring at his and how his bottom lip pouts more than his top lip. They probably feel as soft as they look.

Shaking my head, I push the thought away and say, "Lead the way."

Instead of heading into Celeste Montgomery's exhibit, he surprises me by guiding me out of the building. The pavilion chatters with life as people stroll from building to building, some choosing to hang out at the metal tables near the lampposts.

"What are we doing?" I ask when Cole stops in front of the Urban Light piece.

"If you had agreed to hang out with me, this is the first place I would have brought you since I was hoping this would be our art night," he says.

"Still can be," I say with a smile.

"And let you off so easily?" He takes my hands as he asks.

I fake pout my bottom lip. "Oh, come on."

A moment later, the lamps flick on in unison, fighting the light from the setting sun. Smiling, I tilt my head up and stare at the antique fixtures and how magical they look with the palm trees towering behind them.

"How can I resist with the way you look right now," Cole says, grinning at me.

"Like a dork?" I ask, laughing.

He shakes his head. "No, like you love the lights. It's why I brought you here. That's exactly how you looked when I met you."

"Before I plowed you down."

"I might have let you," he says, lacing his fingers with mine.

I suck in my bottom lip with the way he looks at me. He

steps closer, slowly letting go of one of my hands to tuck stray stands of hair fallen from my ponytail behind my ear. We stare into each other's eyes for a long moment before I close the distance first and brush my lips against his.

He kisses me deeper, sliding his tongue into my mouth in a sweet kiss that tastes like cool mint and watermelon. My heart thrums harder, threatening to leave me breathless. The sound of a camera click pulls my attention away from Cole, and I smile at him as I look around, thankful it was only a tourist with an impressive camera snapping a photo of the lights glowing above us.

"I've wanted to do that since last night," Cole says without letting me go.

I can only smile. "Why didn't you?"

He shrugs. "Because then you might not have been smiling like you are now."

My smile widens, and I'm sure my face beams brighter than the lights. "That was pretty cheesy, but you're cute so I'll let it slide."

He brushes his fingers along my cheek. "And I think you're beautiful, Sage."

Our first kiss, in the spot we first met, couldn't be more amazing. I'd stay out here until the night really set the lamps aglow. But a few camera flashes draw my attention away from Cole. This time, it's definitely not a tourist.

Cole pulls me with him. "Come on. Let's go back inside. He won't follow us."

All I can do is nod, because the paparazzo caught our perfect moment for the world to see, and I'm suddenly feeling sick by the invasion of privacy. But that doesn't matter to the media. As long as we're in public, we're free game. Being seen with the son of a famous singer isn't that big of a deal to me.

"If my parents see that, I'm going to be in trouble," I say.

Cole frowns. "I doubt it. We're not newsworthy."

"You sure?"

He shrugs. "Only if you give them something to talk about."

I guess he's right. At least I hope it isn't.

chapter 6

Shadow Among Stars

I DIDN'T GET to see Cole the last two days because his dad flew into town on a short break from his summer tour. Cole offered to introduce me to his dad, but I suddenly felt nervous and pretended that I had plans of my own. I couldn't help it. I haven't known Cole for long, and even though I really like him, and I'm sure he likes me, I'm afraid something like meeting his dad could mess things up. What if his dad doesn't approve of me? Then what?

The TV hums in front of me, though only my parents watch it. It's one of our things. We sit down together at least once a week to watch a movie, each taking turns to pick one out. Tonight wasn't my night, so instead of watching one of Dad's dark thrillers, I browse through the links Violet texted me of pictures of her from Glitter-Bomb's website. Her parents never follow that kind of thing, so she doesn't have to worry. I doubt either of my parents would look at something like that, but it was better to be safe than sorry, so I didn't let any of the professional photographers take my picture for promo.

My phone buzzes in my hand, and I open up a text from Cole.

Cole: Just dropped my dad off. I want to see you.
Me: How badly?
Cole: I'm dying to see you.

Smiling at my phone for a second, I turn my attention to my parents. Mom rests her head on Dad's shoulder, and he relaxes with his feet propped on the ottoman. They look so comfortable together that I doubt they'd mind if I ditched them during movie night.

I sit up straighter, considering lying and asking them about hanging out with Violet, but I don't want to test my luck again. "Hey, would you mind if I hung out with Cole? I haven't seen him since our date." It's a flat out lie, but they don't have to know that Violet and I didn't actually hang out together alone at the movies like we had told them.

Dad pauses the movie. "So, you still talking to him?"

I nod. "He's been busy since his dad was in town, but he asked to hang out tonight."

"Does his father know you're seeing each other?"

"Dad, why does that matter?" I ask, crossing my arms.

"Because he's a public figure and a parent. We care about that kind of thing," he quips.

I roll my eyes. "I don't know. He invited me to meet him, but I told him I was busy. That's all beside the point. I'm only asking if it's okay to hang out."

"He's welcome to come over tonight," Dad says.

I turn to Mom. "Mom, tell Dad he's being ridiculous. It's not like we're going to hop on some private jet and travel to Paris or something."

Mom purses her lips. "If you invite him over tonight so we can get to know him more, then you can go out the next time. It's the weekend, and the city will be busy."

"It's always busy."

"That's the deal, sweetie," Mom says. "If you plan to keep seeing him, it's only fair."

I groan. They're being unreasonable. They let me go out with him before, but something has changed. "This isn't fair. I'm going to be eighteen in six months."

Dad shrugs. "Then wait six months. The last time you two went out, it ended up online."

"It was a no-name website, and they didn't mention my name." If only they knew that some creep paparazzo, waiting for someone bigger to show up at the Celeste Montgomery exhibit, snapped a picture of us kissing at the LACMA.

"But they could've. We already told you how we feel about fame."

I glare daggers at Dad before turning to gaze at my phone. I consider making an excuse to Cole, so I can make a plan with Violet to sneak behind my parents' backs, but then another text message pops up on my screen.

Cole: Please say you can.

Me: The wardens say we have to hang out here. If you want, I can lie and say I'm going out with Violet tomorrow.

Cole: I'm coming over.

Nerves bunch in my stomach, a mixture of anxiety and excitement.

Me: You sure?

Cole: See you in twenty.

"So, you're into art," Dad says, setting his dirty plate in the sink. It's a stupid statement because we all already know that.

"Yes, sir. Photography is my thing, though I'll occasionally help my mom with her ceramics—sculptures mostly. She's the real artist. She has pieces in a dozen art galleries in New York. A few here in LA, too." Like Dad, Sandra Vettel has art pieces in several galleries in both LA and New York City. Probably more, but I didn't spend as much time internet stalking her as I did Cole.

When I told my parents that Cole agreed to come over, Dad ordered takeout from a burger place down the street for all of us. Sitting on a barstool next to Cole, I watch him while taking another bite of my burger.

"I've met your mom a few times over the years. I had no idea she was ever married to Beau," Dad says.

Cole leans on his elbow. "They never were."

I set my half-eaten burger on my plate. "Seriously, Dad? Can't you ask him what his favorite color is or something?"

Cole rests his hand on my leg under the counter. "It's fine. I don't mind answering anyone's questions."

I meet Dad's smirking gaze. "But I do."

Dad raises his hands up, moving away from the counter. From the living room, Mom's voice drifts in as she chats on her phone. She never even made it through the whole movie before something work-related drew her away.

"Sorry, kiddo. I was just trying to get to know your boyfriend." I look at Cole to see his reaction to Dad calling him my boyfriend, but he only smiles at me. "Now, if you two will excuse me, I'm going to try to pry the phone from Julie's hand before it becomes a part of her."

"Thanks for dinner, Isaac," Cole says. "And for letting me hang out."

Dad offers a warm smile. "You're always welcome here. Stay as late as you want." He turns to look at me. "Your door stays open."

I blow out a breath. "Yes, Dad."

When he leaves the kitchen, I lean forward and rest my head on Cole's shoulder, groaning. He shakes as he laughs, and then he reaches out and tucks the hair veiling my face behind my ear. It's the first time we've been alone all night. I release a breath, glad Dad got whatever parental need it is he carries out of his system.

"I'm sorry about all that. My parents are a little crazy." I release a sigh. "You're so lucky that your parents are laid back and let you do whatever. I bet they don't watch you every second of the day."

"Yeah, but a whole bunch of strangers try," he says, crinkling his nose with a smile.

I lean closer. "Still not as bad as the wardens."

Our gazes lock, and Cole closes the distance between us, brushing his lips against mine. He kisses me sweetly, sliding his hand around my shoulders to pull me even closer. I cup his face, feeling prickly stubble under my fingers. We kiss each other for a long moment even though my parents could walk in at any second.

Thankfully, they don't.

Cole slowly pulls away, and I quickly kiss him once more. I could spend the rest of the night kissing him. He smiles at me like I'm one of the art pieces that fascinate him, and my neck flushes with warmth from being under such an intense stare.

I link my fingers through his and stand. "Want to hang out in my room?" I ask. It's better than staying in the kitchen. Even if my parents do go upstairs, my bedroom is across the house from theirs. They'd have to go out of their way to constantly check on us, if they even do.

He nods, and I guide him back toward the stairs that lead up to the front door where another set of stairs will take us up to where the bedrooms are in our split level house. I don't bother flicking on the lights as I navigate the dark hallway to my room that sits at one end of the hall with two bedrooms in between mine and my parents'.

I pull Cole into my room, kissing him in the darkness for a moment before I cross the room and turn on my bedside lamp. It lights the room just enough that we can see without it being as harsh as the light from my ceiling fan. Sheer curtains hang over my windows, and in the center between the windows is a glass door that leads out to my balcony that overlooks Los Angeles.

Cole strolls toward the door, his fingers still locked around mine, and I let him guide me outside. The summer night wraps around us, a balmy breeze playing with my hair. City lights sprawl out for miles, and downtown LA glows like a beacon, drawing all the traffic in its direction. Eerie clouds hover over the moon, giving the city a ghostly feel, but it doesn't make the lights any less beautiful. They actually look brighter, the usual smog not as heavy tonight.

I rest both hands on the cool metal railing, staring out into the glittering distance. From here, on the Hollywood hillside, it's easy to forget that underneath the lights the city is grimy and not something made of fairytales.

"I could stare at the city lights all night," I say. "I used to think the night was magical when I was a kid. That each light belonged to a fairy, and they lit up every night so I could never be afraid of the dark."

Cole grins at me but doesn't say anything.

"It's silly, I know," I add.

"I think it's cute," he says, pulling me into a hug.

We move toward the small cushioned bench seat and sit together, fingers locked, my head on his shoulder and his head against mine. A comforting quiet falls between us, and Cole pulls his phone from his pocket to take a picture of the city. He then holds it in front of us and takes another one of the two of us. The darkness obscures our faces, but the city lights behind us glow brightly like we're a shadow among stars. It's kind of how I feel since meeting Cole.

"Think your parents will ban me from ever seeing you again if I post it?" he asks, staring at the screen of his phone.

"It's not like the world will know who I am," I say.

"You don't even know how badly I want to show you off, Sage," he says. "I want to tell everyone about you."

I can feel his gaze lingering on my face, and I draw my attention away from his glowing phone to look at him. "They'll be disappointed."

He frowns. "Why do you say that?"

"Because I'm no one. If anything, I'll just always be seen as your girlfriend." The words don't come out how I intend, and it sounds like being his girlfriend isn't a good thing.

"Like I'm Beau Bradford's son?" He smiles as he says it.

I purse my lips. "I didn't mean it like a bad thing. It's just, I want to be known for me, you know."

"So, you don't want to be my girlfriend?" he asks, his crooked smile sending my heart racing.

Warmth burns my cheeks. I'm so glad it's dark on my balcony. His teasing is leaving me flustered, and I kind of wish I could run inside for a second to get control over myself.

"No, I—" I pause. "I mean, yes. Oh, my God." I do the only thing I can think of. I lean over and kiss his teasing smile right off his face, brushing my lips against his before I slide from the spot next to him and onto his lap.

He moans into my mouth, trailing his lips over my jaw and down my neck. His breath tickles my skin, and goosebumps prickle over me. My hands slide into his jacket and I run my fingers up his chest over his shirt and then over his shoulders to the short hair on the back of his head.

"I should tease you more often," he says, breathing heavily against my shoulder for a moment before looking into my brown eyes.

I suck my bottom lip between my teeth, smiling. "I'm going to try not to worry what the world thinks. I don't care if they call me a mystery girl either, because I like you, Cole."

He laces his fingers around my neck, looking up at me as I sit in his lap. "So, you'll be my girlfriend?"

I nod, beaming my most brilliant smile. I can't believe this is really happening. That Cole likes me enough to want the whole world to know about our new relationship. I doubt my parents would allow me to show up at any award shows or whatever with him, but knowing that he's interested in being serious makes my heart race and butterflies swirl in my stomach.

His eyes light up, shining in the dim glow coming through the glass door to my room. And then he kisses me again. We stay together on the balcony long after my parents tell us good-night, just spending the night talking and getting to know each other better. It's not until after the sun rises and the city lights blink off and disappear, that we move. If my parents wouldn't freak out that Cole stayed here all night, I might never leave the spot next to him.

The morning sun shines streaks of honey in his dark hair, and his blue eyes match the azure, cloudless sky. He pulls me to my feet, kisses my forehead, and then I walk him out to his car parked in my driveway.

He holds me by my hips, pressing my back into the driver's side door. "Sneak out to breakfast with me?"

I almost get in the car. "I wish, but I do want to see you later." My dad told Cole he could stay as late as he wanted, but I'm pretty sure he didn't mean the entire night.

"Tonight?"

I shrug. "I'll let you know."

He kisses my forehead. "I bet I could convince your dad."

I laugh. "I'd love to see that. I think he's warming up to you."

"I'm glad. I'd hate to have one of my favorite artists despise me," he says.

I nestle against his shoulder when he hugs me once more. Standing in the driveway, I watch him reverse and leave. He waves once through his window, and I head back toward my door. My phone chimes from my hoodie pocket, and I smile when I see that Violet sent me a couple of pictures. She was supposed to go out with Andrew again last night, and I hadn't heard from her.

I enlarge the first picture and frown. It's not of Violet at all. It's one of me and Cole from the other day. From our first kiss.

Violet: Upcoming solo artist Cole Vettel, son of Beau Bradford, spotted kissing Sage Meadows at the Los Angeles County Museum of Art.

I quickly text her back.

Me: It says that?

Violet: Someone must've asked around about you.

Me: Cole didn't tell me he was following his dad's footsteps.

Violet: Maybe he's not.

Me: My parents are going to flip.

Violet: Don't freak. It was one gossip blog.

Me: Come get me?

Violet: On my way.

chapter 7

SO MUCH FOR being a mystery girl.

Mindy Suarez: Please, Cole. You can't have a girl-friend.

Dedre Smith: This pic sucks. Can't see anything.

Polly Hopkins: Where was this taken?

Josie Tyler: I'm totally jealous.

I swore I wouldn't check the picture Cole posted on his fan page on Friendconn last night, but Violet already had it open on her phone the moment we sat down for breakfast. I only manage to read over a few of the comments before Violet steals her phone back as the server comes to our table.

"Another coffee, please," I ask the server. I'm dead-tired from hanging out with Cole all night, but there was no way I was going to stay at home and risk them hearing us talk. So now, Violet and I sit across from each other at a small Holly-wood diner that only stays open until three and serves breakfast all day.

Violet scoops the last square of her waffle into her mouth. "It's not that bad," she says, chewing behind her hand. "Hell, I'm kind of jealous."

I lean on my elbows. "Cole is great, really. But I'm annoyed he didn't tell me about the music." It wasn't even obvious anywhere, like the news was waiting to be announced.

"Maybe he was working up to it? Making sure you weren't crazy," Violet says.

I shrug. "Possibly. But he had plenty of time last night when we decided to be exclusive."

Her eyes widen. "Already?"

"It just happened. Who knows? I like him a lot, and we have a lot of fun together."

Violet wags her eyebrows. "I take it he's a good kisser?"

"Amazing."

"Well, damn, Sage. Hope your parents don't scare him off like they did with Zeke. I know how much you used to like him," Violet says.

I grimace. I haven't thought about Zeke Buchannan since the last day of school, now that I haven't had to see him every day. We were together for three months, but then he suddenly broke up with me after a fundraiser Shine So Bright threw. He swore it had nothing to do with me and all him, but really, everyone knows that's a lie. A week later, Violet found out that

Dad basically cornered him and grilled him about his life—kind of how he did with Cole—but I wasn't there to save him. He didn't think I was worth the trouble of dealing with my parents. Whatever.

"I doubt it. Cole's more mature than Zeke and used to the scrutiny. Plus, Dad is one of his idols. It's weird, really."

"Yeah, I don't know how I'd feel if Andrew or Roman looked up to either of my parents like that," Violet says, smiling when my eyebrows shoot up.

"Roman?"

"It's just lunch."

I laugh. "You're definitely going to be more famous than me."

"That's the plan."

The server pours me another cup of coffee, and I nearly gulp it down. Violet's always been obsessed with the celebrity lifestyle, the beautiful people of LA, and I have to admit I have been, too. But it's crazy to think that people might start recognizing us. Violet can get away with doing what she wants because her actions won't reflect on her parents' reputations. Not like mine. Mom would die of embarrassment if I did anything to mess up her image. She's well respected. Dad, too. While they're not famous like actors or musicians, they're still well-known among the elite.

My phone buzzes on the table, drawing my attention away from Violet. A few notifications from my Friendconn page pop up on the screen from people I don't know. Violet leans over to peer at my phone as I clear the notifications, and then a few more pop up.

"Seriously?" I ask. I can barely unlock my phone fast enough.

"Uh-oh," Violet says from across from me.

"What?" I'm about to throw my phone across the diner.

"I think you're going to have to shut those off." She snatches my cell from my fingers and clicks through a few buttons. It stops vibrating, and she sets it back on the table in front of me. "And I also think you're going to have to change your name."

I groan into my hands. I'm too exhausted to deal with this right now. "I'm not even special."

She leans forward and shakes my shoulders. "Oh, shut up. You so are, and people know it. You caught the eye of Cole Vettel. They're going to want to know everything about you...like who your best friend is."

I whip my head up. "Violet, please tell me that you didn't do this."

She laughs, grinning. "Oh, come on. Don't look like I just told the world your deepest, darkest secret. We've dreamed about this."

"My parents are going to freak out."

"They'll get over it. It's fine," she says. "It'll be worth it."

I groan again. "I'm going to kill you."

"That's one way to give them something to talk about." She bounces in her chair, still grinning like what she did was for my own good. But I'm not sure she realizes how bad this could turn out.

What if my parents put me on lockdown? Sure, I'll be eighteen in six months, but I don't graduate for a year. I'm pretty sure just because I'll be legally an adult that it wouldn't stop them from controlling my life. I've heard of people getting kicked out for not obeying their parents. While I highly doubt mine would ever do that, I don't want to test my luck.

I press my lips into a thin line. "Vi, you should've told me you were going to do this."

"You're mad," she says, pointing out the obvious.

I don't meet her gaze. "I swear if this messes things up for me—"

"It won't. Just think about it," she says. "You won't have to constantly worry about whether or not people will find out about you. I've saved you a massive amount of stress and anxiety. Plus, I'm here. I'll take the attention off you."

She makes a point but still. "Violet."

"Oh, come on, Sagie. This is going to be awesome. Just wait."

"We'll see. Now, hurry up and finish. I need you to take me to Cole's."

Violet parks along the curb but doesn't shut off her engine. She taps her fingers on the wheel nervously and waits for me to call Cole.

He answers on the third ring. "Hey, what's up?" His voice

sounds low, almost breathless.

"Did I wake you up?" I ask.

"Yeah, but it's fine. I like hearing your voice."

I hide my smile. "What about seeing me? I'm outside."

Static hums through the phone as he shifts. "Is something wrong?"

"No, I just—can we talk?"

I open the passenger's side door when the gate to his house whines open. Stepping out, I wave at Violet, who drives away without waiting to see if Cole actually appears or not. Me? She can handle. I'm pretty sure she's starting to realize that her big mouth doesn't only affect us but Cole as well.

I stroll toward the open gate and right into Cole's arms the moment I see him. He's shirtless, showing off his muscular body, and I rest my head on his shoulder. He wraps me in a warm hug, setting my heart racing. The hug is so comforting that I refuse to be the first one to pull away.

He doesn't pull away either. "You're making me nervous," he whispers into my hair.

"I'm sorry I came here like this. I just knew I wouldn't be able to sleep until I talked to you," I say, breathing in the fresh scent of his bare skin.

"Let's go inside. People are always trying to get a shot of my house," he says.

I link my fingers with his and let him lead the way. The last thing I need is to be caught hugging him in front of his house at nine in the morning, especially considering that he's shirtless. That would be enough to embarrass my parents.

Instead of leading me to the front door of his grand estate, Cole guides me around the side of the massive smoothed stucco mansion to a door that leads to a set of hardwood stairs. Cole doesn't just have a room; he has an entire wing—one that is basically like a two bedroom apartment with his bedroom and an office, a small living room, a gigantic walk-in closet, spa-worthy bathroom, and a small kitchenette.

He leads the way to a plush gray couch that sits in front of an eighty-inch TV hung on the wall with a glass entertainment center below it. The moment I sit down, I lean back and feel my body relax, begging me to close my eyes just for a second. And I do. I can't help it. It's so comfortable that it basically cuddles me.

"Sage?" Cole asks, smiling when I snap my eyes open.

I blink a few times and laugh. "I haven't slept yet, sorry. Violet called me this morning, and we went out to breakfast because she found this."

Cole takes my phone from me and gazes over the image of our first kiss with the caption that includes my name. His lips tilt down, and he stares at the screen a moment longer before he hands me back the phone.

"It's because I posted that picture last night," he says. "I'm sure someone spent a while investigating who you were. They probably found someone at LACMA to give them the information."

"It was Violet," I blurt. "She has it in her mind that we're destined to be famous or something."

His brows furrow together, anger sweeping across his expression. "What kind of friend does that?"

I suck in my top lip for a moment before I say, "Don't be mad at Violet. She has the wild idea—"

"You're going to tell me that you're not mad at her?" he asks.

I shrug. "Sure, but she—"

"How can you trust her?"

I'm stunned speechless. The last thing I expected was for Cole to actually get pissed off. He doesn't know Violet like I do, and she wouldn't intentionally hurt me. She's one of the few people that I do trust. It's not like she was handing out my diary to the highest bidder or something.

I reach out my arm and rest my hand on his leg. He automatically takes my hand between his and holds it.

Instead of defending Violet, I decide to try to take the focus off her. "That's not what this is about," I finally manage to say. "When were you going to tell me that you're working on an album?"

His angry eyes soften, and he suddenly looks worried. "I don't know. I haven't really been thinking about it. I don't start recording for another month."

"Oh." I'm not sure what else to say. "I suppose this is one way to get out of your dad's shadow, huh?"

He moves closer to slide his arm around my back. "Does this change things between us?"

I lift and drop my shoulder. "I don't know honestly."

"Sage, I really like you. You have no idea."

But I do know, because I feel the same. I graze my lips against his in a soft kiss. "I guess we'll see how this plays out. My parents might lock me away, you know. They're really against all this. You sure you want to go through all that effort?"

He kisses me again. "For you? Definitely."

I smile into his lips, letting him push me back into the couch. His fingers brush through my hair as he leans over me, kissing me like we haven't seen each other in days instead of hours. My hands travel up the muscles of his stomach and to his shoulders where I trace over the smoothness of his skin.

I pull away, breathless, and look into his deep blue eyes. "We should stop," I whisper, though I don't want to. But I know if I don't, this could lead to another level where I'm not exactly ready to go with Cole. I'm not a virgin, but I'm not going to throw myself at him and risk hurting my heart when everything is so new and uncertain. What if I do turn out to be too much trouble for him? What if I decide that maybe his celebrity status is too much for me? I want things to be perfect, and not because the moment arose because my parents think I'm out with Violet instead of alone in Cole's bedroom.

He rests his head next to mine, breathing into my shoulder. "Yeah, okay. You're right." He shifts off me so that we're next to each other. "I'll follow your lead."

I smile, giving him a peck on the cheek. "Thanks. I should probably get home. Would you mind taking me? Or I could text for a car service to pick me up."

He twists his lips to the side. "You just got here. Stay for a bit?"

I yawn. "Okay," I say, resting against him.

He breathes softly, and I lie with him on the couch, just listening to the sound of our beating hearts.

chapter 8

MY PHONE RINGING startles me awake. Disoriented, I shift and fall to the soft carpet, the landing enough to jolt some sense into me. Cole jerks up on the couch, swinging his legs over the side to bend down to look into my face.

"Are you okay?" he asks, giving me a once over before helping me back on the couch.

I laugh off my nerves. "Yeah, my phone scared me awake. I forgot where I was."

Feeling around the couch, I find my phone tucked between one of the cushions. I frown when I see two missed calls from Mom and a text message from Violet telling me that Mom called her, too.

I quickly hit *call back,* and Mom picks up on the first ring. "Hey, sorry I missed your call. What's up, Mom?"

She breathes into the phone, and my heart kicks into overdrive, thinking that she knows about Violet leaking my name. "I was just wondering if you were coming home for dinner. I think your dad wants to go to Palm Bonita."

Palm Bonita is a swanky little restaurant owned by renowned chef, Edmund Rivera, on Beverly Drive in Beverly Hills. It's not too far from Cole's house, which is nestled in the Trousdale Estates near the legendary Greystone Mansion. Maybe ten minutes without traffic.

I eye Cole. "No, probably not. You and Dad go without me."

"What are your plans?" Mom asks.

My mind goes blank, and I squeeze my eyes shut for a moment. "Not sure. I'll text you and let you know."

"Okay, see you later, sweetie," she says.

We hang up, and I lean back on the couch and blow rose-gold tinted blond hair from my face. Cole rubs his hand over my bare knee, and I snuggle against him, considering going back to sleep.

"Does this mean I get you again tonight?" he asks with a smile.

"If you want," I say. "Otherwise, I'm going to have to fend for myself. But if we do go out, I need to call Violet and have her bring me something to wear."

He tilts his head to the side. "You look fine. Beautiful, really."

His fondness of me must blind him to the fact that my

makeup is from last night, my hair is a mess, and my one-piece shorts jumper is wrinkled from sleeping on the couch with him. There's no way in hell I'd risk being seen in public, especially if there is even the tiniest possibility that we'll run into some paparazzi or something.

I crinkle my nose. "I guess we're going to stay in."

He laughs. "Call Violet. I promise to be nice."

I give him a peck on the lips. "You're the best."

Violet shows up an hour later while Cole's in the shower, and I invite her inside his house. Her wide eyes look around his room, which is full of different art pieces, framed movie posters, posters of some of Cole's favorite bands, and a wide variety of instruments and photography gear.

"You sure he's not going to make a big deal?" Violet asks, plopping down on the couch before hitting a button to extend the leg rest. She hits a few more buttons to turn on the massager, and a soft hum sounds out.

"Yeah, I'm sure. I can't promise he won't if my parents find out, though," I say.

She rolls her eyes. "You act like Julie and Isaac will hide you away like some princess or send you to boarding school or something." As if Sunset Prep isn't bad enough.

My mouth falls agape. The thought freaks me out. I highly doubt my parents would do something like that. I have a year left, and I'm an honor student. It's not like they'll find me wasted in our driveway or anything.

The door to Cole's bathroom creaks open, and I can't stop the smile crossing my face when Cole steps out. His black jeans hang low on his hips while he buttons a dress shirt before rolling up the sleeves. Running his hand over his shower-dampened hair, he combs it back with his fingers.

"Hi, Cole," Violet says from the couch. "Before things get really awkward, I just wanted to say sorry for my big mouth. Forgive me?"

Cole blinks a few times, his gaze drawing to mine before turning back to Violet. I guess he didn't realize how awesome my BFF is and how it's really hard to stay mad at her when she'll admit to being wrong. If Violet and I ever fight, we usually make up pretty quickly.

Cole strolls forward to the back of the couch. "Yeah, it's all good."

I smile. "Awesome. Why don't you guys hang out while I get ready?"

After a quick shower, I get dressed and apply the makeup Violet brought for me along with a dark red-patterned lace and mesh mini dress. The sheer mesh fabric of the jewel neckline and torso give it a two-piece illusion, and it fits a little tight since I'm a size bigger than Violet. There's no way I can bend down either, but it's this or the wrinkled romper, so Violet's fashion choice wins. She's lucky I love it.

I tie my hair from my face in a sleek bun on the crown of my head and pull a few pieces free to frame my face with my too long bangs. Spinning around, I stare at myself in the mirror for a moment before waltzing from the huge bathroom to find Violet and Cole both staring at Violet's phone.

Cole notices me first, and the way his eyes travel from my neck to my hemline, I feel so sexy that I want to give Violet a hug for coming through like always. She claps her hands, squealing, and hops from the couch.

"Babe! You look hot!" Violet practically yells, her sweet voice turning high. She glances at Cole. "Doesn't she look hot? Like, I'm jealous she's with you."

Cole stands up, closing the distance between us, and brushes strands of hair behind my ears that sparkle with diamond studs. "You look incredible."

I slide my hands over his shoulders and kiss him. "Thanks," I whisper into his lips.

"Hey, I'm still here," Violet says. "And we have things to discuss."

I pull away from Cole and frown. "Things?"

"Yeah, like whether or not you want to join me on a super secret, possibly life-altering adventure tonight." Violet nearly jogs over, waving her phone in my face. "Andrew invited me to some private event someone paid Ariel to perform at. Super exclusive. Legit, the best of the best. And of course, since I'm all of those, Andrew thought it would be fun if I went with him."

I take her phone and read over the text message. "I'm pretty sure he wants only you."

Her eyes sparkle as she smiles. "Well, yeah, but guess who also got invited?"

I turn to Cole.

"Your boyfriend of course," she says before Cole can even open his mouth. This is one of the reasons Violet ended up at Andrew's table at the gala in the first place. She loves to talk, and if she can't get a word in, she's over it.

"Oh," I say.

"Oh? That's all you have to say, Sage? You cannot tell me that you don't want to show off your hot self in that dress to LA's A-listers?" She glares at Cole. "Have you been brainwashing my best friend? Turning her off of fun?"

He raises his hands in surrender.

I shake the surprise off my face and force excitement into my voice. "Don't be stupid, of course he didn't, and of course I want to go."

"You sure?" Cole asks.

Violet lightly slaps his arms. "Don't give her an excuse to say no. She'll regret it."

I smile weakly at Cole. She's right about that. I just hope I don't regret letting her drag me deeper into a world where the lights aren't always beautiful—a world where the lights can blind you.

"Is this place for real?" Violet asks Andrew. A mansion in Holmby Hills was the last place we were expecting. "We're going to someone's house?"

"Lele Rose owns the place." Andrew holds out his arm for her to take. "It's her sixtieth birthday, but don't tell her I told you. She's claiming forty tonight." Lele is a legendary designer, one that everyone speaks about on all the red carpets. She's probably dressed everyone in Hollywood. It makes me feel weird that we're attending her birthday party.

"Should we have brought her something?" Violet glances around. "What would you get Lele Rose, anyway?"

Andrew laughs, shaking his head. "The only thing Lele wants is good company."

"I think Violet can handle that," I say, smiling at my best friend.

Strolling in front of us and up the stairs of a circular entrance, Violet and Andrew head to the door of the enormous mansion made of granite, stone, and glass. It's something you'd see in movies, and has probably been rented out for such, with how gaudy and extravagant everything looks.

I stand at the bottom of the short stairs with Cole for a moment, my nerves making me want to flag down the valet that drove off to park Cole's car. Music and voices hum from the doorway, though we're the only two outside.

"So, you're friends with Lele, huh? Is there anyone you don't know?" I ask, pretending like I'm taking in everything to avoid going up and into the mansion. White pillars hold up a dome-shaped covering over the entrance, a square pattern giving the place an artistic feel.

Cole hooks his fingers on my hip, digging them in slightly to pull me close to him. My chest presses against his, our mouths a few inches apart. "You know, we don't have to go inside if you don't want to. I wasn't planning on coming in the first place, but Violet really doesn't like to hear no."

I laugh, raising my hands to hold his scruffy face before I kiss him. "You really want to risk the wrath of my best friend if we ditch her without saying anything?"

"Might be worth it," he whispers against my lips.

"Sage? Are you coming?" Violet asks from near the door. "You're not going to believe where Ariel is playing. It's ridiculous."

I frown. "What do you mean? Here, right?"

She laughs. "Hurry up."

I slowly pull away from Cole and clasp his hand. This time, it's me who leads him up to follow Violet. She moves so fast through the elaborate house that all I have a chance to notice is the circular marble staircase and gleaming floors shiny enough to see my own reflection. A wide glass door leads out to a decorative tiled backyard with a U-shaped pool. Behind it, a pillar and sculpted stone gazebo with twinkling lights strung around it glows like a beacon in the middle of the backyard.

Dozens of people, scattered around the yard, drink from champagne flutes and glass tumblers. My eyes light up every time I see someone I recognize, which is basically everyone. Unfortunately, I don't recognize them because I know them personally but because I've seen them on TV or heard them on the radio, maybe even watched a few at the sporting events Violet's dad loves to go to, forcing Violet along with her younger brother.

Cole nods and shakes a few hands, introducing me to a number of people I wish I could stop and talk to instead of following Violet wherever it is she's taking us. I grin at Elijah Rousseau, who holds the hand of his girlfriend, Nora, who writes a blog I love to follow. I don't know them personally, but they're as young as we are compared to some of the people here.

Violet suddenly stops, and I expect to see a stage set up in the back, but all I see is what looks like a cellar door. It's the strangest thing, but people convert basements all the time, though it's strange that it's way out here in the backyard and away from the house.

Violet spins to face me. "It's a nightclub."

"Really?"

"Called Sirens," she says, beaming me a smile while laughing. "But don't confuse it with Glitter-Bomb. I'm pretty sure this would be somewhere our parents would hang out when they were young."

Violet leads the way down the stairs, and Cole follows behind me with his hands on my shoulders. Music hums through the air, and people hang out in front of a lively bar with a huge assortment of alcohol neatly arranged on glass shelves. Fish tanks glow from in front of dark blue walls, and a giant neon sign showcases the name *Sirens*, casting a soft bluish-green light through the room set up with a few cocktail tables.

Andrew comes to us holding two champagne flutes and offers one to me, but I decline because the last thing I need is to go home tonight smelling like I've been partying. Mom would know in an instant that I lied to her about watching another movie and going to eat somewhere at the LA Farmer's Market near The Grove.

In the corner of the room is another set of stairs that leads deeper underground. We leave Andrew and Violet at the bar and head down where a DJ is set up near a platform. I spot Ariel immediately as she talks with who I'm almost certain is Lele, though it's hard to tell with the long, red-hot wig that swings back and forth with her movement.

Ariel smiles and waves, and Lele turns around, doing the same. We cut through the small crowd of dancing people.

Cole lets go of me to give Lele a hug before she kisses him, smudging vibrant red lipstick on his cheek. "My boy, Cole. What a surprise! I thought you'd come up with an excuse not to show so you could take me to dinner instead."

Cole shakes his head, grinning, and if it weren't for the lipstick smeared on his face or the dim lighting, I'm pretty sure he'd be blushing. "Happy birthday, Lele," Cole says. "I thought I'd mix it up this year, though I'd still love to take you out. How about to Hillside?"

She tips her head back and laughs before patting his shoulder. "Don't get a lady's hopes up, kid."

"I wouldn't think of it," he says. "You know my dad would never let me get away with disappointing you."

She laughs again before drawing her attention to me. "And who's this pretty little darling and why have you been keeping her away from me? I can already think of a million things I'd like to dress her up in."

I stand awkwardly as she talks about me to Cole. I hold my hand out. "It's an honor to meet you, Lele. I'm Sage."

"It's nice to meet you, Sage. And I wasn't kidding about dressing you up. You have an agent?"

I shake my head. "No agent."

"Well, I know a few. I'll send them your way." She turns back to Cole. "No more hiding her, okay?" She kisses him on his other cheek before excusing herself to mingle with the other partygoers here in her honor.

Ariel hands Cole her cocktail napkin from her drink, and I help him get the lipstick off his cheeks. "Don't think Lele's being polite, Sage. She doesn't lie about that kind of stuff. If you have ever considered modeling, this is your chance."

I shrug. Modeling? I do love being in front of the lens, but I know what my parents would say. "My parents would flip out. They already have a list of colleges picked out that we're going through."

"It doesn't have to be one or the other," Ariel says, sipping her water.

I doubt my parents would ever see her point. "I guess it doesn't hurt to look into it," I say instead of telling her my thoughts.

"Good," Ariel says. "That's one thing you'll learn about Hollywood. Never give up a good opportunity."

After talking with Ariel a bit more, we excuse ourselves to allow her to get ready for her performance. Cole twirls me on the dance floor, and I lose myself in the music. Camera flashes light up the room like tiny strobes as people capture every moment, carefully setting up pictures to show the world. I almost can't wait to see the pictures posted online. Looking at pictures of celebrity parties has always been a favorite pastime of mine and Violet's. It's surreal that we're at one where my parents aren't involved.

"Smile," someone says from behind us, and Cole spins me around to face a guy with a professional camera. Before I can argue, he snaps a picture, and then another when I give him my brightest smile because I don't know what else to do.

"I'll ask Lele to make sure none of us gets posted on her website or social media, okay?" Cole asks, reading my mind.

But then I frown and remember what Ariel said about taking opportunities when they arise. I'll be eighteen soon enough, and I'm not going to be taken care of by my parents forever. I haven't thought about what I wanted to be, but what if meeting Lele was fate? What if Violet was right, and we're meant for this?

I lean in close, brushing my lips against his ear. "No, it's okay. It's not that big of a deal. If my parents find out, I'll just tell them it was a last minute thing and blame it on Violet."

Cole laughs. "I like the sound of that."

The room buzzes with life as the once nearly empty space fills up with some of the most famous faces. Ariel takes the microphone from the DJ and wishes Lele a happy birthday before we all sing. Ariel sings some of her most popular songs while servers pass around cake, and the nerves finally leave me enough that I actually enjoy myself.

Cole hands our empty plates to a server when he catches me swaying to the music. "I'm glad you wanted to come," he says into my ear.

I nod. "Me, too."

I don't pay attention to the time as we dance the night away. I don't even care. After a few songs, Ariel stops singing and makes an announcement that Lele has requested she sing with a special guest.

When she announces Cole's name and the crowd cheers, I push him toward the small stage. A small spotlight sets both him and Ariel aglow as one of my favorite songs starts to play, and they sing it as a duet.

Cole's eyes never leave mine as his voice carries me away—deep and sultry, not unlike his father, but different. It's the kind of voice lead singers of rock bands have—the voice that sinks deep into your soul and leaves you humming for days. And it's like he's singing just for me.

I sway to the music, a smile cutting across my entire face, and I can't believe the turn my life has taken. I can't believe how perfect it's become.

Violet was right. This is how I want my life to be. The sparkle of lights on my skin, the pop of camera flashes, the haze of magic that only comes from moments that don't seem real.

The song ends, and Cole thanks the crowd through loud cheers. He meets me in my spot in the middle of the dance floor, and I wrap my arms around him.

"You know I'm going to want to hear you sing more, right?" I tell him, smiling. I could really listen to him all day. "You are really amazing."

He spins me around once, lifting me off my feet. "I can say the same about you."

I fake a smile into his lips but don't say anything. Because I don't feel amazing. Not compared to Cole. I feel like a fraud. Like someone who doesn't really belong here even though I want so badly to fit in.

He pulls away, slightly frowning, but doesn't ask me what's wrong. Instead, he says, "Why don't we get out of here?"

I can only nod. "I'd like that."

chapter 9

The World's a Brutal Place

I POSTED PICTURES on my Friendconn page. I couldn't resist. I just blocked my parents from seeing them.

Violet Jensen: God, we're hot! You better tell everyone I picked out that dress.

Sadie Riggs: What, no invite? Too good to call us mere mortals now?

Sage Meadows: It was last minute and invite only. Plus, didn't think you could fly in from Boston. ;)

Sadie Riggs: Ugh, my stupid dad and his stupid summer plans. Miss you!

Carlos Garcia: What about me?

Sadie Riggs: Always, Carlos.

Violet Jensen: Just hook up already!

Sage Meadows: Agree!

I smile and continue to click through pictures, forcing myself to not click on Cole's fan page though I really, really want to. And by some miracle, Mom and Dad have no idea that people, while not many, are starting to talk about me. I haven't been brave enough to read any more of the comments on Cole's fan page, but Violet claims that most of them are just full of intrigue. They want to know about the mysterious Sage Meadows who has won the attention of Cole Vettel. I much prefer to just talk with my friends from Sunset Prep, who have all abandoned me and Violet for the summer.

Even after three days, Violet still brings up Lele's party and how amazing it was. I haven't told her that Lele showed interest in me, because I'm sure she'd be the first one to jump on it and start planning my headshots. Violet loves the idea of fame, but it's not just for recognition. It's to be able to experience the glamorous life. She couldn't care less about what she was famous for to an extent—since murders and sex tapes definitely don't count—but she'd gladly be known as the girlfriend or friend of someone famous. Like Mom says, fame by association is still fame.

My phone buzzes from next to me as I click through the pictures Violet posted on her page. I pick up my cell, and Cole's smiling face comes up on the screen to greet me.

Cole: I miss you.

Me: You saw me yesterday.

Cole: Not for long.

Me: The wardens are gone. Pick me up?

Cole: Pack a swimsuit.
Me: Where we going?
Cole: Surprise.

I'm technically not supposed to leave the house since Mom had to go out of town for the night and Dad went with her, but there's no way I'm going to pass up the opportunity to hang out with Cole. We could stay here, but it'd probably be worse for my parents to find out we stayed in alone instead of going somewhere.

I slip into my favorite light gray and pale pink bikini, shimmy into a baby doll sundress and flip-flops, and then pack a bag with a change of clothes, sunscreen, and a towel just in case. The moment I zip it up, the doorbell rings. Cole grins at me from the enclosed patio, and I greet him with a kiss to show him how much I've missed him, too.

Sliding his arm around me, he pulls me with him toward his black Porsche. I take in his casual clothes—jeans and a simple black T-shirt—but he looks good no matter what he's wearing. His hair sticks up on the back since he didn't use any product, and dark sunglasses hide his endless blue eyes.

I pull my own sunglasses from my bag and pop them on before tying my hair up with the elastic band from my wrist. Cole reverses and navigates down my narrow street that'll take us into West Hollywood. He continues on Fairfax, and it only takes me a minute to realize we're not going to his house like I had assumed. He gets on the I-10 freeway, which luckily has only mild traffic this time of day.

"We're going to the beach?" I ask, sitting straighter in my seat.

He merges over a few lanes to exit Lincoln Boulevard. As we draw near Santa Monica, traffic slows to a crawl. This is one of the reasons I hate coming to this particular beach, because it's a massive tourist spot and shopping area, but the smile shining on Cole's face stops me from admitting that. It's been years since I've been to the pier. Violet and I usually prefer pools to the ocean, but if we really, really wanted to go to the beach, we usually head to Big Dume Beach in Malibu. It's not only a nice hike, but on good wave days, there is a ton of eye-candy because surfers like the area.

Cole parks in a public lot right next to the pier and shuts off the engine. He turns in his seat, still smiling. His enthusiasm snuffs out any and all displeasure I felt the moment we got off the freeway.

We both get out, and Cole strips out of his jeans and shirt right next to the car to reveal a pair of dark blue board shorts. I gape at him for a minute, just taking in the curves of his muscles. He watches me watch him, and I suck my bottom lip between my teeth while smiling.

Cole unpacks the car and carries the bags and ice chest, and we head straight for the sand instead of the busy pier. Bright sunshine cuts through the hazy clouds overhead, making the sky and water look slightly gray. Soft sand clings to my feet the moment I step into it, and I hold Cole's arm as we meander down a cement path that ends before the water.

From his bag, he pulls out a huge beach blanket and umbrella, and we set up our spot a little way down from the pier near a lifeguard tower. Sea breezes play with my hair, pulling it from my messy bun. I sit in front of Cole at the edge of the blanket, using him as a backrest while I bury my feet in the sand.

"I haven't been on this beach since I was a kid. Only to the Promenade," I say, leaning against his warm, sun-kissed shoulder. The hairs on his arms sparkle against his tanned skin, and I rub my fingers down them until I rest my hands on top of his.

He locks our fingers together, tapping my bent knees. "My dad has a condo down the road from here. Been a while since I've been there," Cole says.

It doesn't surprise me. My parents own a place in San Diego that we'll occasionally go to when Mom manages to ever take a day off.

"Show me later?" I ask, watching the foamy water crash into the shore. Some people play in the wet sand while others jump the waves. A couple of surfers float on their boards a bit farther out, and hundreds of people walk the pier where the Ferris wheel in Pacific Park spins and people scream from the small rollercoaster.

Cole trails his lips over my shoulder to my neck. "That was the plan."

The hazy clouds break free, and the hot sun beats against my skin. I pull my dress over my head, and Cole runs his fingers over my bare stomach. His quick intake of breath doesn't go unnoticed, and I shiver because even though we're on a crowded beach full of people, revealing myself in my bikini is the least amount of clothes he's ever seen me in.

I get to my feet, spinning in the sand, and he leans back on his elbows, gazing at me like I'm the best thing he's seen all day—I hope I am.

"Do you think Lele was right? That I could make it in the fashion world?" I ask, placing one hand on my hip to pose like you see starlets do on the red carpet.

Cole tilts his head, shading his eyes to block the sun. "I know you mentioned it before, but is it something you'd really want? Like if your parents would let you?"

I lift and drop a shoulder. "I hadn't really thought about it until she said something. Dad uses me as his model for a lot of his projects, and I do love fashion. But does it even matter? I can just imagine what my mom would say. She'd claim that I'm too young and the world is too brutal."

"But is it something *you'd* want?" he asks again, leaning over to dig into his bag. He pulls out a black case and unzips it to reveal his camera. He twists on the lens, presses a few buttons, and aims it at me. He doesn't give me warning when he snaps a picture.

I glare at him from my place in the sand. "Think I could make it?" I ask again instead of answering his question.

"It doesn't matter what I think." Cole puts the camera around his neck before he stands.

He offers me his hand and guides me toward the water until we're out of the shade cast from the lifeguard tower. With a touch of his hand, he tilts my head until I'm looking over the beach and away from him. He snaps another picture.

"It might not matter, but I'd still like to hear," I say, letting him pose me again. I only let him take one more before I turn away from him and face the water. I look over my shoulder.

The camera clicks again, and then he closes the distance between us, lacing his fingers around my stomach. His hot chest presses into my back with the camera to the side, and he rests his chin in the crook of my neck, breathing softly against my warm skin.

"You definitely have the looks, Sage," he muses.

"But?"

"But I don't think you'll go through with it."

"Yeah?"

He kisses my cheek. "Like you said, the world's a brutal place. I see your hesitation."

I spin around to face him, surprised by his words. It's almost like he's daring me. "Those aren't my words. I think the world can be beautiful." And it can. I mostly hesitate because I don't want to hear my parents' complaints. I don't want them to start taking away the freedom they've given me over the last year.

"Like you," he says, leaning in to kiss me.

He positions his camera and manages to snap a picture of us while I kiss his cheek. Slowly pulling away, I saunter toward the waves as he looks at me. Something about his words digs deep into my mind, consuming my thoughts. Maybe I don't have what it takes to make my mark on the glamorous life of the rich and famous. *Shut up. You can do anything you want.*

I *can* do anything I want. My parents have told me that all my life, though they'd probably never thought that I would ever want to be a model, to put myself out there for the world to judge me. But I'm not going to let those things stop me. I know I'd regret it if I didn't at least try.

Saltwater rushes my legs, pulling the sand beneath my feet back into the ocean. The one thing that might stop me from succeeding is my parents, but maybe if they see that this is what I want to do, what I was meant to do, maybe they'll change their minds. I still believe it was fate that I ended up in front of Lele Rose. Hell, it might've been fate that I knocked Cole off his feet.

I dip under the water before strolling back to Cole, who continues to photograph my every move. He sets his camera back in its case and laughs when I pelt him with ocean water. Cupping his face in my hands, I gaze intently into his eyes long enough to make him tilt his head slightly in question.

"You know, I can go through with it. I will go through with it," I say. "And I'll prove it."

He grins against my lips. "How so?"

"I want you to post some of those pictures of me," I say. "Because I can totally handle it."

"But your—"

I rub my thumb over his lips to cut him off. "Then give

them to me."

His eyebrows peak on his forehead. "You sure?"

"Yeah, completely," I say, whispering in his lips. I push away all the nerves that try to convince me to change my mind.

He leans back in and kisses me for a moment longer. "The world's going to love you, Sage. They're going to see what I see."

I just hope he's right.

Cole drapes his arm over my shoulders while we sit on the wooden stadium seating at the end of the pier to watch the sunset. Dozens of people crowd the railing, but the best spot is right where I'm sitting next to Cole. A few seagulls fly around, looking for anything to steal from unsuspecting people, and boats pepper the sea, looking picturesque on the horizon. Music hums over the ocean as a woman with long wavy hair strums a guitar while singing in a microphone, the pier her unofficial stage.

The heat of the day sinks with the setting sun, casting reds, golds, and oranges against trails of clouds. It's a perfect end to a perfect day with Cole. The moment the sun disappears into the horizon, I turn my head and catch Cole watching me.

He stands up, locks his fingers with mine, and pulls me down the stairs without giving me a chance to protest.

"Come on. You don't want to miss this," he says, navigating us through the crowded pier. When we pass the restaurant, he guides me to another short set of stairs that go down to a looking deck with a mechanical set of binoculars you can pay to use for a better look at the beach.

He holds his hand out and points at the Ferris wheel that suddenly erupts in colorful light. All the rides at Pacific Park light up along with the lampposts that line the entire pier. I grin, suddenly dazzled by the rainbow lights that haven't even had a chance to outshine the twilight sky.

"You and your lights," Cole says, chuckling. "It's a sure way to make you smile."

I laugh, shaking my head. A few tendrils of my pinkish hair fall around my face from my messy bun. "I don't know what it is. I just like how they light up the world."

"And I like how they light up your eyes."

I giggle—and I mean full on giggle—at the cheesiness of his words. My phone rings from my bag, cutting off my response, and I only look at it in case it's Mom or Dad calling. It's Violet, though.

I let it go to voicemail but get a text a moment later.

Violet: You did not just ignore my call.

Me: Yeah, I'm with Cole.

Violet: In Santa Monica?

I turn my head, gazing around the crowd for Violet but don't see her anywhere.

Me: How'd you know?

Violet: Lola's Star Guide posted some pics. You're hot btw.

A second later, a link pops through. I click on it to see a

few photos of me and Cole sitting on the sand, and another that had to be taken minutes ago while we watched the setting sun. It creeps me the hell out that somewhere in the crowd, someone is taking pictures of me. They might be doing it even this second.

I hold up my phone to Cole. "We're being stalked."

He frowns as he zooms in on the pictures. "We can leave."

"No, I'm not going to let it get to me. It's just weird. Any one of these people could be snapping pictures of us and uploading them right now."

"You should tell Violet to stop following all the tabloids or at least stop sending them to you. It'll just drive you crazy." Cole turns me so I have to meet his eyes. "I mean it, Sage."

But how can I resist? I do want to know these things. I don't admit it, though. Instead, I say, "You're right. I'll tell her."

"Good. Now, why don't we get some dinner, and I can show you the condo? We can eat there and watch a movie or something."

I nod. "That sounds perfect."

As he holds my hand and we stroll down the pier, I can't help but look at everyone we pass with suspicion. I can't help wondering what they all think of me.

I guess I'll find out eventually.

chapter 10

"WHOA, WHERE WERE these taken?" Violet asks, spinning my laptop in her lap so I can look at the screen.

I pale, feeling sick to my stomach. In a picture article with the heading, "What's New in Love and Heartache," are a few shots of me and Cole heading into his dad's condo which is part of a small complex directly on the beach. That's not the bad thing, though. The fact that there is one of us leaving, and I'm clearly wearing the change of clothes I had brought but also a hoodie of Cole's, makes it look worse.

"If you guys are sleeping together and you didn't tell me, I'm—"

"Violet!" I snap, slamming my laptop closed before tossing it onto the bed. "We just went there to eat dinner and watch TV. I can't believe you just assumed..." I release an angry breath. "We're not having sex yet."

She stares at me with wide eyes. "Jeez, sorry. It's not like it's a big deal. This isn't the fifties."

I roll my eyes. "I just—" Ugh. I don't know how I feel about the fact that people will just assume. I don't know why I care so much either. I know the truth. And it's not like it's anyone's business. *Try telling that to Mom.*

I can see my budding, well, soon-to-be budding, modeling career explode in flames before it even has a chance to take off. I haven't even talked to Lele yet. Cole had arranged a dinner with her that was supposed to happen in a few days when Mom and Dad flew to New York for some art event featuring Dad. If they find out what the world knows, they'll make me go with them. And I don't want to lose my summer freedom.

"Relax, Sage," Violet says, touching my knee. "You're freaking out for nothing. Everyone knows how the media twists the truth to make better stories. There isn't anything interesting about you and Cole having dinner. The story is in the speculation of what happens when the door closes."

I sigh. "You're right, but it still drives me crazy."

"Come on," she says. "Isn't it fun, though? You looked hot. At least it isn't you guys actually eating dinner where you're mid bite or something."

I laugh. "Or the sneezing pictures."

Violet snorts. "Oh, God. Could you imagine? That's when you know you're famous. When it's interesting to get a picture of you sneezing or coughing or something."

Violet shifts from my bed and gets to her feet before pulling me to mine. I consider texting Cole immediately to tell him what we found online, but then think better of it. He warned me about how it'll all drive me crazy, and he'll tell me that he told me so. But he doesn't get it. He's used to the attention. He doesn't face the same standards I do either. It sucks.

We stroll downstairs and find my parents both eating lunch at the bar in the kitchen. Dad waves toward the array of sandwich stuff on the counter in front of them.

Violet glances from the food to the phone in her hand. "No, thanks, Isaac. Sage and I are going to grab lunch at Ariel's house. She's invited us swimming."

I furrow my eyebrows. "What? When?"

She flashes her phone at me before waving it at Dad, who obviously wants to see the proof without having to ask.

"Right now. Just a small gathering."

"Do you mean Ariel Marin?" Mom asks, setting down her half-eaten sandwich on her plate. "I didn't know you knew each other."

"We met at the gala when I—" Violet stops mid-sentence. "We met at the gala." If Mom knew Violet switched tables, she'd probably ban her from the next event as punishment. It wouldn't be the first time either of us has been banned. It's been at least a year though.

"Yeah," I say. "She's super nice."

"I don't know," Mom says.

"Sorry, Sage," Violet says. "I guess I'll see you later."

I glare at her. "Please, Mom. It's not a big deal."

She purses her lips together and sighs. "You said it was at her house, Violet?"

Violet nods. "Yeah."

Mom looks at Dad for a minute. If only they knew that we've been to Ariel's before. After a long, silent minute where they converse through gazes that I can't even decipher and almost make me believe they can read each other's minds, Mom finally says, "Okay, you can go. But be smart about it, girls. No drugs."

"No alcohol," Dad says.

I roll my eyes. "Are you going to remind me to apply sunscreen, too?"

My parents look at each other and laugh. "Sorry, sweetie," Mom says. "I have to remind myself you're not a kid anymore."

I sling my arms around each of my parents' shoulders. "Thanks. You guys are the best."

Violet and I run back upstairs where we sort through a dozen of my bathing suits to pick out the perfect ones. There's no way I'm going to wear the one I wore to Santa Monica, because that'd be the first thing people point out, like it's a sin to wear the same thing a few times.

Instead, I pick out a black bikini bottom with double straps that make it look like it has cutouts to show off my hips and a geometric-patterned halter-styled top that pushes my boobs together to give me nice cleavage. Violet picks out the white tie-string bikini she keeps here in case we want to go swimming and strips down to put it on.

"We look hot," Violet says, looking at us in my wall mirror.

I grin. "Totally."

Snapping a quick picture of our reflections, I text it to Cole before sliding my phone into my tote bag. I never thought in a million years that I'd be invited to a pool party at Ariel Marin's house, but I also never in a million years dreamed someone like Cole Vettel would be my boyfriend.

Twenty minutes later, Violet pulls her Audi onto the winding driveway in front of the huge garage. The moment I open my door, I catch sight of a familiar Porsche. I wasn't expecting Cole to be here, but I was hoping. He knew I was hanging out with Violet today, and it's probably why he didn't ask me if I wanted to come. He might've known I'd come regardless since Violet has been seeing more of Andrew lately. She saw pictures of Roman with a few different girls online and decided to cancel their second date, claiming that Andrew is more fun anyway. I don't blame her.

Andrew waits for Violet in the doorway of the house and wraps his arms around her, lifting her from her feet. I smile at the sound of my best friend's squeal and how happy she looks. Andrew looks pretty happy himself. His long hair hangs over his shoulders, and Violet runs her fingers through it while kissing him.

I say hi to Andrew, slide around them, and head toward the glass doors that lead out to the pool where Andrew says everyone is hanging out. The scent of barbeque wafts through the air as a guy in a chef's jacket stands in front of a giant grill built into an outdoor kitchen under a covering I didn't notice the first time I was here, probably because it was too dark. Some people swim, some lay out in lounge chairs, and the rest sit in the shade and talk under the wide palms.

"Sage, you made it!" Ariel calls from her place on a raft the size of a mattress. "Get in. The water's perfect."

I peer around once but don't see Cole and would rather get in the water than stand here looking like a lost little girl since the only other people besides Ariel that I know are still somewhere inside.

Setting my bag near a chair and far enough away from the pool to stay dry, I kick off my sandals before shimmying out of my white cotton dress. I saunter to the edge of the pool where the stairs lead to the shallow end.

The moment I step on the first step, cool water encompassing my feet. Strong hands grab me by the waist, and I'm lifted into the air. Cole laughs, jumping into the water with me in his arms. A wave splashes over us, and I bury my face into his neck as water soaks my hair. He doesn't even give me a moment to breathe before his lips meet mine. He kisses me, water dripping from his face, and I smile into his mouth.

He walks deeper into the water, only shifting me so I can wrap my legs around his waist. "I was hoping you'd come."

"And if I didn't?" I ask.

"I'd have shown up at your house because then I'd have

known Violet ditched you," he says, smirking.

I rest my forehead against his. "Sneaky. You planned this."

He kisses my nose. "Actually, you can thank Andrew. It just happened to work in my favor, too."

Like he was waiting for someone to mention him, Andrew strolls from the house with his hands glued to Violet's hips. She beams me a smile, and I blow her a kiss from over Cole's shoulder. Ariel smiles at me from her raft, and I push off from Cole, flipping backward and underwater. When I pop up, I swim toward Ariel and rest my elbows on her raft.

"Thanks for inviting me," I say, kicking my legs to stay afloat.

"Of course. I love making new friends when I can. It's so hard being on the road all the time that it's nice to have people to come back to when I'm home. Especially because you never know who you can trust." Ariel slides over on her raft and motions for me to climb on while she holds onto the wall.

Cole helps me up, and I manage not to flip us off, though I doubt Ariel would care. She's nothing like I imagined. She's easygoing. Sweet. Nothing like what you read online or in the magazines. My old obsession with the tabloids has already morphed into disgust over them, especially after what I found this morning.

"I guess I'll find out sooner or later," I say. "Did Cole tell you that we're having dinner with Lele?"

"That's great!" Ariel says. "She's so wonderful to work with. She designed the dress I wore to the Grammys."

Cole stands next to the raft, dripping water on my stomach. "Sage will be amazing. She's a natural."

I crinkle my nose, smiling. "You think so?"

"Totally," Ariel says. "I saw the picture he shared of you on Friendconn."

I shift on the raft, making it wobble. "You did it already?"

He shrugs. "I can take it down if you've changed your mind."

I shake my head. "No, it's just—you didn't show me."

He leans over and kisses my forehead. "Don't worry. I picked the best one. Trust me."

I tilt my head and look at him for a moment, his blue eyes shining in the sunlight, a smirk playing on his lips. I do trust him. I trust him completely. I didn't know it until this moment, but I know that whatever he shares of me with the world would be how he sees me.

"I do," I say quietly.

Ariel pulls her phone from a cup holder on the raft. "Take a look for yourself."

"That's way better than what I saw online," I say, cringing when the words leave my mouth. Cole frowns at me but doesn't say what he's thinking in front of Ariel.

"They always are. You can only control what you post yourself, so you have to make sure it's always more entertaining than what the paparazzi post. Give the world something better to look at. They don't actually care about pictures of you walking on the street. They want to see what it's like in a day in the life of Sage Meadows from you," Ariel says, holding her phone out to Cole. "Now pose so he can take a picture."

Cole snaps a few shots of us faking a candid photo, like he caught us sunbathing. Ariel smiles as she looks at the pictures.

I point to my favorite one. "This one is perfect."

She nods. "Can I post it?"

I think about it for a moment and say, "Definitely."

With a picture of me and Ariel online, it'll take the focus off the ones of me and Cole at the condo from the other day. Ariel is right. I have to create an image that people want to look at so they don't pay attention to everything out of my control.

"Will you take one of us now?" I add, sliding from the raft.

Cole lets me get on his back, and I smile brightly for Ariel. All the worry I had this morning is now gone from my mind, and all I can think about is how much better things will be now that I've decided to take things into my own hands instead of just hoping for the best.

Ariel snaps another picture with her phone. "This is the one."

I stare at it from over Cole's shoulder. It's an actual candid photo where my arms hug Cole, and he's staring at me as I smile away from the camera. She's right. It is perfect. Cole's perfect.

"I love it."

Cole flips me off his back and into his arms. "Good. Now enough with the pictures. Let's have some fun."

The glow of the fire pit casts golden light and shadows across Cole's face. He sings along with Ariel as she strums her guitar, playing a song I haven't heard before. The excitement of the day has turned into a calm night. Violet and Andrew disappeared into the house over an hour ago, and I'm pretty sure I won't see her again tonight.

"Loving you is like loving the lights. You light up my world. You shine in the night. With you around, I can clearly see, how perfect you are. How you belong with me," Cole sings, drawing my attention to him. He smiles, watching my face, and I rest my head on my hands, just listening. I could listen to either of them sing all night. I almost hope they do. Cole sings in the car, but something about him singing right now, like he's singing especially for me, sends my heart racing.

When the song is over, Ariel props her guitar against a chair. "What'd you think?" she asks me.

"I loved it. I think it might be my favorite song out of everything I've heard of yours," I say.

Ariel grins. "Cole wrote it. I'm going to pitch it for my next album as a duet."

My eyes widen, and Cole smirks at me. Next to him, I feel like a talentless fake. But I'm also in awe over how amazing he is. "It was beautiful."

"It was about you," he says, watching me for a moment, gauging my reaction.

Without saying a word, I get up from my spot and cross the distance to slide onto his lap and kiss him. The chorus hums in my mind over and over, and I snuggle against him.

I turn to Ariel. "I'm awake, right? This isn't some dream?"

She laughs. "I ask myself that every day." Standing, Ariel stretches her arms over her head, showing off her perfect stomach, and then grabs her guitar to head inside. "You're welcome to crash here or hang out as long as you want, but I have a flight to catch in the morning."

I nod, waving. "Thanks, Ariel."

"Good luck with Lele."

Ariel passes Andrew and Violet, who have surprisingly found their way back outside. Violet glances at me, a funny look on her face. She nearly rushes over to me and yanks my arms so I'm forced to get out of Cole's lap.

"Did Ariel just wish you luck with Lele," she half-whispers, half hisses. "As in Lele Rose?" Her turquoise hair hangs over her shoulders, half covering her face when she leans close enough that I can feel the warmth of her minty breath.

Cole watches us from the other side of the pool where Andrew arranges the chairs to prop his feet up. Our eyes lock and worry creases his brows. He would never admit it, but he's still wary of Violet and her sometimes big mouth.

"It's not a big deal. Cole and I are having dinner with her. She's a close friend of his family," I say.

Violet squeezes my hand. "You're lying, Sage. I know you are because you never do."

I stiffen. "It's really not a big deal. I don't want you to freak out if it turns out to be nothing."

"Freak out in a good or bad way?" she asks.

I shrug. "Lele mentioned she'd like to see me in some of her designs. Told me she can refer me to some agents."

I didn't think it was possible for Violet's eyes to go wider than their usually big, beautiful roundness, but they do. A few indecipherable emotions cross her face before she grabs my shoulders, shaking me while squealing and grinning.

"I can't believe you kept this from me!" Her voice rings through the air. "This is huge!"

I laugh, the world jerking around as she continues to shake me. "It's nothing yet."

"Are you kidding? My BFF is going to be famous. I'm going to be famous."

"You have to swear not to tell anyone, okay? I don't want my parents to find out until they absolutely have to," I say.

"Ugh. I want to tell the world," she says, a whine to her voice.

"Violet," I say.

She pulls her hands from my shoulders and raises them in the air. "Okay, okay. I get it. My lips are sealed."

"Good, because I really don't want to be famous for murder," I say.

She laughs, pulling me back toward the guys. Andrew smiles at Violet in his easy-going way, his long hair pulled back into a messy bun better than anything I can ever pull off. Instead of sitting with him, Violet takes his hands and pulls him to his feet.

She glances at Cole. "I'm entrusting Sage with you for the rest of the night."

I snort, covering my face with my hand at the seriousness in her voice, like Cole hasn't been hanging out with me all night while she kept herself occupied.

Cole gets to his feet, wrapping his arms around me in a hug. "Yes, ma'am."

Violet grins, blows me a kiss, and heads back inside with Andrew trailing behind her.

I rest my head on Cole's shoulder, letting him hug me in the light of the fire pit. Warmth radiates through the balmy air, and he rocks me back and forth. Stars sprinkle the sky above us like tiny pinpricks fighting against the light pollution from the city. The sudden quiet calm of the air, the sturdiness of Cole embracing me, his warm lips on my forehead—all of it digs into me, filling me with something I haven't ever felt before. I've liked other boys before, but this is different. This feels real. This is love.

I don't dare say the words, but the thought sits heavy on my mind, just simmering, warming me like this hot summer night.

"Want to get out of here?" Cole asks, whispering into my ear before brushing his lips against my cheek.

I meet him for a kiss. "I don't want to go home."

"My place?"

"Think it's a good idea? I'm still not ready..." My voice trails off. I kind of feel lame for saying it but going back to his house this time of night, knowing that Mom and Dad think that I'm crashing at Violet's. The opportunity is there. Cole knows it. I know it. The thought has crossed my mind.

"Sage, I told you I'd follow your lead. No pressure from me. Promise," he says, gazing into my eyes. Golden light shines against the blue depths of his like the sun setting on the ocean.

I finally nod. "Okay. I'd like that."

chapter 11

MY PHONE BUZZES from Cole's bedside table, and I shift on my side to glance at my glowing screen with a dozen text messages from Violet. Cole sleeps quietly next to me, his warm, bare side against my back, and I can't stop the smile from crossing my lips.

We watched a few movies in bed last night after I checked in with Mom and told her we had made it back to Violet's. She didn't question me or anything like usual. It's not unlike me and Violet to switch off houses, even during the school year.

I turn my gaze away from Cole and to my phone. Violet's been busy this morning. She sent me a few pictures of her and Andrew in what I'm assuming was his room and another of him at a stove in a gigantic kitchen. After at least a dozen pictures, I finally see her text.

Violet: Go on Friendconn. The pic Ariel posted of you two was liked by 77k people.

I quickly text her back, eyes wide.

Me: Seriously?

Violet: No joke. It's viral.

Me: Whoa.

My fingers shake. Fear sneaks up on me, and I tremble, looking at my home screen. I want so desperately to see what Violet's talking about, but another part of me is terrified. Seventy-seven thousand people have seen my picture with Ariel. I'm sure it was all Ariel's fans but still. This is huge.

My gaze flickers to Cole again. He looks so cute, sleeping on his back, his bare chest rising and falling with every soft breath. I raise my phone and snap a picture to remember the moment. Or maybe I'm stalling. Either way, I force myself to open up Friendconn and click on Ariel's fan page.

Our picture, the one of us floating on the raft in the pool, pops up first. It's now at eighty thousand likes, ten thousand comments, and six thousand shares. I blink a few times to see if I'm just imagining it all in my head, but it doesn't go away. The most popular comments pop-up on the top, mostly fans saying how much they love Ariel. Some ask who I am.

I release a breath and click on the next picture, the one of me and Cole. I expect a dozen of the same comments, which there are, with a couple random ones with hashtags like #hairgoals, #lovecole, and #lifegoals.

I click through a couple more, seeing some of the other

partygoers, including one of Violet and Andrew before I stop on one of Cole and Ariel singing together. They look at each other with smiles, Ariel holding her guitar, and the firelight glowing across their faces. It's a really great photo of the two of them before they sang the song that Cole wrote while the crowd was still hanging around.

My gaze flicks to the comments, and I wish with everything in me that I didn't look at them. Because apparently a ton of people love them together. There are comments begging and wishing for them to be in love. And then, there are some that mention that Cole is with me with long threads of people questioning why, what he sees in me, how much Ariel is better than me. She's prettier, has nicer hair, better body—everything they claim I don't have. All the things that make me undeserving of Cole's attention.

Jennifer Richards: God, I love them!

Samantha Johnson: Aricole is life.

Quinton Rogers: Bet Cole's banging them both. Damn him.

Carissa Flynn: Pick Ariel, Cole! She's way hotter and talented. You guys rock together!

Shawna White: Ew, that pink-haired chick can't even compare to Goddess Ariel. She should just get out of the way.

I click my phone off and toss it at the floor. It clunks onto the carpet before banging against the wall. Tears drip onto my hands, and I suck in a shuddering breath, trying my best not to make any noise.

The bed shifts beneath me. Cole slides his hands around my waist, attempting to pull me back to lie down with him again. But I stay frozen in my spot with my legs hanging off the bed and my head hung low.

"Sage?" Cole asks. "You okay?"

I wipe my face with the back of my hand. "Yeah, I'll be right back." My voice quivers, the words sticking in my throat. Standing, I cross the room and head toward the bathroom without looking at Cole.

I need to pull myself together, but I can't stop thinking about everything that I saw online. It makes me question what I'm doing. Who am I kidding? They're probably all right. I'm no one. I'm definitely not Ariel Marin. She's on a level I'll never find myself on no matter how high I try to jump.

Sitting on the edge of the tub, I quietly cry into a wad of tissues from the dispenser on the long, granite counter with a his-and-hers sink. I regret tossing my phone, because now I can't call Violet to talk to her.

A knock sounds on the door, and I wish Cole wouldn't check on me. I know I've been in here for at least twenty minutes, and he either thinks I'm horribly sick or that something is wrong. I consider saying I'm sick but embarrassment holds me back.

"Sage," he calls, knocking again.

"I need a minute," I say. "Please."

He doesn't knock again, but I'm pretty sure he hasn't left

the door. Hurrying to the sink, I splash cool water on my face to wash away my tears, run my fingers through my soft waves, and then take a deep breath before heading to the door.

Just as I suspected, Cole stands a few feet away, arms crossed over his chest. He gives me a once over, and I force myself to smile the best I can though all I want to do is to text for a car service to pick me up.

His brows furrow, and I know I'm busted. There's no denying I've been crying with my stupid red, puffy eyes. He closes the distance and brings his hands to my face to cup my cheeks. I blink away my self-doubt, forcing myself to quit acting like other people's opinions matter. And while they don't— shouldn't—matter, it doesn't make them any less hurtful.

"What happened?" he asks, gazing into my eyes.

I look away. "It's nothing. I'm fine."

He drops one of his hands and reaches into the pocket of his athletic shorts. Pulling out my phone, he holds it out to me. "You cracked your screen."

I sigh. "It's all so stupid. I know you told me not to pay attention to anything, but then Violet told me how many people liked the photo Ariel posted, and—" I snap my mouth shut. I can't even manage to spit the words out. Squeezing my eyes shut, I lean forward and rest my head on Cole's shoulder. His arms circle around me, pulling me to him, and he holds me without a word.

I break despite how hard I try to keep it together. Sobs wrack my chest, and I cry against him, pelting his bare shoulder with my tears. He lifts me off my feet and moves me back to the bedroom, gently setting me on the bed. He leaves for a second and returns with a box of tissues.

I laugh through my tears. Not because it's funny, but because I'm embarrassed. Mortified. I expect Cole to tell me he told me so at any second, but he sits silently next to me and rubs his hand over my back while half-hugging me.

I suck in a deep, shuddering breath, calming my nerves enough to look him in the eyes. "Go ahead and say it. Get it over with."

He frowns. "What do you mean?"

"Tell me you warned me. Tell me you told me to ignore whatever is posted online," I say.

Pouting his lip in the most adorable way, he shakes his head before kissing me despite my sticky, tear-dampened face. "No," he says, pushing tendrils of hair away from my face. "But I want to know what I can do to make you smile again."

An unexpected smile crosses my face, but a pout soon follows because he's almost too perfect. "Cole," I say, ignoring his statement. "What do you see in me?"

Pressing his lips into a thin line and tilting his head, he gives me a long look, like he's half expecting me to start laughing and tell him I'm just joking around. But I'm not. I don't care if it makes me seem insecure or like I'm begging for a compliment, because the online comments really clawed into my head and latched onto me.

I'm not some talented, interesting, perfect person. I'm just me—a girl with no idea what she wants from life just that I know I don't exactly want what my parents expect from me. That's no reason to like me. Maybe he only sees what Lele Rose sees. A pretty girl to dress and parade around. *That's not all that there is to modeling...*

After a minute he says, "You're serious." It's not a question.

I straighten my shoulders and meet his gaze. "Very."

He sighs and rubs his chin. "Well, you're beautiful to start."

I get up. I can't help it. "I need to leave."

I don't make it halfway across the room before he locks his fingers around my arm to stop me. When I spin to face him, he drops his hand to his side, giving me a foot of space.

"Sage, I feel like anything I say right now will be the wrong answer and will upset you," he says.

I swipe my hand across my cheek as another tear spills. "I'm sorry, Cole. I just—" I glance at the door. "I'm going to call for a ride."

"At least let me take you home," he says. "Please?"

But I'm afraid that if I let him, he'll make me laugh or smile, do something to forget how different we really are. I don't need him to try to make me smile or feel better about myself. I need to think about what will make me feel better on my own. I need to figure out if I want to even do this, put myself through this. If life in the public eye is even worth it to me.

I thought it would be. But I don't know.

All I know is that I want to go home and be alone.

"I'm sorry, Cole," I say, giving him a quick kiss before grabbing my phone and bag. "I'll call you later. I promise."

"Sage," he says.

I run from his house, and just when I think I'm trapped at the front gate, and that Cole will corner me to talk to him, it whines open. A woman driving a silver Mercedes waits on the other side, and all I do is smile and wave as I jog away.

chapter 12

So Many Haters

I LIE IN bed for the third day in a row with my laptop open on the pillow next to me. The empty plate from breakfast sits on my nightstand with the one from dinner, and I just stare at comment after comment on the picture Ariel posted of me and Cole.

Kody Tilt: I'd do her. She looks wild. Good for Cole.

Stacey Cho: So many haters. Cole deserves happiness. Get lives, people.

Gloria Ramirez: Hate her. Hope it doesn't last.

Joann Perez: I love you, Cole!

Brent Smith: Why do you care about some nobody?

Randy Weston: Why? No, Cole!

Tara Luachrain: More with Ariel!

Jessika Johnston: Love it!

Cara Flounders: Y'all are crazy. She's gorgeous.

After the first hundred or so comments, I wanted to break my laptop. I wanted to reply to each and every person saying something bad about me and defend myself. But I just couldn't do it. I didn't want to show how much they got to me.

Now? After reading comment number seven hundred and four, I'm numb. It doesn't even feel like they're talking about me but just some girl who looks like me hugging a boy I've basically pushed away for no other reason than because of these people who want to see me break.

My phone rings from next to my laptop, and I stare at Cole's smiling face. He's called at least a dozen times since I ran out on him, and every time, I don't answer. I just respond with a text. It's easier to tell him I'm sick instead of feeling like my world will implode at any second.

He doesn't leave a voicemail but sends a text.

Cole: I miss you.

Me: I miss you, too. :)

Cole: Can I see you today?

Me: I'm sick.

Cole: I don't care.

Me: Tomorrow?

Cole: Promise? I really want to talk to you in person about the other day.

Me: K.

He's going to break up with me. I know it. I've gone all melt-down mental on him, and he has had plenty of time to think about what he sees in me and probably came up with nothing just like I expected. And I hate it. I hate myself for it, too. All I'm good at are boring classes at school, but anyone can get good grades. I don't act or sing or paint. I don't have a good eye for photography, and the closest I've gotten to creative writing was a few bad poems I would never dare show the world. I'm just ordinary, boring Sage Meadows.

A knock sounds on the door, and Mom strolls in without asking if it's okay. She never does. Crossing her arms, she takes one look at me and strides to my bed to sit on the edge. Her blond hair, a color similar to my natural hair color, twirls in a neat bun at the nape of her neck. She looks like she's come home from the office for lunch to check on me while Dad is busy at his studio in Culver City.

"Ms. Meyer called me. She wanted to know if you could go in this afternoon for a few hours. One of the other volunteers had to cancel," she says.

I turn on my side and shut my computer. "I still feel sick."

She reaches over and gently touches my forehead. "You don't feel warm, and you seem to be eating fine. Is everything okay with Cole? You haven't asked to hang out with him in days."

I shrug. "It's fine."

"Something happen with Violet? She hasn't been around either."

"She has a new boyfriend." Violet and Andrew haven't defined their relationship or anything, but he's probably the only reason she's allowing me to ignore her.

"Come on, Sage. You can talk to me. I know something is wrong," Mom says. "Whatever it is, maybe I can help you."

Like ban me from ever going online again or from seeing Cole when I get the nerve to face him again? No, thanks.

I sigh and sit up. "Actually, I'm feeling much better. I'll call Ms. Meyer and confirm."

Mom pats my leg but doesn't argue. "I'll be busy at the office, so if Dad's not home, go ahead and call for a ride."

I hug her before she stands. "Okay."

She brushes my knotted hair from my face. "And my offer still stands. You really can talk to me. About anything. If you really don't want to, give your Aunt Jamie a call, okay? You know how much she loves talking to you."

Aunt Jamie is Mom's younger sister by eleven years and has felt more like a friend to me over the last few years. But she lives so far, and I'm afraid she'd go to Mom if I told her. It goes beyond aunt duty. If it were boy problems—which it kind of is but not really—then maybe. This is more, though.

"Thanks, Mom," I say, letting her stand.

She bends down and kisses me on the forehead and then heads toward the door. Before she leaves, she says, "There's still time to buy you a ticket if you want to go to New York with us tomorrow. It could be fun. We could see another show on Broadway. Do some shopping. Find some cool Fourth of July event. I hate that we won't be here for that. A week and a half seems like forever."

I shake my head. "Mom, no offense, but I want to spend it here. I'll be fine. Violet is coming over and we're going to catch up on our shows, swim, maybe go to The Grove."

"And on the fourth?"

I shrug. "Nothing crazy. Maybe rent a super yacht, break into your liquor cabinet, party all night—"

She rolls her eyes at my sarcasm. "Okay, okay. Just check in with us. I'll leave you some extra cash on the counter in case we're asleep when you get home," she says. "And I'll wake you up before we leave in the morning, okay?"

I nod. "Okay."

Without another word, Mom leaves my room. I open my computer again and continue to browse until I force myself to get up and shower. *Today will be a normal day. You're doing normal things. This is who you are.*

I push the thought away. I'm not so sure anymore.

"Oregano! Where've ya been?" Old Man Felix greets me the moment I walk into the Hammer Building. One of the volunteers from the children's gallery, where kids can make their own works of art and participate in story time, called in sick, so that's where I'm helping out.

"I've been around. Violet's been keeping me busy," I say, bumping my closed hand against Felix's outstretched fist.

Seeing Felix, hearing him purposely call me whatever herb he thinks of from the top of his head, makes this feel normal and pulls me from my bad mood. "Well, you need to make time for us. Summer's been complaining that she misses her friend. And you know how much I hate listening to that girl whine. Almost as much as I hate when people walk in here with giant backpacks on, ready to knock everything down."

I laugh. "Where's she working tonight?"

"Where do you think?" he asks with a smile.

Somehow, Summer always manages to get me wherever she's assigned for her shift.

I haven't been here since the Celeste exhibit, where Cole and I shared our first kiss, but that memory feels like so long ago. Standing in front of the old man who likes to tease me, who lights up and greets me like I'm worth his time, reminds me that I'm not only Cole Vettel's girlfriend, the girl both worthy and unworthy of him depending on who you ask, but I'm more than that. And for the next few hours, the only thing I'm going to be is a girl here to make sure the kids are having fun.

"I'll see you later, Felix," I say, heading toward the children's gallery that consists of wall-to-wall art supplies and long tables to work at with round stools.

Summer grins through the glass doors when she sees me strolling past the walls of miniature bottles with beautiful artwork painted inside the glass instead of on it. She opens the door for me and basically pulls me in by the hand.

Only a few kids and their parents sit at the rectangular tables, some painting while others draw with markers on cream paper. It's not even busy enough for two people, but Ms. Meyer likes to make sure there are plenty of people on hand just in case there is a sudden rush.

"I texted you yesterday," Summer says, standing next to me, pretending to show me something on the sign-up clipboard.

I purse my lips. I ignored almost all texts apart from the one I sent Cole to stop him from showing up at my door. "I know, and I'm sorry. I've been sick."

"Bullshit, Sage. You'd be on your deathbed and still be texting," she says.

I roll my eyes. "It's been a crazy week."

"I know." She smirks, wagging her eyebrows. "So, you're with the hottie who came to the Celeste event? Cole Vettel, right? I had no idea he was Beau Bradford's son. Why didn't you tell me?"

I shrug, wishing she'd just drop all the conversation about him. I glance over the room, hoping that maybe one of the kids will need more paper or spill paint all over—something, anything, so I won't have to talk about this now.

"I didn't really think about it. I had just met him," I say.

"And now you're BFFs with Ariel Marin?" she asks, digging for all the juicy details.

I shake my head with another eye roll. "Violet's dating her cousin."

"What? Damn, Sage. You need to invite me to hang out with you sometime. And not to your house, unless Ariel is over or something. Does Cole have an older brother?"

I laugh. "Okay, and no. He's an only child."

"That's a shame."

One of the younger kids, a toddler, starts suddenly scream-crying, pulling our conversation away from each other. The girl throws a fit right at the table before dropping to the floor in a way I wish I could if people wouldn't think a tantrum from me would be unacceptable. The mom scoops the little girl up, apologizes, and leaves everything at the table.

Summer jumps into action, cleaning up the mess, and I perch on a stool near the door, waiting to be of some use.

A small family with two elementary school-aged boys comes into the gallery, and I greet them with a smile and help get them situated to paint at one of the tables. I show them a few of the brushes and a mixing palette, and wait for them to begin.

"Sage," Summer says from across the room. "Isn't that Cole? Did you tell him you were going to be here? I swear, no bailing on me tonight."

I cross the room to where she peers through the glass wall that leads to the exhibit outside our small room. Cole raises his eyebrows when our gazes lock through the glass, and heat trails up my neck to set my cheeks ablaze. I told him I was sick. Now, here I am, standing in the children's gallery, totally not sick.

The second he smiles, I grip the table because my knees weaken and everything I've created in my head suddenly melts away. None of this is his fault. He doesn't deserve my sudden avoidance. He deserves so, so much more. If he breaks up with me, I'll deserve it. I hope he doesn't, though. I really like him.

More than like him.

I expect him to come my way, but instead, he just stands there, probably thinking I've gone crazy or I'm going to break up with him. My lips tilt downward, and I frown. His expression shifts to match mine. Now, we're stuck in a staring match to see who makes the first move.

Summer comes up next to me and waves her arm, making the move for both of us. Cole relents, meandering to the glass doors that I hit the button to automatically open for him. His hands hide in his pockets, and he doesn't even attempt to hug me, sending my heart sliding into my feet.

"It's nice to see you again, Cole," Summer says, clearly sensing the uncomfortable awkwardness between us.

Cole offers her his hand. "Summer, right?"

She beams, clearly taken aback that he knows her name. "Yup. Sage and I are in charge of the littles tonight. It's pretty slow, but you can't steal her away."

His blue eyes flicker to mine. "Think I could pass as a kid?"

Summer shrugs. "Oh, I don't care if you hang out. Pick any seat you want. Sage can set you up."

"Yeah, sure. Let me get some supplies." I couldn't sound more awkward if I tried. I want him to be here, I do, but I have so much on my mind that it's making me feel like a jerk. It doesn't help that he wanted to talk to me about the other night. About the freak out I want nothing more than to forget.

Cole picks a stool right where I'd stand to greet anyone who comes in. He's clearly too big for it, and looks adorably ridiculous. If people wouldn't think I was weird, I'd pull out my still cracked phone and take a picture.

While I get a few bottles of paint to take to the table instead of pouring them onto a palette, Summer busies herself with cleaning up the brushes. She leaves me, and then plops down at the table with the two boys and their parents to help them out.

Cole gazes at me during the short distance I stroll from the counter to his table. Instead of just setting stuff down in front of him, I perch on the stool next to him, brushing my arm against his as I arrange our supplies. There's no way I'm going to stand there and just watch him.

I create a few brush strokes in dark green paint across my cream-colored paper, avoiding his eyes. "I'm really sorry, Cole."

"You look better," he says instead of accepting my apology. It hurts, but I've clearly hurt him.

I frown, continuing to paint sage leaves as a border to my paper. I've always thought it was cool that my name was something I could put on paper as more than words. Cole watches me paint for a second before starting on his own paper.

"I'm sorry I lied," I say a little late. "And for avoiding you."

"So, you are avoiding me," he says.

"I was really planning on seeing you tomorrow. I didn't know you'd be here tonight," I say.

He doesn't look at me. "I come here when I want to get my mind off things, but all I could think about was you."

My bottom lip puckers at his admission. I've ruined the

museum for him. Awesome. "I feel awful. I swear none of this is about you."

"Sure seems like it. You ran out on me and refuse to talk to me. It's like I've done something wrong, but I can't think of anything. I thought everything was going great."

"It was—it is," I say. I refuse to talk about us in past-tense. "I'm just—"

The glass door swings open as a large group of kids rush in with their parents trailing behind them. I have no choice but to cut off my conversation with Cole. He remains in his spot without looking at me, still focused on his paper like he's creating a masterpiece. Maybe he is. I wouldn't put it past him.

It's like the universe is on my side today. A rush of people come in, keeping me from sitting back down next to Cole long enough to talk about things I don't want to discuss around others. Things I don't really want to discuss with him.

After two hours of helping kids paint and color and twenty minutes of story time, we say goodbye to the last kid as we close down the children's gallery for the evening. Cole quietly helps Summer and me clean up the mess and get things back in order.

Summer locks up the room and waves goodbye, swearing at me to make sure I invite her the next time I find myself somewhere cool, and Cole smirks at her, holding a few dozen sheets of paper in his hands. He doesn't let me look at them, though. My sage leaf border picture remains on top of his stack.

We exit the building together, and warm summer air wraps around us. The sun won't set for at least another hour, so I don't bother heading toward the front to look at the lampposts. I hold out my hand for Cole, and he takes it, lacing his fingers with mine without a word. His eyes soften with the action, and he strolls next to me for a moment before letting go of me to slide his arm around my back.

Stopping before the tall escalator, I turn and hug him, burying my face into the crook of his neck, breathing in his light, citrusy cologne.

"Come on. Let's go to the look-out deck," I say, pulling him toward the steep, vibrant red escalator I'd usually avoid to take the elevator inside the BCAM building.

We ride it up where it ends at a cement deck that gives us a breathtaking view of the Hollywood sign and Hollywood Hills. I can't see my house, but I can guess where it sits nestled on the hillside. The city sprawls out before us, a mixture of buildings and greenery. From up here, I can see the tops of the tall palm trees.

I pull Cole to the guardrail a few dozen feet from the entrance to the third level of the building and just soak in the view. We're alone up here, and for a minute, I can forget about everything except for me and Cole.

"Sage," Cole says, pulling my attention away from the hills.

I turn to face him, tucking my hair behind my ears to stop it from catching on the warm breeze. "You want an explanation."

"Did something happen? I thought everything was fine after Ariel's party," he says.

I press my lips into a thin line for a moment. "Can I just say that I really like you? Like, I seriously hate myself right now because I can tell I hurt you. It wasn't my intention, but I just—"

"So, this isn't something I did?" he asks, interrupting. "You're not planning to break up with me."

I puff air through my lips. "No, definitely not. It's all my fault. I did something stupid."

He stiffens but doesn't say anything. Ugh. He's probably thinking the worst.

"I read the comments on the photos Ariel posted," I add quickly, before he can think of a million horrible things I could possibly do.

He tilts his head, a smirk crossing his lips, and then he releases a breathless laugh. "Sage," he says, pulling me to him in a hug.

"I know you warned me, and I know I shouldn't have," I say, cutting him off. "But Violet said that it was basically going viral, and I had to see for myself."

"You didn't like what you read," he says, still holding me.

I shake my head. "Some people were nice, but people don't get what you see in me. They want you and Ariel to be together. All of it got me thinking."

Cole sighs into my ear. "That's why you asked me what I saw in you."

I nod. "Because I don't get it either. You are this amazingly, unbelievably perfect guy. I'm no one."

He shifts back, adjusting the stack of papers in his hand. "You're ridiculous, Sage, and now you're making me nervous because I'm not perfect. I don't want to disappoint you."

I sigh, pulling away to look at the Hollywood sign again. "I know. I'm stupid. I get it. You wouldn't understand."

"Sage, please look at me," he pleads.

I slowly turn to face him.

"You know other people's opinions of us don't matter to me, right? It's not going to change how I feel about you." He shifts on his feet. "And I don't know how to convince you of this. You want some grand list, but I can't give you one."

"Because you don't even know why."

Hurt sweeps across his face, and he rubs his hand over his neck. "Seriously?"

I shrug. "It shouldn't be this hard."

"And I shouldn't have to defend my feelings for you."

He's right. This is so messed up. I let a bunch of mean strangers get into my head. They're getting what they want by ruining me, by destroying what I saw in myself.

Tears trickle down my cheeks. "I'm sorry."

He closes the distance, wrapping his arms around me. "Sage, seeing you like this kills me, you know. I want to go online and delete every bad thing before you can ever see it."

I smile through my tears. "I wish you could. I wish I could just pretend it doesn't exist."

"You can. I do," he says. "They don't matter."

If it were only that easy. "I know, but this is all so new to me. I'm not even sure I want to have dinner with Lele now."

"I'm not going to tell you it's going to be easy or that you can't let them stop you from trying to do something I know you want to do, but if you don't do it because the assholes online can't keep their opinions to themselves about something that has nothing to do with them, then they win," he says.

I dry my eyes on my sleeve. "This was what I was talking about. How perfect you are."

He shakes his head. "No way. If you call me perfect one more time I'm going to—"

"Kiss me?" I ask, now smiling.

A smile lights up his face, and he leans in and brushes his lips against mine. The stack of papers slip from his hands, scattering across the deck, and I freeze when I catch sight of them. On every sheet Cole wrote both our names, decorating them with the markers. It's something I'd do in my notebook during a boring class.

I collect a few of the papers from the floor before they blow off the deck. "This is what you've been doing the last two hours?"

It's the first time I've ever seen him blush. "For only about thirty minutes. I spent the rest of the time watching you light up the faces of all those little kids."

I laugh. "It was the activity that made them smile. Not me."

"The pictures say otherwise." He holds up his phone, showing a photo of me kneeling next to a toddler I was showing how to hold a paintbrush. The little girl is smiling while looking at me.

"You're as bad as the paparazzi," I say.

He raises his phone and snaps a photo of me. "There's a difference. Their pictures are meaningless. Mine, well, I want to remember how I'm feeling in this moment."

"And how's that?"

"Like you're the best thing that's ever happened to me."

chapter 13

 Change of Plans

Patricia Collins: She's so fake.

Julian McGee: Who is she again?

Viktor Munoz: Sexy.

Hazel May: Trashy! Another famous for no reason slut.

Ruben Flores: Lot of shit talkers here.

Rebecca Sal: Good, maybe Cole will get a clue and stop posting crap we don't wanna see.

Vicky Reyes: Don't let the haters get you down, Sage! They're jealous!

Cole snatches my phone from my hand, glances at the screen once, and then shoves it into the pocket of his jeans. I no longer want to bury myself in my bed to never be seen from again anymore, but reading comments on the last photo Cole posted of me and him still makes me want to throw up.

"Okay, that's it. I'm not sharing any more of us," Cole says, studying my face for a long moment.

I sigh. "I don't get why they hate me so much."

"No one hates you," he says.

I raise an eyebrow. He can't possibly know that. He doesn't read what people say like I do. I guess growing up in his dad's spotlight made it easier for him to just let things roll off his back, but he also doesn't have people trying to slut shame him, belittle him, or make him feel like all he has going for him are his looks. That actually might be the case for me. I'm tall, pretty enough, and fit the mold to have Lele Rose wanting to dress me like one of her little dolls. But after looking at photos from her last runway show, I'm not even sure I can make the cut. I don't have flawless skin; freckles splatter my face and shoulders. I'm more muscular than thin because of all the hiking I do with Violet when it's not so hot out. And I don't even want to think about how it's possible that I might not be thin enough.

"What?" Cole asks, challenging me with his own raised eyebrow. "No one who matters to us hates you."

"Just the millions of others."

"Not millions."

"Thousands."

"Sage."

I sigh. "Sorry."

Cole rests his hands on my shoulders, peering into my eyes. "You can't control what they say, but you can control how it affects you."

In moments like this, he sounds way too wise, like he's years older than me instead of just months. "Do I need to tease you about your perfection again?"

He chuckles. "Definitely not. That's something my dad told me a while ago."

"Ugh, your dad. He's going to already have an opinion of me before meeting me."

"My dad already likes you and can't wait to meet you. Plus, you're not the one who's going to face the wrath of the Meadows's. Your parents are going to think I'm Satan. I'm surprised they haven't noticed that you've gone public with me."

"They won't be mad at you," I say. "It'll come back to me. And it's not like they can do much. They don't have time."

I'm not surprised by my parents not noticing. The best word to describe both my parents is busy. Mom works too many hours to count, even when she's home, she's working. And Dad? He's started working on his next art installation. When he gets in his zone, he loses track of the day of the week. His process makes him cut himself off from the world. He once didn't leave his studio for a week. Mom checked on him every day to make sure he was at least eating.

They care. They're overprotective. But they're also oblivious more often than not. I just hope they don't catch on until it's too late for them to even do anything. As long as I'm not brought home in a police car and no one informs them, they won't realize anything. Cole and I show up in places they wouldn't look unless they happen to just stumble upon it.

Cole leans forward and kisses me. "I hope you're right, because sneaking around is hard to do when you're me."

I laugh against his mouth. "Afraid of the challenge?"

"Not if it means being with you."

Cole's phone rings, cutting through the sound of our soft breathing. He pulls it from his pocket, glances at the screen, and then puts it to his ear. His blue eyes hold mine. I stand close enough that I can hear the masculine voice cutting through the line, and Cole does nothing to try to hide the conversation.

"Really? That sucks, but I can't say I'm not happy," Cole says. He listens for a few seconds as the other person says more. Then he responds with, "No, I don't mind. I'll let Sage know there has been a change of plans. I can't wait for you to meet her." More listening. My eyes widen, hearing Cole make some sort of plans without asking me. "Okay. See you in a bit." He hangs up the phone and smiles at me.

"A change of plans? You mean we're not staying in tonight?" I ask, butterflies swarming my stomach.

"Lele wants to move dinner to tonight," he says.

I take a breath. I thought it was going to be something else. But then I remember he was talking to a man. Maybe an assistant? "Okay, but she's already met me. Who else are you excited to introduce me to?"

He sucks in his bottom lip. "Don't be mad. I know you're already nervous, but I promise it's going to be fine."

I squeeze my eyes shut. "Cole…"

He kisses my forehead. "My dad's Florida shows were postponed due to weather, so he's back in town through the fifth."

"And he's joining us tonight with Lele?"

He nods. "Stop panicking. It'll be fine."

Any other time I'd be freaking out but only because I'd be excited. But this time is different. Beau Bradford isn't just some iconic singer. He's my boyfriend's father. What if he hates me like the rest of the world seems to? Then what?

Me: I'm going to throw up.

Violet: Suck it up, babe. I'll crash dinner if you want.

Me: Cole would kill you.

Violet: He hates me, huh?

Me: No, but if you crash dinner, he might. This isn't a party. I'm meeting his dad.

Violet: We can make it a party. I'm dying to meet Beau.

Me: I'll ask Cole.

Violet: Love you. Send pics.

Me: If I don't die first.

A warm hand slides over my bare knee, and I draw my attention from my phone. Cole leans closer, pursing his lips when he sees me texting with Violet. I can't help it. I need her moral support more than anything. Beau Bradford is Cole's dad. Cole would never understand how intimidating that is for me. He swears it's all going to be fine, but I'm still afraid.

He trails his fingers up my leg, stopping at the hemline of my dress. "No more phone, okay?"

"It's my security blanket." I sigh, shoving it into my glittery clutch purse that complements my pearl and taupe sheath dress with capped sleeves, bateau neckline, and V-back. An embroidered floral pattern gives me an innocent look perfect to meet my boyfriend's dad. It's a far cry from the sexy mini-dress I borrowed from Violet the night I met Lele, but the last thing I want is to make a bad impression.

"I didn't get a security blanket when the only way I could see you was if I spent the evening with your parents on our third date." He smiles as he says it, keeping his eyes on the road.

"My dad is like a kitten compared to yours," I say, shifting in the front seat of Cole's car as he drives down Fairfax to Wilshire toward a restaurant called The Sky, which is only a few blocks from the LACMA.

"At least you're not a huge fan of mine," he says.

I laugh. "Are you making this a competition? Because I'll win."

"I might let you win if it continues to make you smile like that," he says, watching me in his peripheral vision. "I thought I was going to turn left instead of right for a quick detour." He doesn't have to tell me where the detour would lead, because the lampposts would be lighting the dark right about now.

I consider telling him to do it, to take me there, but then I don't want to keep anyone waiting. I wish I would've snuck some of Mom's wine before we had left my house. It's what Violet would've done, but she also can keep herself more composed than I can with alcohol.

Puckering out my bottom lip, I fake a pout. "No more smiles for you until we leave."

He chuckles, pulling to the curb in front of a skyscraper where a few people dressed in tuxedos wait near a podium under a bright red awning. A valet opens my door and offers me his hand before Cole even has a chance to respond to me. Cole hands a woman his key before joining me on the sidewalk. We watch the valet drive his car away and around the corner.

Neither of us moves for a minute, and I tilt my head up and look at the shining lights glowing through the windows of the building. They're not as pretty up close with the hum of traffic blaring from the streets, the sirens in the distance, the smell of something coming from the trash in the gutters, and the sudden flash of a camera that surprises me from a few feet away.

A paparazzo snaps another photo from his place on the corner, far enough away that he won't get hassled by the valets who whisper too quietly to hear. I expect Cole to rush me inside, but he doesn't. He watches me turn away from the camera to look around the lively city for a moment.

"You'd really rather stand out here and have your picture end up in a tabloid rather than go inside and meet my dad?" he questions, amusement playing on his face. Most people in his position might be insulted. He finds it funny, thankfully. Because he's right.

"I just need a minute longer," I say, lacing my fingers with his.

He slides his arms around my waist, running fingers up my back to where my skin peeks through my rose-gold hair I've left cascading to my waist in soft ringlets. He kisses me despite the fact that I'm wearing dark purple lipstick, a bold statement compared to my nude-colored eyeshadow and thin black liner.

Another camera flash pulls me away from him, and I finally force myself to let him guide me inside the building. My platform pumps tap against the tiled floor of the lobby as we walk toward an elevator. I've never been to The Sky before, but I've read about it in a few magazines. It's supposed to be amazing.

The wall-to-wall mirrored elevator is run by a man in a suit, and he hits the button for the twenty-fifth floor. I gaze at Cole in the mirror, my heels making me almost his height. The elevator opens to a small lobby with a woman who stands at a podium. She greets Cole with a smile and guides us to another elevator that takes us up to the roof.

A warm breeze plays with my hair, and the first thing I do when I step from the elevator is pull Cole to the glass partition that gives us a view of the city around us. We're on top of one of the taller buildings in the area so the lights glow below us for what looks like forever. The waxing moon shines brightly in the cloudless sky above, and the open-air restaurant really feels like we're going to be dining in the sky.

Big, comfortable booths line the perimeter, giving every table a different view of the city. In the center, there's a large fire pit that illuminates the place in a soft glow. Twinkling lights strung overhead light the rest of the place just enough to see but not bright enough to take away from the breathtaking view. Every table is already full, the place being reservation-only. With a name like Beau Bradford, I'm sure it was easy making arrangements.

Cole clasps my hand, pulling me along to follow the hostess to a table in the corner of the roof. Lele sits next to Beau at the circular booth, quietly chatting with their heads leaning close to each other in a quiet conversation.

My fingers grip Cole's in a death hold that's probably cutting off the circulation in his hand, but he doesn't pull away or complain. Instead, he offers me a wide smile, one that shows me how excited he is that I'm here with him and about to meet his dad.

My heart speeds up the moment Beau catches sight of us. He slides from the booth and stands, grinning at Cole before turning his gaze to me. I can't tell what he's thinking, but something flickers in his eyes as he tries to figure out what he thinks of me before I even have a chance to open my mouth.

"Cole, I've missed you," Beau says, wrapping his son in a warm hug.

I twine my hands together and smile at Lele, who remains seated. She reaches out and takes my hand between hers, but before she can even greet me, Beau releases Cole and turns his attention to me.

"Dad, this is Sage," Cole says, introducing us.

I offer my hand out to Beau, but he doesn't take it. Instead, he gives me a hug as well, surprising me. I laugh, letting him rock me on my feet for a moment. "It's so nice to meet you, Mr. Bradford."

"None of that formal stuff. Call me Beau." He leans back and smiles at me. "And I'm so happy you could make it tonight. Cole talks about you all the time."

The more he talks, the less nervous I feel. He sounds just like any other person I'd meet and talk to at one of Mom's events. It's sometimes hard to remember that just because someone's famous, doesn't mean they won't treat you like you're on the same level, even if they are legendary.

I smile at Cole. "Hopefully nothing embarrassing."

"Like how I cushioned your fall when you were too busy looking at the lights?" Cole asks, pulling me to the booth to slide in first.

"Sounds straight out of a movie," Lele says. She reaches over and pats my hand. "I'm so happy you had my Cole boy call me, doll. I've wanted to badger him about you since my birthday." I wonder if she calls all her models that.

"Oh, Lele. Give me a chance to get to know Sage before you turn this into a business meeting," Beau says.

Lele bumps her shoulder against Beau's. "I'll make it quick." She turns her focus on me. "I meant what I said when I first met you. You would look perfect in my new Fall/Winter collection, and it so happens that one of my models had to pull out of a private, client-only show this weekend. I'd like you to audition for me tomorrow."

I blink. Tomorrow? Whoa. I wasn't expecting something to happen so quickly. "I—"

"Don't say no."

"Okay," I say. "But I have to warn you. I've never walked a runway in my life."

She shrugs. "I hadn't either before my first show."

Cole squeezes my knee under the table, and it takes everything in me not to jump up and down in my seat. While it's not a sure thing, it's still an audition. It's one step closer to doing something I've had my heart set on doing despite all the negativity that has surrounded me the last week.

"So is it a yes?" Lele adds.

I nod. "I'd love to audition. Thank you."

"I'll have my assistant call you first thing in the morning," she says.

Beau clears his throat. "Now that that's all settled, I want to know more about you, Sage."

I shift in my seat. Where do I even begin?

chapter 14

Dead Girl Catwalking

Cole: You've been invited for dinner again tonight.

Me: So you weren't lying about your dad liking me?

Cole: He wants to invite your parents over when they return.

Me: Oh, boy.

Cole: I heard him talking to his lawyer about a possible betrothal.

Me: Haha. We could be the next teen Hollywood scandal.

Cole: How about we start with just dinner again?

Me: I'll call you.

Cole: Invite Violet.

Me: You must really want to see me.

Cole: Always. :)

The screen on my phone changes as an unfamiliar number pops up. Taking a breath, I quickly swipe my finger to answer it. I'm expecting a call from Lele's assistant about my audition today. As much as I wanted to scream about it to the world, to tell Violet so she could come help prepare me, I haven't said a word to anyone. Even when Cole brought it up last night on the way to my house, I refused to talk about it because of nerves. I also turned down his offer for a ride to Lele's.

"This is Sage Meadows," I say when the line clicks on.

"Hi, Sage! This is Shane Martinez calling for Lele Rose," a masculine voice says. "She wants to see if you could swing by her home in an hour. I know it's short notice, but with the up-coming holiday and the show, we need to get you in as soon as possible."

I shift the phone on my ear. "That works perfectly for me."

"Fabulous." Voices hum through the line. It sounds like he's shuffling paper. "I know everything isn't final, but I figured I'd save us some time and tell you that you're already ninety-nine percent the model Lele wants to replace Andrina this show. If everything works out, I bet you'll be offered a contract in no time."

My heart pounds in my ears at his admittance. "That would be amazing," I say.

"For your time, Lele is offering you a stipend of two grand. Is that acceptable? I'll have the paperwork ready when you arrive."

Two grand? Whoa. I don't know why getting paid surprises

me.

"You are old enough to work, right?" he asks.

"I—"

"Hold on, Sage," he says, cutting me off. Static buzzes through the line. It sounds like he's moving around a lot. "Okay, sorry about that. Anyway, that about does it. Wear something you can easily get in and out of since you'll be getting measurements done. Don't worry about dressing up for Lele. She likes to do all that."

I smile into the phone. "Okay, sounds great."

"We'll see you in an hour."

Shane hangs up the phone before I even have a chance to say anything. Flopping back on my bed, I stare at my ceiling fan for a moment before my phone buzzes in my hand. Talking to Shane took away a lot of my fear. This is happening. It's really happening.

I release an excited scream, glad my parents aren't home. This was fate's doing, and she totally rocks.

Cole: You there?

Me: Sry. Lele's assistant called.

Cole: And?

Me: Tell you later.

Cole: Let me take you.

Me: Already scheduled a ride.

Cole: Can I pick you up?

Me: I'll let you know. I g2g.

Cole: Good luck! :)

Me: Thanks! :-*

Forty-five minutes later, I tip the pretty brunette woman who drops me off in front of Lele Rose's mansion. I watch the Toyota Prius drive back out the gate of the mansion for a moment. Gathering my confidence, I stroll toward the set of stairs to the wraparound entrance of the magnificent mansion. With the sun shining, I can't see into the wall of windows around the grand door.

A guy with a neatly trimmed beard, wearing a summery blue dress shirt and gray cotton pants, greets me from the already opened door. His eyes trail from my ballerina bun to my strappy sandals, and then he smiles.

"You look just like your pictures. I would've bet my last paycheck that they'd all been edited," the guy says.

I'm taken aback by his remark but catch myself before I stare blankly at him. "Thanks, I think. You must be Shane."

He nods his head, sweeping his arm out so that I step inside the house in front of him. Not much has changed since I was last here, except now I can take a moment to really let it all sink in compared to when Violet made me tear through the place to the odd underground club in the backyard.

The grand staircase leads to a balcony that overlooks a huge living room filled with the kind of furniture that you don't want to sit on because it was made for aesthetics rather than comfort. Dozens of framed fashion sketches are hung throughout the house, and photographs of some of the most renowned models line the walls in the huge upstairs hallway off the balcony.

A brown and burgundy floor runner directs us to a thick, dark wood door that is opened to show what I can only describe as a beautifully chaotic workspace. Swatches of what looks like a million different fabrics clutter a glass table fit to seat twenty if it had any chairs. Long racks take up a good portion of wall space with so many pieces of clothing, it looks like something from a store, except each piece is different. A floor-to-ceiling mirror sits behind the black desk Lele hunches over without sitting in the leather desk chair behind her. Dozens of sketches sit on the surface and a large flat screen TV projects what's on Lele's monitor, which is only a photo collage screensaver at the moment.

"Sage, welcome! Sorry the place is a mess. I'd have had you go to my office downtown, but it's a madhouse there at the moment." Lele straightens her back and glides around her desk to greet me with a hug.

"This is fine. Great, actually," I say, gazing at how detailed the sketches are on her desk. I wish I had an ounce of her talent.

Her warm smile lights up her face. "Now, Shane told me that he went over everything with you already. What I want to do is get your measurements so I can send them to my team."

"Okay, would you like to see me walk?" I ask.

She chuckles. "I've seen you walk. You're a natural. Confident. I like it. We'll have a rehearsal to prep, and my choreographer will make sure everything goes smoothly."

This is really happening. I almost don't believe it. "That

sounds good." My voice quivers a little.

Lele slides her arm over my shoulder. "Don't be nervous, doll. It's a small show, just a handful of my clients and business associates. Maybe fifty people tops. It's not New York Fashion Week. Possibly next year, though."

"Wow, really?" I ask.

"We'll see how this weekend goes. I have a good feeling about you, Sage. I might have to have my lawyers draw up a proposal for you next week. Once people see you in my designs, I might have some competition."

I consider telling her that my parents would probably refuse any proposal, but I end up keeping my mouth shut because she asks Shane to get to work. I go through the motions of everything, acting like the perfect doll for Lele as she sees her own visions unfold.

After an hour, I sign a few forms for Shane, change back into my summer dress and sandals, and wait for Cole to pick me up. Everything happened so quickly, it only takes seeing Cole to realize that my life is changing. I'm no longer going to be only Cole's girlfriend. I'm going to find a name for myself. I've never been more certain of anything.

"So?" Cole asks me from the front seat of his car. Lele only had a moment to say hello before Shane swept her away to head downtown. All Cole heard was that she'd see me soon.

I tap my fingers on my knee. "I'm officially going to walk the runway."

"Congrats, Sage!" he says, leaning over to kiss me. "You'll

be amazing."

"She even mentioned coming up with a proposal," I say.

His eyes light up. "I knew she would. Why don't you sound like it's a good thing?"

"My parents won't ever agree to it."

He frowns. "You never know. They might surprise you."

"Or they might just kill my career before it even has a chance to start."

"Try these," Violet says, handing me the fourth pair of heels she brought from her enormous collection. "They're the tallest ones I have. If you survive a walk down the hall in these, you'll survive in any pair of shoes they hand you."

I don't know who was more excited about the show this weekend: Me or Violet. The moment I texted her that I got the gig, she must've flown to Cole's house, because she was already waiting there before we even arrived, and she came armed to help me.

The platform stilettos are so tall that Violet has to strap them for me. When I stand, I tower over her by what feels like a foot. She's more petite, not even five and a half feet, which is one of the reasons she hasn't begged me to talk to Lele for her. Plus, she'd much rather act than anything else, though the only acting she does is when she lies to both our parents.

I wobble on my feet. "Whoa. I'm doomed if they hand me something this high. I'll either fall and die from embarrassment or fall and die from a broken neck."

She holds out her hand to me. "Come on, little toddler. You can learn to walk."

I laugh, taking an ungraceful step forward, proving Violet correct with her nickname. I look like I'm about to step on a mine at any second and blow myself up with the tiny steps I'm managing.

The door to Cole's suite opens, and I meet Cole's amused smile. Straightening my shoulders, I let go of Violet and strut across the room to him like I was taught to walk in heels. His arms slide around me, rocking me on my feet, and I topple sideways with a yelp. I don't hit the floor. Cole manages to grip my waist and pull me onto his shoulder. My hair swings back and forth, the world jerking as he carries me upside down to the couch.

"That didn't go exactly as I planned," I say, smiling up at Cole from the cushion.

Violet plops down by my head. "You worked it, babe. Only took trying to impress a guy to get it out of you."

Warmth blossoms in my cheeks. "Yet I still managed to fall. I'm a dead girl catwalking."

Violet snorts. "You have two days. You'll blow them away."

"Or embarrass myself."

Cole reaches his hands out to pull me back to my feet. "Violet's right. You'll be perfect. And guess who got two tickets to attend said show?"

My serious expression lights with a smile. "Really? I was going to ask Lele, but she said it was exclusive."

He raises an eyebrow. "She's my godmother. I'm family."

"The second ticket is for me, right? 'Cause I'm willing to fight for it," Violet says, raising her fists.

"I'd like to see that," Cole says, teasingly.

I laugh. "Watch out. She fights dirty."

A knock sounds on the door, and Beau peeks his head in. Violet jumps to her feet, nearly running as she crosses the room. Beau was out when we arrived, so she hasn't had the chance to meet him, and seeing her rush Cole's dad makes me want to tackle her and intercept.

Violet holds out her hand to Beau. "I don't know if Cole told you about me, but I'm Violet, Sage's best friend."

Beau laughs, smiling at Violet like he knows how to handle her kind of crazy. He shakes her hand. "It's a pleasure to meet the infamous Violet. Cole might have mentioned you a time or two."

Violet grins over her shoulder. "Don't trust anything he says."

Beau laughs again. "Don't worry. It's all good." He turns his attention to his son. "So, is everyone ready?"

Cole pulls me to my feet, and I wobble. "As soon as Sage finds shoes she can walk in."

Beau glances down at the pile of shoes on the floor. "Oh, boy. I'll go ahead and wait in the car." He chuckles, closing the door.

I bend my knee, attempting to unbuckle the strap of my shoe unsuccessfully. Cole stands over me, smirking, and I lightly kick him. "Help? Unless you just want to carry me."

Violet makes a gagging sound. "Your dad had the right idea. I'm going to wait in the car." Without waiting for a response, she leaves us alone in Cole's suite.

Cole bends down and picks me up off the couch.

"What are you doing?" I ask, breathing lightly against his neck.

"You're the one who made the suggestion," he says, turning his head to kiss me.

"Violet's about to be alone with your dad. She might harass him for a bunch of selfies," I say.

He brushes his lips against mine again but doesn't set me down. "She wouldn't."

"Do you hear yourself?"

He sets me back on the couch and holds my feet on his knee, helping me unbuckle the straps. "You're right. We better hurry. She might ask him for an invite to Thanksgiving or something."

"And Christmas," I say with a laugh.

I kick off the shoes and step into a pair of wedged, backless sandals. They're taller than the ones I wore to my meeting with Lele but short enough that I don't have to worry about falling on my face. Cole helps me to my feet, and we take the back entrance out of his room and to the garage large enough for ten vehicles, though his dad only owns three and Cole has one.

Beau's already waiting in the circular drive with Violet in the front seat next to him. Music hums from the stereo and the two of them bob their heads to the beat. Violet's brown eyes shine in the light from a small fixture on the garage, and she looks like she's having the best time of her life. It's totally something she'd do with her own dad, just hang out and sing.

Cole joins along, motioning me to slide across the leather seat of his dad's black Mercedes-Benz G-Class SUV. I'm the odd man out, definitely not feeling the need to belt it out to Watchful Fox's latest single. It doesn't stop me from dancing in my seat though.

Less than fifteen minutes later, Beau pulls into the parking lot of a restaurant that has been converted from a mansion not far from the Beverly Hills Hotel. I had no idea that Frank's Oasis even existed. Surrounded by tall hedges, it's almost completely secluded and away from the prying eyes of the media. With a security guard manning the only entrance, there's no way paparazzi could bother any of us here unless they snuck into one of the surrounding mansions and took pictures with a long focus lens.

A man in a red bowtie and blazer opens the door for Violet before opening my door. He helps me to my feet and takes the keys from Beau to park the car for us. The maître d' greets us from his position at a counter in the grand entrance filled with shiny gold ornate fixtures, gleaming tiles, shimmering chandeliers, and artwork worthy of LACMA.

Beau speaks a few warm words with the man, calling him Bentley, and then we're shown to a clothed table near a window with a view of a glowing fountain with color-changing lights outside. A bartender mans a bar behind us along the back wall and a few people in business wear sip drinks and chat, some even eating a meal alone.

Violet sits to my right and Cole to my left, with Beau sitting directly across from me. A server comes by and offers Beau wine while pouring the rest of us sparkling water, and then Cole asks for a carafe of lemonade, because he knows how much I hate sparkling water.

When the server leaves, Beau shifts in his chair, glancing at Cole before turning his eyes toward me. The way he looks at me, with a seriousness I have yet to see on him, makes me incredibly nervous. He doesn't even have to say anything for me to know he's a man on a mission with things he wants to say.

He clears his throat. "This is one of my favorite places to eat."

I reach out and grab Cole's hand under the table. This isn't the first serious conversation an adult has had with me. He sounds like my mom did last summer when she had finally agreed to let me stay home while she and Dad went out of town. That conversation included a ton of rules and a whole lot of warning. This feels exactly like that.

"I can see why," I say. "It's private."

"You seem to be quite aware of things, Sage. I like that," Beau says. "When you're in my line of work, things can get quite complicated. You never know what to expect being in the public eye. Don't get me wrong, I love my career and love performing, but it isn't always good."

Uh-oh. I stiffen in my seat and straighten my shoulders. Violet kicks me under the table, but I don't take my eyes off Beau even though I want to slink down and hide under the table.

"I know," I say quietly, because I'm afraid the nerves twisting in my stomach will cause my voice to crack.

"I figured you did, but since my son mentioned something to me yesterday, I felt like I had to just get that out in the open. You're going to be under a lot of scrutiny dating Cole. People are going to try to narrate and speculate on everything you do, so it's important to try your best and not give them something to talk about," he says. "I care about Cole and all his friends. I know he didn't choose this lifestyle, but I'm doing my best to let him take a go at things on his own. But I want to just be clear that your lives need to stay private." He shifts to look at Violet. "This includes you."

Violet shrinks down in her chair. I doubt that Cole told his dad that Violet leaked my name to the press, but it sure feels like he knows it was her.

"Dad," Cole says with a sigh. "If I had known you invited my girlfriend and her friend to just tell them that they need to keep away from the press about our affairs, I could've saved you the trouble."

I lick my lips. "It's fine, Cole." I turn to Beau. "You don't have to worry about us. I wouldn't do anything to jeopardize you or Cole."

Beau nods his head. "Thank you, Sage. I'm sure your parents would feel the same way."

Ugh. I wish he'd have never brought them up. I force myself to smile. "Oh, they do."

Beau's cell phone rings from his jacket pocket, and he excuses himself from the table to answer it. Violet leans her elbows on the table, glaring at Cole, and he winces. I'm pretty sure she might've kicked him under the table.

"This was not what I had in mind for a nice dinner," she hiss-whispers.

Cole raises his hands in surrender. "I didn't know. I swear."

"Yeah, right," she says.

It's my turn to kick Violet. "Quit it, will you? Beau said what he needed to say. He'll move on, and we can get this dinner over with and head back to my place for some fun."

She bares her teeth at me in a fake smile. "Eat fast." Turning to Cole, she points at him. "And you owe me."

I sigh. "Don't listen to her."

Cole laughs. "And have her hang this over my head? Name what you want, Violet."

She tosses her hair over her shoulder. "I want you to post a picture of me and Sage on your Friendconn page."

I palm my forehead, covering my eyes. "Seriously?"

"Deal," Cole says, not giving me the chance to argue with my best friend, who I'm pretty sure lives in a rainbow bubble with how unfazed by the world she is. If only I had her confidence. "But it has to be now or never."

Violet scoots her chair closer to mine. "Hurry before your

dad gets back."

Cole holds up his phone. "Smile."

"No, fake laugh with me. Pretend we're having a good time," Violet says.

I roll my eyes. "You're ridiculous."

"Just do it."

I tilt my head toward hers, and Violet lets out a fake laugh, causing me to really laugh. Cole snaps a couple photos, and Violet gets the honor of picking the picture she likes best.

"Done," Cole whispers, tucking his phone into his pocket.

Violet shakes my shoulder. "Now we wait."

"I hate you," I whisper.

"Shut up. You love me."

If only everyone else in the world loved us, too.

chapter 15

Don't Need to be Saved

I CAN'T SLEEP. Violet bailed on me over an hour ago when Andrew texted her that he was back in town. We were supposed to spend the week together until my parents came back, but I'm pretty sure I'll be having a lot of boring alone time every night, which sucks. I've found myself spiraling into a black abyss made of hundreds of comments about the photo Cole posted of me and Violet.

Benny Holt: Bet they have threesomes.

Alice Gibbons: New girl is way prettier.

Kelley Dobs: Cole needs to ditch them for me and my bestie.

Lane Towns: These bitches better leave my boyfriend alone!

Jorge Carranza: Mmm...sexy.

Freddy Quinton: Whores. Gotta love them.

Leaving my laptop open next to me, I lie back on my pillow and rub my eyes. I have to be at Lele's rehearsal at one in the afternoon. Shane said it might take a few hours, then comes hair and makeup, followed by the show itself at nine. My mind whirls with so much negativity that I'm starting to think it's unintentionally sabotaging me.

I roll over and grab my phone from my nightstand and glance at the broken screen. It's already close to two, and I doubt Cole's even awake, but I send him a text anyway.

Me: You awake?

Me: Violet bailed on me.

Me: Can't sleep. Hate being alone.

I wait for Cole to respond, staring at my phone for a good fifteen minutes. The second I give up and set it on my nightstand, it buzzes.

Cole: I'm here.

Me: Did I wake you?

Cole: No, but you should answer the door before someone thinks I'm creeping.

A smile crosses my face as I jump from my bed. I didn't realize he was actually outside. Had I known he was just going to show up, I'd have cleaned up my room. His place always looks so neat. I kick my scattered clothes into a pile near the closet, dim the lights some, and jog down the stairs to the front door.

I unlock it without looking through the peephole. Cole offers me a crooked smile, his hands hiding in the front pockets of his hoodie that he has covering his hair. I step out of the way to let him inside, and we stand in the foyer.

"I hope it's okay I came," he says, leaning in to kiss me.

"Won't your dad miss you?" I ask between kisses.

"He won't even notice."

My heartbeat speeds up when I look between the stairs that lead down to the kitchen and living room and the ones that lead to my bedroom. It only takes me a second to decide to guide Cole up to my room. It's not the first time we've spent the night together, but something feels different this time.

Cole trails behind me, his fingers grazing my hips, his chest nearly pressing into my back. I stroll right to my bed and climb onto it. He pauses, taking in the view of the glowing city through my sheer curtains for a second before turning his attention back to me.

I pick up my computer. "Mind setting this on my desk?"

He takes it from me, glancing at the glowing screen for a second. "I can see why you can't sleep." I wish I had closed my computer before handing it to him.

I lean back on my bed, thinking about pulling my pillow over my face. "They're a mixture of good and downright awful. It doesn't bother me as much though. I think I'm becoming immune."

He sets my laptop on the desk and returns to me. I slide over so he can sit down. Taking my hand, he holds it between his while looking at me with his crystalline eyes.

"I hate that you put yourself through this, Sage," he says,

his bottom lip pouting.

I glance down at my gray comforter. "I can't help it."

"You have to promise not to let it get to you again, okay? Not like the last time."

"I'll try," I say. "I just hate that some people are so against us for no reason."

He sighs. "They don't matter. What matters is that you're the most amazing girl I know, and I love you."

Cole goes quiet, and I can feel him staring at me. His words dance around in my mind. I knew I had feelings for him way beyond just liking him, but I wasn't sure he felt the same. And I'm afraid he's going to take those three words back because he might've only said them to make a point.

"You love me?" I ask, forcing myself to meet his intense gaze.

I wish I didn't just ask him that. Because I don't need the confirmation with the way he's looking at me. His hand moves up to my face, and he pushes my hair behind my ear.

"Yeah," he says quietly. "It's the reason my dad said all those things to you the other night. I know it has only been a few weeks, but I can't deny that I've fallen in love with you. And seeing how terrible people are online kills me. But what kills me more is that there's nothing I can do to save you from all that."

"I don't need to be saved," I say.

"I wish my dad wasn't famous or that I could somehow be one of those anonymous musicians, you know?" he continues.

"I'd do anything to—"

I cut off his words with a kiss. "Be quiet. I wouldn't change anything about you or your life. I might not like the way people are, but I love the way you are and the way things are going. And you know what?"

He pulls away a few inches. "What?"

"I love you, too."

He grins as he kisses me, sliding his hand around my back to pull me closer. Our smiles fade into something more intense, and I roll over and on top of him, straddling him while I lean over, kissing him deeper. My hair veils over us, blocking us from the world. Goosebumps prickle up my arms, his fingers running to my lower back and up my shirt.

I don't stop him when he pulls it up and over my head. He now sits up slightly with me on his lap with my legs curled behind him. His lips move from mine, and he brushes them against my jaw to my neck and then along my bare shoulder, nudging my bra strap to fall onto my arm.

My breathing quickens, feeling the heat of his lips against my cool skin. I help him tug his hoodie and plain black T-shirt off and toss it onto the floor with mine. Taking in the sinewy muscles of his taut shoulders and chest, I run my fingers across his warm skin to link them behind his neck.

"We should stop," he whispers after another long kiss.

I pout my lip, and he kisses it. "Only if you want to," I whisper.

He shakes his head. "I don't."

A thousand thoughts fly through my head, gazing into Cole's blue eyes. I'm ready to take things to the next level with him, and I know he is definitely ready, but it still doesn't stop nerves from making me hesitate. This would be the second time I've ever had sex, but the first time I'd be doing it with someone I love. Someone who loves me.

"Me either," I finally say. "I want this."

He responds with a kiss, gently rolling me over onto my back so he can peer down at me. He trails his fingers over the curves of my waist and my stomach, and I suck in my bottom lip between my teeth. Slowly, he takes off my pajama shorts and gazes at me for a long moment in the dim lighting. Desire lights his blue eyes, and he kisses me again.

He breathes into my hair, propping up on his elbow, half lying on me so our bare skin touches. "I love you," he says again for the third time tonight. "You're perfect, you know."

I smile without a word. Instead, I lose myself in all that Cole is, in all that we are together.

Bright sunshine streams in through my curtains, setting my room aglow in hazy light. A heavy arm rests on my waist, and Cole softly breathes against my neck. His warm skin presses against mine, and if I don't move, I can feel his heartbeat against my back.

My phone buzzes on my nightstand, and I reach over and grab it. Cole remains asleep against me, so I stay on my side and read the string of text messages from Violet. I swear that girl never sleeps, though it's already past ten.

Violet: I'm famous.

Violet: Did you see?

Violet: People think I'm dating a legend.

Violet: I'm going to be Cole's step-mom hahaha.

Violet: Andrew thinks it's hilarious.

Violet: Wake your ass up, Sage!

My eyes widen as I open a link she attached with a photo from the other day. Someone snuck a picture of us when we were at dinner with Beau. It's a terrible picture due to the low lighting at Frank's Oasis, but it sort of looks like Violet is Beau's date. The caption calls her a mystery woman, but it acknowledges both me and Cole.

Violet: I could be your mom-in-law one day.

I sigh at her text message. Only Violet would get a kick out of this. Beau's thirty years older than her, and here she is excited that she wound up in the press instead of grossed out that people assume that she's with a man our dads' ages.

Me: Gross, Violet. You just had to ruin my good morning.

Violet: When you see Cole, tell him he better start being nicer to me.

Me: He's here.

Violet: What!

The only reason I tell her over a text message is to get her to shut up. The last thing I need is for her to take things too far and text Cole herself. She'd do something like that, and I'm pretty sure Cole might not find it as funny as she does. I really want them to get along today so they can go to the show together, because I could use the moral support.

Me: He said he loved me.

Violet: OMG! I knew it! Did you sleep together?

Me: Violet...

Violet: Yes! How was it?

Me: Amazing. :)

Cole's hand slides up my side. He leans closer, kissing my bare shoulder. I set my phone down and roll over to face him. He smiles at me, his blue eyes bright in the morning light, and he wraps his arms around me to squeeze me against him.

"How long have you been up?" he asks into my hair.

I snuggle into him. "Only a few minutes. Violet woke me up."

"What now?"

"It's just Violet being Violet. If you thought I was obsessive, you have no idea."

"Why do I have a bad feeling?" Cole studies me for a second. I can tell he wants me to just tell him what is going on with Violet, but I really don't want to ruin our morning.

"It has nothing to do with us," I say, hoping he'll give up.

Narrowing his eyes, he fake glares at me. "Then why won't you tell me?"

I sigh. "It's not a big deal."

"Sage..."

I breathe into the crook of his neck. "Someone snuck a picture of us at dinner with your dad and assumed Violet was his new girlfriend."

He groans. "I bet she's loving this."

I laugh. "Prepare yourself for the step-mom jokes today."

"Okay, she's uninvited to your show."

Pulling back, I stare into his eyes with a pout on my lips. "But I need both of your support."

He kisses the pout right off my face until I smile again. "Fine, but I'm going to clear the record."

"She'll be heartbroken," I say.

He chuckles. "I'm sure she'll recover."

An hour later, I'm dressed and ready to go. Cole sits on my bed with my laptop on his legs, and he glances up from the screen to take me in. My hair hangs loosely down my back, and I'm wearing plain yoga pants, a white tank top, and sneakers. Shane said to come dressed comfortable, since a lot of the rehearsal will just be me hanging around and doing whatever it is the choreographer and Lele want.

"You ready to go?" Cole asks from my bed.

I puff air through my lips. "I guess so. I wish I weren't so nervous."

He slides from his spot and closes the distance between us. "You'll be amazing. If you weren't, I doubt Lele would've ever taken notice of you."

"I hope I don't let her down," I say. "I want this more than anything. I hope this will convince my parents that I'm meant for this."

"That's why you'll do great, because you want this for you," he says.

Ten minutes to one, Cole pulls into the parking lot of an old, red brick building on Hollywood Boulevard. It's only a few blocks from Glitter-Bomb, the club he took me to before, and I'm pretty sure this place is usually used as a nightclub, but Lele must've rented it out for the night.

A security guard sits on a stool near a propped open back door. I swipe my bag with my spare pair of heels I'll use to practice in off the floor of the car. Leaning over, Cole kisses my cheek before I turn to face him and kiss his lips.

"Look for me in the front row," he says, kissing me once more.

I exit the car and head toward the security guard. He checks me off his list, and I head inside the bustling room. People run around with headsets and clipboards while a few people work on the décor around the stage. The opaque glass of the runway changes colors as a few people walk across it, sensing their weight. Each footstep leaves behind a starburst for a few seconds. A man in all black pulls cloth covers over metal chairs, and huge pieces of fabric are strung across the walls, turning everything black so that the main focus is the runway.

"Sage?" a masculine voice calls out. "Over here."

I turn my gaze away from the runway and to Shane, who stands in front of hanging black fabric in front of the stage. He slides his arm over my shoulder and guides me from the hectic room behind the curtain where two dozen models, both male and female, hang out on a few couches and chairs. I recognize quite a few, and my mouth nearly drops open when I see Eva Devereaux and Penelope Plessen. They're the biggest names in the room, and I can't believe I'm going to be sharing a runway with them. The thought excites me all while making me queasy.

I take a seat on the end of a couch next to a guy with a shaved head and cheekbones I envy. He smiles at me before introducing himself as Delano. My attention is quickly drawn away when Lele claps her hands, smiling at the group of us.

"Thank you all for being here to debut my fall/winter line," Lele says, dancing in her spot from her own excitement. A few more people join the rest of the group, and a woman with a pixie cut, wearing athletic wear, strolls up beside Lele, putting her arm around the designer's shoulders. "Some of you know Betty Francis, but for those of you who don't, Betty has been the choreographer for all my shows over the last five years. What she says, goes, so please listen and pay attention. She'll make sure everything goes perfectly, and that you all will look stunning, debuting my upcoming line."

Betty nods her head. "Tonight's show's going to be a breeze. I know all you beautiful people will do us proud."

After saying that, Betty goes over her list and introduces herself to each of us individually. We're split off into groups by Lele, who works with Betty in making sure their pre-planned arrangements work while adjusting things accordingly.

"I haven't seen you at one of Lele's shows before," a feminine voice says, coming up to my side. "You look nervous.

Don't be. Lele could feature a toddler line and have the whole thing run smoothly."

I shift my focus from watching Lele and Betty talking to a group of guys for the men's line to the girl next to me. Shante Graham has graced the covers of a dozen magazines, including *Sparkle*, one of the world's top fashion magazines.

"I'm that obvious? This is my first show," I say.

Shante raises her eyebrows. "You must have an amazing agent. It took me a year to even get on the runway of someone like Lele."

"I don't," I say. "I actually met Lele at her birthday. She asked me to audition for her since someone dropped out, and now here I am." I kind of wish I had made up a story, because what if Shante thinks I'm undeserving to be here? I am technically someone Lele basically pulled off the street.

"She must see something special in you." She points to a girl with bright red hair. "Destiny's career started like that. Lele loves discovering people herself. I'm Shante, by the way."

I almost tell her that I know exactly who she is but manage to keep myself together and say, "Sage."

Before we can continue our conversation, Betty interrupts us with a wave of her hand. "Sage, Shante, you two will be pairing up with Delano and Sam accordingly for the couples' walk."

Delano grins at me, coming up next to me. "Hey, again."

"Sage, may I have a quick word," Lele says from next to me before I have a chance to greet Delano again.

I offer Delano a quick smirk and let Lele pull me away. She

takes me in, looking me up and down, and then nods to herself like she's having an internal conversation.

"Betty made a few suggestions to adjust the choreography we had worked on, but I wanted to run it by you first as a courtesy. You were originally supposed to be limited to the couples' walk due to your inexperience, but I've decided to split up one of the couples' lines, so you'll be doing a solo. Are you okay with that?"

"Yeah, of course," I say. It's not like I was going to tell Lele Rose no anyway.

"Perfect."

Lele flutters away, leaving me with Delano and Betty as she goes over the choreography. Thankfully, it's a lot less scary than I imagined, and everything is set down to the second. All I have to do is make sure I don't fall, only smile at the end of the runway at Delano, and keep my pacing to the music that Betty turns on to practice to.

It takes more than two hours to get everyone situated, and I spend most of the time just listening and watching everyone. Shante gives me a few tips while we wait, and I manage to take a ton of photos for Violet.

Sitting back on one of the couches, I pick at a salad that was catered. Delano sits next to me, chatting about a shoot he did in Paris for a Tilly Pop men's fragrance, and my phone buzzes from my pocket.

Violet: OMG, Sage. You're with Delano Crews?
Me: How'd you know?

Violet: Saw it online. He posted a pic. You guys are so cute.

Me: Thanks, but don't tell me any more. I'm so nervous.

Violet: You're hot.

"Sage, they're ready for you in hair and makeup," Shane says, offering his hand out to me to help me from the couch.

"See you backstage," Delano calls from behind me.

I smile and wave over my shoulder. The moment I sit in front of the makeup table, the lights shining in my eyes, everything sinks in. This is really happening.

And I couldn't be happier.

chapter 16

"FIVE MINUTES!" SHANE calls out.

Music hums through the air, loud enough that it's hard to even hear myself think. Standing in front of the wall mirror, I gaze at my reflection as one of Lele's team members snaps the final button on my mid-calf wedged boots. Burgundy, plum, and lilac patterned tights stand out compared to the steel gray mini dress that flows around my thighs. A faux fur vest drapes over my shoulders, and my now lavender hair hangs stick straight down my back with a part in the middle. I haven't worn my hair parted like this since I was a kid, and it's hard to get used to it. Glittering rhinestones cover my eyebrows and bold plum lipstick pops compared to my overly highlighted face.

I'd never go out like this in public, but this is a show, and

I'm here to embody Lele's vision. With how big she's smiling, preparing to make her grand entrance to welcome her guests, I'm sure she's satisfied with the outcome of her dolls.

Betty motions me over to the line of models the moment one of the assistants does a final wardrobe check, and I take my place next to Delano. He's wearing pants of the same color as my dress, but his shirt matches my tights and instead of a vest, he's wearing some weird furry scarf. His eyebrows have also been covered with rhinestones, making his serious face appear a lot more expressive.

He smiles when he sees me. "Damn, baby girl. Now this is what I'm talking about." He waves at one of the assistants. "Hey, Georgie, take a pic of us, would you?"

The assistant pulls her cell phone from her pocket and holds it up. "No smiling," she says, snapping a few.

Delano wags his eyebrows when she's through. "I'll text those to you later," he says.

I consider asking him not to post them, but I don't want to be that girl, the one who wants to approve every little thing. Delano is super sweet and friendly, and I know he's doing it out of excitement. Being photographed is his life. Maybe it'll be mine, too. It's just hard to shake the nerves.

The sound of Lele's voice erupts through the air, coming in from the stage, and I bounce in place, rolling my shoulders to push away the remaining jitters. The first fall line is a solo walk with Eva Devereaux leading the way. Once the women's line is featured, then will come the men's, and then the couples. I'll have two more wardrobe changes and then I'll be done. It's crazy to think about how much time goes into my look for less than a minute on stage each time.

"Don't let me fall," I say to Delano next to me. He's supposed to walk me down the runway with his arm first draped over my shoulder and then we break apart to have me walk in front of him on the way back.

He slides his arm over my shoulders. "Don't think about falling, and if you do, you just get back up and pretend it didn't happen."

That's easy enough for him to say. He's not the one who'll flash the audience his underwear on the way down.

"He's right, Sage," Shante says from behind me. "It happens, but the worst thing you can do is let it stop you."

Now that they've both put falling in my head, I'm pretty sure I'm going to. My knees shake with every step, and my ankles aren't doing any better even though I've walked in higher shoes than the boots I'm wearing.

"Go," Betty says to the two models in front of us. I think their names were Kiera and Giovanni.

Delano guides me forward. My heart thuds against the thin fabric of my dress, and I take a deep breath, straightening my back and shoulders. *Think good thoughts. Think good thoughts. Think good thoughts.*

"Go," Betty says, motioning to me and Delano.

Wrapping my arm around Delano's waist, I stride toward the entrance to the runway. The blaring music intensifies, and lights nearly blind me when we step out onto the glowing platform. I couldn't see the audience if I wanted to because the room is so dark apart from the stage lights sparking like a starburst with every step I take and the spotlights overhead.

As instructed, I hold a serious expression, strutting down the catwalk like I'm the coolest person in the world, though I don't actually feel cool. All I feel is terrified that I'll stumble on an imaginary crack. It doesn't stop me, though. My confidence boosts with every step I take.

At the end of the runway, Delano releases me. I place my hand on my hip like Betty wanted and smile at Delano as he removes his scarf to hang it on one of his shoulders. I count to five, turn once, and then head back in the direction I came.

The second I'm backstage, an assistant starts undressing me before I have a chance to let my first walk on the runway sink in. It all happened so fast that it almost feels like it didn't happen at all. I'm handed a bottle of water, and I take a sip even though I'm not thirsty.

Lele flutters around, checking wardrobes and making sure everything is coming together how she imagined. I'm helped into a high-waisted mini-skirt in a deep purple color that complements the lavender of my hair. A lacy, V-neck top with a bodice decorated in matte gray sequins, shiny black tights, and chunky ankle boots complete the outfit. The assistant adds a rope necklace that swings between my breasts, and the cold metal sends goosebumps over my skin. The hair and makeup team swap my plum lips for a silver gloss, and I'm directed back to the line where I meet with Delano again.

He looks much more casual with dark purple jeans, a gray shirt and dark gray suede jacket, though his rhinestone eyebrows still match mine. A few minutes later, we're off again. This time, Delano strolls ahead of me where he spins and smiles as I catch up to him. I spin once, gliding next to him, and then he presses his hand into my lower back, and we walk back up the runway together.

"You're a natural, Sage," Lele says, smiling as she takes me in. "I'm never wrong about these things, you know."

"Thank you," I say. Her team is already at work undressing me. I'd normally be embarrassed by getting almost naked in front of strangers, but everyone's been so professional and quick, that I never have the chance to really think about it. This is work for everyone, and now including me.

Lele tilts her head sideways, gazing at me. I step into a pair of skinny dark washed jeans that are rolled up just above my ankles. A cozy, open front sweater covers the nearly sheer, long-sleeved top with a floral embroidered pattern in the same gray I've been in all night. Platform, lace-up heels give me a good five inches of height, and I stand as still as possible as the hair-stylist pulls my long tresses back into a severe ponytail that gives me a slight headache. The makeup artist touches up my makeup once more, and I'm ushered back into place.

Lele follows me, staring at me with intense eyes. Rubbing her hands together, she peers at my shoes and works her way up my jeans and to my jacket. I get nervous under the weight of her inspection, and I half expect for her to pull me from my solo walk.

The line toward the catwalk shortens, and only two girls remain ahead of me.

"Go," Betty says to the first model.

"Lose the sweater," Lele finally says.

I don't even have a chance to respond when one of the stylists pulls the jacket off me.

"Go," Betty says to the next model.

I glance down, the lights overhead shining on me, and my heart sinks into my stomach, threatening to splatter on the floor. In the dressing area, the top looked great, especially with the sweater. But now, as the stage lights shine down on me, I realize that the top's more see-through than I thought. The moment I get on that stage, everyone will see my boobs, and there's nothing I can do about it.

"Go," Betty says, motioning to me.

I hesitate.

"Go!" Betty says, waving me forward.

Swallowing my nerves, I steel myself and strut forward onto the runway. Bright lights shine in my eyes, and I keep my chin raised, not looking around the dark perimeter. Heat burns in my chest and crawls up my neck the farther I get down the runway until I'm forced to stop at the end.

Camera flashes sparkle like stars. I didn't notice them before because I was too concerned about falling. Now, they're all I can see. In this moment, I hate the lights. I wish an earthquake would suddenly erupt under my feet and cause everyone to drop their cameras onto the hard floor. I almost wish the stage would collapse and take me with it.

Turning, I strut back down the runway, forcing my legs not to run. The moment I'm off the stage and back in the dressing area, I blink unwanted tears from my eyes. I've never been more embarrassed in my life. Had I gotten a chance to psych myself up and brace myself, it might not have been so bad, but now all I can think about is an audience full of strangers probably thinking about how they could see right through my top.

And then there's Cole. How am I going to face him after having to bare myself like that? What if he's mortified? What if this changes things between us? I can't stand the thought of something like this messing everything up especially after I gave myself to him last night.

"It's Sage, right?" a feminine voice says from beside me.

I glance over, surprise peaking my brows as I come face to face with Eva Devereaux. The gorgeous model's usual strawberry blond hair has been dyed a pale blue that matches the color of her blue-gray eyes. Her thick, expressive brows lower, creating a crinkle between them.

"Oh, hey, Eva. You were amazing out there," I say, sucking in a breath so I don't sniffle.

"So were you," she says. "Lele said this was your first show, but I don't believe it."

I nod, forcing myself to smile. "It was."

"Did you love it?" she asks.

I shrug. I can't help it. "I did at first."

"What do you mean at first?" she asks.

I drop my arms, showing the sheer top I'm still wearing. "This was supposed to have a sweater, but Lele changed her mind at the last minute."

Eva glances at my top, head tilted. "What's wrong with it? You look stunning. I might have to convince Lele to give it to me."

"You could see underneath it in the lights," I say.

Eva's lips tilt downward. "That's what's bothering you?"

She makes it seem like it isn't a big deal. "Sort of."

She pats my arm. "Well, knock it off. You were amazing, everyone loved you and the outfits, and if someone cares that you wore a sheer top on the runway, then they have a lot bigger problems in their life because they obviously have nothing better to do than worry about things that don't concern them."

Her words sink in, making me smile. "I guess you're right."

"I *know* I'm right. I've been doing this since I was your age. You learn a thing or two about people. And you know what? The only thing that matters is how you feel about yourself." Eva pulls me along with her back toward the stage. "Now, come on. We have the final walk, and then we can get out of here. You're coming to the after party, right?"

"The after party?" I ask.

"Yeah, it's at my favorite rooftop club downtown. You have to come."

"Okay," I say.

"Great! Now, show the world what you got."

The lobby of the McGregor Tower buzzes with life. Eva and a small group of the models from the show enter the elevator that'll take them up to the rooftop bar. I didn't want to keep Cole and Violet waiting, so I told them to meet here an hour after the show ended to give me time to get ready. Riding in the limo with Eva, Shante, Delano, and a few others was seriously a party in itself. We toasted our success with champagne, and now that I've recovered from my embarrassment, I'm really enjoying myself. I haven't even checked to see what people are saying online. I don't want to ruin the amazing feeling that's taken hold of me.

"Sage!" Violet yells, yanking Cole by the arm to make him keep up with her. "Oh, my God!"

I hold up my hand. "Say one word about my boobs, and you'll be waiting in the car."

She laughs, rolling her eyes. "Hey! I was so not going to mention how brave you were. But I was going to say that you were amazing. I'm so proud of you."

Cole slides his arm around my waist, kissing my cheek. "She's right, Sage. You looked incredibly sexy even with the weird eyebrow bling."

I laugh. "Thanks. It was a lot of fun. I can't wait to introduce you to the other models."

Linking my fingers with Cole's, I pull him toward the elevator. Violet waltzes on the other side of me, her phone glued to her hand, and she takes a few pictures of the three of us in the blurry, dark metal walls of the elevator.

Colorful lights and music greet us when we exit the elevator. People dance on a small dance floor in the middle of the rooftop bar. Small standing tables with a few barstools line the perimeter, and along the far side is a long bench that a couple sits on, looking at the surrounding city. It's a better view of the city lights being immersed within them where Los Angeles sprawls all around us like it goes on for infinity.

"Look," Violet whispers. "It's Hugo Gutierrez and Elijah Rousseau. I wonder where their girlfriends are. I saw Alexandra and Nora at the fashion show. They sat a few seats over from me. I even snuck a selfie." She holds up her phone and swipes through until she shows me a picture of her head with Elijah and Nora cuddling up behind her.

"She almost lost her phone to security for that one," Cole says, smirking.

"It would've been worth it," Violet says.

"Sage!" A feminine voice yells from near the bar. Eva twirls her hand, motioning for me to go over to her. Both Cole and Violet follow me, and Eva gives me two air kisses, one on each cheek. She already smells like alcohol and smiles widely. "Are you really dating Beau Bradford's son?" she asks, swaying as she tries to half hug Cole.

"You were stunning tonight, Eva," Cole says, laughing while righting the model.

She tilts her head toward the sky and grins. "Everyone was

gorgeous. Perfect." Her attention turns to Violet. "Are you a friend of Sage's?"

"This is Violet," I say, introducing the two. "She's a huge fan."

"I love that!" She pulls Violet into a hug, causing my best friend to beam a smile brighter than the sun.

"Eva," a feminine voice says from behind us. "You were stunning tonight as always."

"Jen!" Eva squeals. "You made it! And you brought Nora! This makes me so happy."

A woman with light brown hair smiles as the model hugs her. I recognize the girl next to her from one of Violet's many celebrity crushes fan pages that we both follow. Nora Novak is the girlfriend of Elijah Rousseau, who's on the show *Creatures of Slaughter Creek*.

"Of course I did. I'd never miss one of your parties, Eva," Jen says, pulling back from the model. She turns her attention to me and offers her hand. "You must be Sage Meadows. I'm Jen Novak. You were incredible tonight. Lele Rose called me up yesterday with a million wonderful things to say about you. I work for a lot of her talent and would be happy to meet with you sometime if you're interested." Without missing a beat, she pulls a business card from her clutch and hands it to me.

I stare at it for a moment. Lele had mentioned something about wanting to negotiate a contract with me. I didn't realize it'd be so soon. I'm so awestruck that it takes me a moment to smile and acknowledge Jen. "I'd love to. I'll definitely give you a call."

Eva heaves a sigh. "Enough business! We're here to have some fun!"

Jen looks at her niece. "But not too much fun. If it starts getting out of control like last time, I want you and Elijah to leave, okay?"

Eva flutters off, greeting her other guests with Jen trailing behind her. Violet bounces on her feet, squealing like we've just had the most fun ever. Cole takes the business card from my hand and tucks it into his pocket since I'm without a pocket or bag.

"There you are, Nora."

Violet nearly spits out the champagne she took right off the bar when none other than Elijah Rousseau comes up behind Nora and wraps his hands around her waist. I reach out and grab Violet's hand before she can even consider tackling them for a selfie where she's not a total creep.

"Hey, Cole. I was surprised to see you at the show tonight," Elijah says, turning to my boyfriend.

Violet's hand flies to her mouth. "Cole, you didn't say you knew Elijah!"

I bump Violet with my shoulder. "Reel it in or we're leaving."

She glares at me.

Nora laughs. "It's totally okay. If you ever met my best friend, you'd realize that Eli's used to this kind of thing." She turns to her boyfriend. "Sage was a model tonight and is a potential client of Aunt Jen's."

Elijah nods his head. "It was a great show. Lele Rose has a wild imagination, huh?"

"It was a lot of fun," I say.

Elijah and Nora excuse themselves, and Violet wanders off to check out who is here. The DJ puts on a song by Ariel, and Cole guides me toward the dance floor. The music takes me away, and I dance in Cole's arms amid a crowd of the most beautiful people I've ever seen. Cameras flash and people clink glasses. I'm dizzy on excitement and champagne but in a good way.

After a few songs, Cole pulls me away from the throng of dancing people and toward the glass wall protecting us from the wind and from falling over the ledge. City lights sparkle in Cole's eyes and he kisses me under the nearly full moon.

"Sage!" Violet calls, waving her phone toward me. "Sage!"

Cole shakes his head. "Not tonight, Violet. We're here to have fun, remember?"

Violet glares daggers at Cole. "Well, then you can be the one to answer the phone. It's Julie. She texted me twice."

"Let it go to voicemail," I say after a moment of watching Mom's name flash on Violet's phone. The last thing I need to explain is that we're at some rooftop party celebrating my fall into fame.

When it goes to voicemail, I quickly send a text telling Mom we're at a movie and I'll call her later.

She replies a second later.

Mom: Okay, you girls have fun. XOXO

Me: Call you tomorrow. Love you!

Mom: Dad loves you, too.

Violet pushes her turquoise hair from her face and smiles at me. She holds up another glass of champagne. "Here's to my best friend in the whole world and what could possibly be her last night of freedom."

I laugh, stealing the glass from her to take a sip. "Here's to us."

Cole kisses my temple. "To us."

chapter 17

BALMY AIR LIFTS tendrils of my still lavender hair from my neck. The hot sun beats down, warming my skin. The scent of a charcoal grill mingles with the tropical fruitiness of the pineapple, coconut, and mango chunks that sit on a plate on the table next to my lounge chair.

A loud splash draws my attention away from my phone, and cool water peppers my legs. Cole swims a lap in his rectangular pool that's twice the size of mine. The strums of a guitar fill the air with familiar music as Beau plays one of his older songs.

I haven't been home in two days since the show, and Beau hasn't even mentioned it once. He's more laid back than my parents. They'd freak out had they known I was spending the night with Cole alone in his wing. We're basically alone in the gigantic estate since Beau's suite is on the opposite end of the U-shaped mansion. From my spot on the loungers, I can see at least seven rooms on the second story. I've never asked how big the place was, though. I haven't even been farther than the kitchen.

"Big brother!" a woman calls, startling me. Beau sets his guitar down to greet the woman.

Cole hops from the pool, sopping wet, and rushes her despite her yells to stay back because she doesn't want to get wet. No one has to introduce me for me to know that the woman is Cole's Aunt Michelle, who I nearly ran into the first time I slept over.

She bats Cole away with her purse, her perfect smile spreading across her face. Light brown strands of hair hang around her face, purposely pulled from her topknot, and she looks like she's in her mid-twenties. She's either had a lot of work done or has a big age gap like my aunt and mom do. I can never tell with people in Hollywood.

Swinging my legs over the lounge chair, I slide into my flip flops and pull my bathing suit cover on to introduce myself.

"Where's Christy?" Michelle asks. "I didn't see her when I passed by her room."

"Vacation until tomorrow when I head back out," Beau says, talking about Cole's live-in housekeeper I still haven't met yet.

The woman pouts. "I wish I had gotten a flight sooner. It seems we're always just passing by each other these days."

Beau slides his arm over his sister's shoulder. "We'll plan something as soon as my tour is over."

"You better."

Cole spots me strolling in their direction and rushes to drape his dripping arm across my shoulders. "Aunt Michelle, this is Sage."

I half expect her to comment on my speedy exit the only time I've seen her, but instead, she surprises me with a hug, putting her arms around both me and Cole.

She pulls away, her eyes crinkling in the corners as she grins and says, "Your hair is different than in all the pictures Cole always sends me. I like the lavender. It's pretty."

"You can thank Lele for that," Cole says. "Sage walked in her fall/winter line debut."

"Oh, Cole didn't say you were a model," she says.

"I'm not. Well, not really. I'd like to be," I say.

"With the way Lele was talking, I think you'll be signed with her by the end of the week if she has her way," Beau comments. "But don't let her pressure you."

Beau excuses himself, pulling his sister away to show her a few things he picked up for her on tour. Cole turns to me and slides his hands around my neck, hugging me against his damp body. His heartbeat pounds against mine; the only thing separating us is the thin fabric of my cover-up. Leaning closer, I brush my lips against his, kissing him softly while sliding my arms up the muscles in his stomach and chest before trailing them to rest on his back.

He moans quietly into my mouth, caressing his tongue against mine, and slowly nudges me away from the door his dad and aunt left through. Cole's hands slide through my hair and to my lower back, and then he moves them lower until he picks me up off my feet, and I wrap my legs around him, letting him carry me toward the entrance to the stairs nearest his suite.

"They'll be busy for a while," he whispers through kisses. "Won't even know we're gone."

I nod, running my fingers through his messy, wet hair. My back presses into the door as he opens it, and he only sets me back on my feet so I can climb the stairs on my own. The second he closes the door to his suite, he picks me back up and carries me across the room and to his bedroom.

Gently setting me on the bed, Cole gazes down at me. His chest rises and falls, his intense blue eyes taking in the fallen straps of my cover-up. It doesn't take long for him to help me from it, and he eases himself onto me, kissing my lips before trailing them to my jaw and down my neck. His fingers tug at the bow tying my bikini top together, and I release a breath when it loosens.

"I love you," he whispers, pulling the strings around my back free.

I smile into his mouth, pressing my head into his pillow that smells of his citrus shampoo. "I love you, too."

Cole's hands travel down my sides to my bikini bottoms, and his fingers play with the hooks on my hips. My cell phone rings from somewhere in the room, making him freeze, and I sigh.

"Cole, wait," I whisper, sitting up, holding my bikini top on. "That's my mom's ring. I have to get it."

"Let it go to voicemail," he says, trailing his cool fingers up my arm and into my hair.

I consider it for a second but then give him a quick kiss before scooting to the edge of the bed to gaze around the room. My phone sits in the middle of the floor, where it must've fallen out of the front pocket of my cover-up when Cole was carrying me.

I scoop it up and let my bikini top fall to the floor with my back to Cole. He makes a noise deep in his throat, and I smile at him from over my shoulder, motioning for him to stay where he is on the bed.

"Hey, Mom. What's up?"

"Dad and I decided to catch an early flight to surprise you," she says.

I frown. "But I'm not at home."

"I know. That's why I'm calling. Where are you?"

I glance at Cole, wishing I had just ignored the phone like he asked. "At Cole's," I finally say. "Violet ditched me to spend the day with her boyfriend. But don't worry, Cole's dad is here. So is his aunt. We're just swimming."

"Oh," Mom says. I can't tell what she's thinking without seeing her, but since she didn't already start yelling, I'm just going to assume that she's not completely mad. "Well, I managed to snag a few tickets aboard the Sunset Siren tonight for dinner and fireworks on the water. I bet I could get a few more. You should invite Cole and his family. I'd love to meet his father."

I grimace. "I don't know."

Cole's chest presses into my back, and before I have a chance to stop him, he snatches my phone away. Pressing it to his ear, he says, "Hi Julie. I hope you had a good trip." He listens for a moment, and I can hear Mom inviting him on an adventure I'd rather neither of us participate in. "That sounds great. My dad would love to meet you and Isaac as well. We'll see you at five then."

He hangs up my phone without letting me say goodbye to my mom.

I shake my head at him. "I was trying to get us out of that."

He shrugs. "And I'm trying to impress your parents."

"They don't need to be impressed," I say.

He laughs. "Oh, they might. Now, come on. This might be the last time I get you alone for a while."

I scrunch my nose, smiling at him. "I love you, you know."

"And I love you."

Violet: I can't believe you abandoned me for family yacht night. It's the Fourth of July!

Me: Thought you were partying with Ariel?

Violet: I am, but you're on a yacht!

Me: You get seasick.

Violet: So what? Famous people on a yacht. You're

ditching me for stardom, huh?

Me: Totally. This is what you get for ditching me all the time.

Violet: :(I miss you.

Me: Liar. And you know I'd trade you places right now. Mom is talking about music with Beau.

Violet: Abandon ship!

Me: I tried, but they left port!

Violet: I love and hate you.

Me: Have fun tonight!

Violet: Don't jump overboard.

Me: Don't do anything I wouldn't do.

Violet: I guess the options are endless.

I roll my eyes and slide my phone back into the pocket of Cole's jacket that I'm wearing. The sun sinks into the horizon, casting a golden glow over the blue-green water. We're far enough from shore that all the beachgoers nearly blend in with the sand and houses lining the beach. We left the harbor at Newport Beach a little after five, and now we're just drifting along the coast until we dock again around eleven tonight.

"You look like you're considering jumping ship." Cole comes up next to me and grips the railing to gaze at the endless ocean.

"I might. Have they gotten into the embarrassing stories yet?" I ask, leaning my head on Cole's shoulder.

The blazing sunset makes his blue eyes almost golden in the light. "Like the time you fainted on stage during your freshman year choir performance?"

I cringe. "They told you that?"

He laughs. "Is that why you don't sing?"

Shaking my head, I let my hair fall into my face. "Nope, that's why I passed out. There was a mix-up on my class schedule that forced me into a semester of choir. I hated it. Fainting actually saved me from even worse embarrassment. I can't stay in tune to save my life."

He slides his arm around me. "I bet you're exaggerating."

Heat claws its way up my neck. I almost expect him to ask me to sing to him, and there's no way that'll ever happen. I'd rather dive into shark infested water. "You'll never find out."

He smirks. "Maybe in fifty years."

I suck my bottom lip between my teeth. I haven't thought past tomorrow let alone fifty years from now, and to think that he's including me in his life in fifty years sends my heart racing. The yacht rises on a small swell, sending my stomach into my throat, and I release a small yelp. Cole pulls me away from the railing, linking his fingers through mine, and we sit together along the bench seating on the bow of the boat.

"There you two are," Mom says, stopping in front of us. "They're serving dinner in the saloon if you are hungry. It's a buffet."

Cole stands, pulling me to my feet. Before we can walk away, Mom grabs my arm, stopping me in place. She looks between me and Cole for a second.

"Can I talk to you for a minute, Sage," she says.

"I'll meet you inside, Cole," I say, wishing that I could just ignore my mom and follow Cole inside.

Mom moves back to the seat and pats the spot next to her. Her serious expression sends knots through my stomach. She looks like she has a lot on her mind, and it doesn't seem all that great if she's decided to interrupt me and Cole on a party yacht to talk with me alone.

"I was kind of surprised that you were with Cole today," she says, staring off into the darkening sky. Lights already decorate the beach in front of us. "When we left, I was sure you stopped seeing him for one reason or another."

I look at my hands. "I told you I was sick."

"You know, I can tell when you're lying," Mom says, touching my chin so I look at her.

"Well, I don't want to talk about it," I say. "I'm over it."

Her lips tilt down in the corners. "Okay, sweetie, but there's something else I wanted to talk to you about."

I sigh. "It can't wait? You guys weren't even supposed to be home, and you hijacked my Fourth of July plans." I don't mean to sound angry, but I kind of am. I was supposed to be having fun, not trapped on a stuffy yacht with a bunch of strangers while my parents get to know my boyfriend's dad. This is like torture more than anything.

"And what plans were those?" she asks.

I turn away. "It doesn't matter."

"It does to me," Mom says. "I learned something pretty interesting from Cole's father tonight. I haven't told Dad yet, but

I think we should all sit down together first thing tomorrow."

Oh, no. I don't like the sound of this. What if Beau mentioned my participation in Lele's show, and the only reason Mom hasn't blown up is because it'd make a scene? This isn't good. I wanted to tell them myself when Lele actually offered me a contract.

My dreams of being a model are slipping through my hands before I've even had a chance.

"Mom, I can explain," I say.

She reaches out and touches my hand. "You don't have to explain, Sage. I remember what it was like to fall in love."

My brows crinkle. "Huh?"

"Beau told me that you and Cole are getting pretty serious," Mom says.

I release a long breath. "Oh, yeah. Please, don't make a huge deal out of this. And no, I don't need to be reminded about sex. You were pretty informative before Junior Prom, remember?" I'll never forget how mortified I was when Mom showed up in my room with a bunch of print-outs she had found online even though Sunset Prep requires Sex-Ed during sophomore year.

Mom tilts her head back and releases a loud laugh. "Okay, okay. I get it, but there's more to this than sex, which I hope you'll come to me with if you have any questions."

"Mom," I say. "I know that. Now what else did you want to tell me?"

She pats my hand again. "We'll talk more tomorrow. There

are going to be some rules with Cole. I just want you to be prepared and not get upset about them. I'll do my best to make sure your dad doesn't go overboard, okay?"

"Really? I'm almost eighteen."

"And until then, you're to respect our wishes for you. Dating regular boys is hard enough, but you fell in love with someone famous. I'm just looking out for you, sweetie."

I stand up and place my hands on my hips. "Is that it?"

"Sage..."

"Mom, it's fine. Whatever. We can all talk about my love life tomorrow."

Not only is this conversation far from what I expected, it's a conversation I don't really want to have. What are my parents going to do? Put me on lockdown until I turn eighteen? It'd be totally unfair.

I turn away and head across the deck to the path that'll take me directly to the stern where I can enter the saloon. I crash right into Cole, nearly knocking him into the wall of the yacht. He steadies me on my feet, smiling, and I press my open palms on his chest.

"Were you eavesdropping?" I whisper.

He shifts his gaze to the ocean. "I was worried. Thought my dad might've said something about your fashion show."

Pulling him by the arm, I lead him away before my mom comes around the corner and sees us. "No, thank God. But he told my mom we were serious."

"You'd think we were getting married tomorrow," he says.

I laugh. "Now that would get us on the front page of all the tabloids."

"And give our parents heart attacks."

Instead of heading into the saloon, we take the stairs up to the sundeck where a few people sit on lounge chairs near an empty, bubbling hot tub. A bartender mans the bar, making a few martinis for a man I recognize from Shine So Bright. He pats my shoulder as I pass, and I offer him a smile and stroll with Cole to the guardrail facing the beach.

The dark waters blend with the shore, and without the sun, the lights on the beach look like dozens of stars, some colorful, but mostly silvery white. A few bonfires light up the sand and set the tiny looking beachgoers aglow as people settle in, waiting for the fireworks show to start.

Cole pulls one of the lounge chairs from the line of them and turns it to face the beach. He lies down and motions for me to climb on with him, and I sit between his legs, resting my back against his chest. My stomach growls, but there's no way I'm going to make an appearance at the buffet. I don't think I can even look at my parents without reddening in the face just thinking about all the possible ways they can ruin my life while they think they're protecting me from the ugliness of fame.

"Want me to get us something and bring it back?" he asks, moving my hair to kiss the side of my neck.

I nod. "Would you? I really don't want to be sociable right now." I move so Cole can stand up.

He leans down and kisses me once more. "I'll be right

back."

Leaning back, I gaze up at the clear night sky. The stars shine brighter than usual without the light pollution of the city. They're pretty but not as stunning as the lights twinkling on shore.

My phone buzzes from Cole's jacket pocket, and I grab it to glance at the screen. It's another message from Violet.

Violet: Still alive?

Me: Yeah. Aren't you supposed to be having fun?

Violet: I am, but I went to post something on my Friendconn page and saw this.

A link pops up on the screen. I'm almost afraid to click it. Violet manages to find some of the best and worst things about me, and I don't know if I should even look at it now. If Cole were here, I wouldn't, but since he might take a minute to come back, I can't resist.

Taking a breath, I tap my finger on the link and wait for the website to load. It takes me to the welcome page of Teen Celebrity Heartthrob where a banner flashes across the screen with the latest gossip.

Too hot to handle? Cole Vettel spotted leaving a Lele Rose fashion show with a mystery girl after Sage Meadows, the next face of Lele Rose, bares it all on the catwalk. Is this the end of SaCole? Was Sage using Cole for a chance at stardom? Maybe she's decided to get cozy with sexy Delano Crews. Who'd blame her? We wouldn't.

After the short article, it mentions the reporter reached out to both me and Cole, but both of us have yet to respond. Except that didn't happen. If they did, they wouldn't have had this speculative article that suggests I used Cole. But that's not even the horrifying part.

Plastered across the page are pictures from the show, including a close up shot from my waist up in the sheer shirt that was supposed to be covered by the sweater Lele decided to ditch at the last second. Thankfully, they don't show my actual boobs, but the tiny black stars get their point across.

I scroll down to the comments and start reading.

Anonymous45: New face of Lele Rose? Yuck.

Bluebirdabc: Shows boobs. Now famous. Slut.

GiaM: Terrible article! Get your facts straight. Cole posted a pic of Sage from after the show.

BoyBond008: Too skanky for both those sexy guys!

HalpoDi: Delano wouldn't ever touch that hoe. He's mine.

Leaning forward, I cover my face with my hands, taking deep breaths to stop myself from crying. I need to let this roll off my back. If Mom ever found out that I'm hurt over what strangers say online, she'd definitely figure out a way to lock me away in my bedroom forever.

"Sage?" Cole's voice wraps around me before his arm does. "You okay?"

I shake my head. "Violet sent me something she found online."

"I thought you were going to stop letting the haters get to you?" he asks, pulling my hands from my face so he can look at me. He puts a plate of food on a table next to us.

"That's easy for you to say. They're not calling you a slut, hoe, or skank," I say. "They're saying I used you to get famous."

His face turns hard as my words sink in. "Let me see it," he says.

With the way he looks like he's about to throw my phone in the ocean, I hesitate for a second before handing it to him. Cole reads the short article speculating our non-existent breakup and closes his eyes for a second when I point out the nasty comments.

"I'm sorry, Sage," he says quietly. "You know none of that is true, right? You're going to be famous by your own doing. I'm not taking any credit for that. You impressed Lele on your own. You were amazing on that runway on your own. And now, you're going to shine brighter than everyone all on your own."

Wrapping both arms around me, Cole squeezes me against him, letting me bury my face into his shirt. He just holds me for a long while, playing with my hair while I compose myself enough to talk without my voice shaking.

"I'm just so tired of pretending all this stuff isn't being said about me, you know?" I say. "I don't want people to just keep assuming they know me."

"Would it make you feel better if I posted something to-night to stop the rumors the best I can and then we can think of something tomorrow?" he asks.

I nod. "I guess so."

Cole turns the flashlight on my phone to give us enough light to take a picture together for him to post. From over his shoulder, I watch him write a few lines.

Happy Fourth to everyone! I've spent the day with my beautiful, amazing girlfriend, Sage, and now we're about to watch some fireworks off the coast of Newport Beach. We both hope you all have an amazing day. He attaches the picture he just took and then closes his phone.

A minute later, a loud screech echoes through the air before a firework explodes overhead in a cascade of sparkling red and purple. Cole's face lights up with the next firework, and he leans in and kisses me softly before pulling me against him to lie back in the lounge.

He picks the plate of food from the table next to us, and I balance it on my lap. We share the plate of chicken and veggies while watching the fireworks, and I wish I could stay in this moment forever without having to worry about what happens tomorrow.

Because I know something's going to happen.

I can feel it in my bones.

My life's about to change by my doing because I'm not keeping quiet anymore. My parents can try all they want to protect me from the world, but I don't want their protection. I want to stand up for myself. I want the world to know who I really am.

I want them to know the real me.

chapter 18

A Good Headline

Kerry Kerr: Ew, Cole. What do you see in her? You could have me.

Penny Frank: Watch, she'll cheat on him with Delano. Who could resist Mr. Gorgeous? Not me.

Deidre Womack: Bet she'll be with Daddy Beau next.

Monika Wells: Bunch of idiots on here. Love you Sage and Cole! #relationshipgoals

Bruce Hey: More body. Less face. Purple hair gotta go.

Yesenia Lopez: I want her to die. Cole's mine!

William Smith: I'll take your leftovers, Cole man.

Scott Verhaegan: Sage is very beautiful. You're a lucky guy.

Trina Gibson: LOL! All the haters are so jealous, like you even have a chance with Cole. Lame asses! You don't even know them.

Sally Denver: I hope she falls off the next runway and breaks her neck.

Sighing, I shut my laptop and get out of bed. If I continue to read through the comments from the photo Cole posted last night, I might decide to hide under my covers for the rest of the day. I keep hoping that the good comments will start outweighing the bad ones, but they're getting worse and worse. How can people want me dead for just existing? It's absolutely insane. If I wasn't afraid of getting attacked online, I'd reply. Instead, I've decided to go a different route.

I've created an official page to share the part of me people don't see in the tabloids or even when Cole or someone like Delano or Ariel shares a photo of me. I've decided to give myself a voice so I'm not just Cole's girlfriend but a hopeful model and a real person. I just hope I get to keep it. My parents would flip out if they saw that I'm purposely letting strangers into my life, but they don't read all the terrible stuff about me.

My phone buzzes from my nightstand, and I expect to see Mom's number, telling me that she and Dad are on their way home from Dad's studio in Culver City. She wanted to talk to him alone without him confronting me. If he's caught in the heat of the moment, he'd just tell me I can't see Cole anymore. Don't get me wrong, Dad is usually a nice guy, but he reacts first before thinking. He's a lot stricter than Mom. We all know it.

I don't recognize the number, and I usually wouldn't answer it, but maybe it's one of the careless reporters trying to get confirmation for their speculative articles in one of the tabloids. It could be Lele or Shane, too. I don't want to miss them if they do call.

"This is Sage," I say, answering my phone.

"Hi, Sage! This is Julian Michaels calling on behalf of Jen Novak from Anderson and Novak Associates."

"Oh, hi," I say. "I'm sorry I haven't had a chance to call Jen."

"No need to apologize, Sage. Jen wanted me to follow up with you in regards to representation. Would you be available to meet with Ms. Novak sometime this week?" he asks.

"I'd love to, and I'm available whenever." I agree despite knowing that this very well might not turn into anything the moment they find out that I won't be eighteen until January. But I want to at least have stuff to bring to Mom and Dad so they can see how serious I am about all this.

"Great! Jen would love to take you out to dinner tonight or tomorrow. There's a great little Italian restaurant on the corner of Canon Drive and Brighton Way in Beverly Hills. We can send a car to pick you up."

I think about it for a moment. It'll be better if I can have something to show sooner than later. Dad might suddenly feel the need to put me on lockdown mode and move his work to the house. Mom's more predictable. I know she'll visit her office downtown, so she won't be the one I have to worry about. Dad's more available, but I know he won't sit around and do nothing, so a trip to his studio would be in order. All I know is that I have to plan for the worst.

"Tonight would be perfect," I finally say.

"Great, I'll arrange a car to pick you up at seven."

I give Julian my address and smile as I hang up my phone. It's not until then that I see a text from Mom.

Mom: Be ready in ten. Cole and Beau are picking you up, and we're all meeting for a bite near LAX to discuss things.

Ugh. *Things* just sound foreboding. My life isn't a thing. My relationship with Cole isn't a thing. Hell, it's not even a family affair. I consider texting her back what I really think about all of this, but I don't have a chance because my doorbell rings.

I fly around my room, changing out of my yoga pants and camisole and into a sleeveless, pale pink taffeta midi-dress with a scoop neck, waist belt, and black sequined flowers blossoming from vines that run from the bodice to the flared skirt. It's definitely what Violet would call a good girl dress, and that's exactly how I want to portray myself going out with Cole and his dad.

The doorbell rings again, and I slip into a pair of black strappy heels before running out of my room while braiding my long locks into a side braid that I tie off with a ponytail band from my wrist.

My phone buzzes in my hand at the same time I fling open the door to find Cole standing on my porch, his hands hidden in his pockets. The look he gives me says a million words, with the way his eyebrows lower over his blue eyes and his bottom lip pouts slightly. He's apologizing without words, and the only thing I can think to do is pout right back at him with a shrug.

Sliding my phone into a hidden pocket on my hip, I step out and lock the door behind me, sticking my house key with my phone.

"Why does this feel like we're going to be on house arrest?" I ask, staying in my spot. "Supervised visits, scheduled outings, monitored phone calls..." My voice trails off as I say what's on my mind.

He smirks at my dramatics. "It can't be that bad. And if it is? We'll figure it out. People need to sleep."

I lean into him and kiss him. "Promise you won't let this be the end of us."

"I promise," he says. "But you have to promise the same. You're the one who might possibly be trading your freedom for me. And I hate that. It's why my dad called your parents. I told him about what you thought they might do."

I grimace. "What is he planning on doing?"

He shrugs. "I don't know. Reassure them that everything is going to be fine. Let them know that we can still have a life."

I sigh. "Maybe he should just cancel and let me handle the wardens."

Cole grips my hips, keeping me close to him. "They might listen to him though. He's dealt with this kind of thing most of his life."

"They might not," I say. "And I'm about to make matters

worse anyway. Whatever he says will just get thrown out because I scheduled a meeting with that lawyer we met at Eva's after party. I'm having dinner with her tonight, and then I have to tell my parents."

He lets go of me and rubs the back of his neck. "They're going to blame me."

I shake my head. "I won't let them. You had nothing to do with it. I did this all on my own."

"They won't see it like that." He might be right, but I don't agree with him.

Instead, I say. "I'll blame Violet. They can't hate her. She's like their adopted daughter."

He chuckles. "I like that plan."

Beau honks the horn of Cole's car from my driveway, drawing our attention away from each other. Pulling apart, we slowly meander away from my house to face what lies ahead of us.

"Maybe they'll surprise us, and we'll have gotten worked up for nothing," Cole says, letting me get into the backseat.

"We can only hope."

Cole pulls into the parking lot of a Mexican and seafood restaurant that's walking distance from the Pacific Ocean in Playa Del Rey. The small building has a courtyard with open air seating, a small indoor dining area, and enough windows to gaze at the sand that leads to the water. Though I can't see the ocean, I can hear the soft hum of the waves when Cole shuts off his engine.

I spot Mom's white Lexus LS 460 parked in the front of the lot near the door. Beau opens his door first, but Cole doesn't move as he stares at me in the rearview mirror. He presses his lips together, trying to silently talk to me, and I know he's just as nervous as I am.

"You two okay?" Beau asks, leaning down to peer at us.

Cole nods his head and opens his door. "Yeah, we're all good."

I respond with a tight-lipped smile. Cole holds his hand out to me and helps me from the backseat before closing the door. The restaurant is pretty empty, with most people already sitting at their tables. I hear a few whispers, people asking if Beau is really *the* Beau Bradford, and someone is gutsy enough to wave, which Cole's dad responds to with a smile.

Mom and Dad sit at a corner table, both facing the dining room, which forces the rest of us to look out the window. I don't mind though. They probably did it that way so a bunch of people won't sneak a ton of selfies with us in the background Violet-style.

They both stand up from the table to greet us, shaking Beau's hand before we all sit down. The server comes over, beaming a smile at the five of us before taking our drink orders. Mom, Dad, and Beau all order margaritas while Cole and I just get glasses of water.

I stuff my face with a few chips when Dad looks at me like he expects me to say something, anything, like I'm already in trouble.

This whole lunch is already so awkward and no one has even said anything yet. I grip Cole's hand under the table in an attempt to stop myself from excusing myself to the bathroom but then just ditching everyone to call for a car home.

The moment the adults' margaritas hit the table, Dad takes a huge sip of his. He clears his throat and finally says, "I know this is awkward for the both of you, and I would have been mortified if my parents sat me down like this, but you have to understand where we're coming from." Dad reaches out and sets his hand on mine.

"Dad, please," I say.

He holds up his hand. "Sage, this is important to us. You know how we feel about being in the spotlight, but we get that you like Cole. And Cole, you're a nice kid and all, and we just want what we feel is best."

"Get to the point. Mom said you two were setting rules for us," I say.

Dad sighs. He glances at Mom and then to Beau before bringing his attention back to me. "We want to limit your exposure as much as possible, meaning we don't want Cole posting about you online."

I frown. "Seriously? It's not even a big deal."

"This isn't up for debate," Mom says. "When you're eighteen and out of our house, then you can do whatever you want, but until then, we want you to keep your life private. The world doesn't need to know every little detail about your lives. I'm sure Beau agrees."

My gaze flicks to Beau's, and I half expect him to reveal to my parents that I'm far beyond protecting, and that I purposefully put myself out there in a fashion show nonetheless. All Beau does is look at me. In this moment, he knows that I went behind my parents' backs, but he's not going to be the one to say anything.

"Mom, Dad," I say. "Are you going to start chaperoning my dates, too? Or am I not allowed to leave the house with Cole?" Sarcasm lines my words.

"Well," Dad says.

My mouth falls open. "You can't be serious."

"Lower your voice," Mom says.

"Julie, Isaac," Beau says. "I fully respect your wishes in regards to your daughter, and I assure you that Cole will follow your rules, but I think there's something you should know."

Oh, no. Cole's Dad is going to rat me out. I can feel it.

"Beau, please," I say, turning my attention to Cole's Dad.

He ignores me and asks, "Are you aware of your daughter's aspirations?"

"What do you mean?" Dad asks. "If you're suggesting that Sage wants to pursue a career in the industry, then no. Sage doesn't sing, and she's never wanted to act."

I groan. "This isn't about me. This is supposed to be about the stupid rules you're making up to ruin my relationship."

"Sweetie," Mom says.

I shake my head. "No. Do you even know how embarrassing this is? You said it yourself, Dad. If Grandma or Grandpa did this, you'd be mortified. And guess what? I am."

The server pops over to our table, and I release a breath at his perfect timing.

"We need just another minute," Dad says.

I stand up. "Not me." I turn to Cole and Beau. "I'm really sorry about this. It would've been better if I dealt with this alone."

"If Cole wants to see you, Sage, it's important he knows," Dad says.

Heat crawls up my neck and blossoms in my cheeks. I've had enough. People from other tables stare at us, and I see someone in the corner take a picture of me. And I lose it. While I don't scream at them, I do glare.

"Sage, sit down," Mom pleads. "Let's just forget about all this and have a nice lunch."

Cole grabs my hand, but I tug away. A million thoughts cross my mind. I know I should sit down so I don't make a scene, but I can't stand to sit here another minute knowing that my parents are being unreasonable.

"I'm going to use the restroom," I say.

"Okay, sweetie," Mom says.

Turning on my heels, I head toward the front of the restaurant in the opposite direction of the bathrooms. I should've done this before we even sat down. I wish Beau never tried to get involved. I wish I wasn't in this stupid restaurant with a dozen people staring at me in the first place.

The moment I step out of the building into the warm

summer air, I hear the click of a camera. And then another one. Word of Beau's presence must've traveled fast because a few paparazzi hover, waiting for their perfect photo opportunity.

"Sage Meadows," a man calls. "Having a nice lunch?"

"Amazing," I say, strolling from the front of the restaurant toward the street that separates us from the stretch of beach. I pull my phone from my pocket to call for a car.

The man follows me. "Where you goin'?"

"For a walk."

"Where's your boyfriend? You two seem inseparable." The man clicks his camera again. He's the only one keeping up with me, and it makes me nervous.

"He's with his dad," I answer. My phone rings from my hand, displaying Mom's picture, but I decline the call. Commotion sounds out from behind me, and I'm pretty sure it's because Beau has exited the restaurant, but I don't look back to confirm.

"You two get in a fight or somethin'? Is this over Delano Crews? You two were looking cozy in the photos from backstage at Lele Rose's show." The man jogs forward and starts walking backward in front of me. He snaps another picture.

"You don't seem like the type to be interested in other people's relationships," I say.

"I'm interested in anything that makes a good headline. Why don't you stop for a minute? This is great lighting. Give me something good to work with and a good headline, and I'll make you famous. Isn't that what you want, Sage?"

I crinkle my nose without responding. He's baiting me, expecting me to give him something that he can misconstrue.

My phone rings again from my hand. This time Cole's calling.

I answer. "Hey, what's up?"

"You left," he says.

I press my lips together. "Sorry. I'll call you later, okay? I'm being followed right now."

"What?" Cole asks.

"Yeah. It's fine. I'm fine."

"Please, come back," he says, begging with his voice.

"Is that Cole?" the paparazzo asks. "You ditched him, didn't you?"

I glare over my shoulder. "You got your pictures now leave me alone."

He stops in front of me, aiming his camera again. "It's a free sidewalk."

I roll my eyes and walk around him.

"Sage, where are you? I'll come get you," Cole says, still staying on the line.

"You need to get your dad to the airport."

"Let me talk to her," I hear my mom say from Cole's end of the line.

"I'll call you later. Promise. I love you," I say. Hanging up, I check my phone to see how long it'll take to get a ride. There's a convenience store about a block away that the driver can meet me at.

"Not even going to give me a hint why you're walking off all alone?" the paparazzo asks.

I shake my head but don't say anything.

"I still think it's about Delano. He told one of my buddies that he thought you were hot, especially in that sheer number." This man is relentless. "I bet that got under Cole's skin, how you showed the goods to the world."

I stop in place and spin to face him. "Are you kidding me? That was a job. I didn't pick out the clothes I wore."

"So, you hated them?"

I shake my head. The last thing I want is to bad talk Lele's designs, especially when she wants me to model for her in the future, but what this man is insinuating makes me uncomfortable. And I hate it. "Lele is amazing, and her designs are so much fun. But what you're saying is gross."

He raises his hand. "Sex sells, you know."

"Leave me alone," I say, picking up pace. "This is harassment."

"Tell you what. I'll leave you alone if you tell me why you ditched Cole. You don't want me to make up a story, do you?" he asks. He snaps another picture. "Maybe he went off on you. You look a little distraught."

"I said leave me alone." Fear trickles down my back when the paparazzo doesn't listen to me. Glancing at my phone, I bring up my keypad to call for help before I step into the street to cross.

A horn blares, startling me, and my heel catches between

the sidewalk and the street. Brakes squeal, the scent of burning rubber making my eyes water, and the car hits me hard enough to send me sprawling across the asphalt. The skin of my palms scrape on the ground and pain bursts on my side.

A woman rushes to my side, and a man yells out at the fleeing paparazzo. "Oh, my God. You're bleeding. Oh, my God. You just jumped into the street. I tried to stop."

I groan, the shock of everything stunning me silent.

"I'm calling for help. You're going to be okay," the woman says.

I can only nod.

"Can you tell me your name?" she asks.

I stare at the blood dripping down a cut on my arm, but I still don't answer.

"Sage!" a familiar voice calls out. Cole stares at me with wide eyes through his open window before he hops out of his car and slams the door. "What happened?"

I start crying. I can't help it.

Cole kneels next to me, trying to move me into his lap.

"Don't move her," the woman says.

"The ground's burning hot," he argues.

The moment he says it, pain radiates through me as my adrenaline dissipates. Too much goes through my mind to register what's going on. A crowd gathers, and I hear my name whispered.

Sirens ring through the air, and a man yells for people to get back. It's not until then that I realize the police have arrived.

I do the only thing I can think of. I hide my face against Cole, letting him hold me until an ambulance arrives to take me away.

chapter 19

Wildest Dreams

DESPITE HOW I'M feeling inside, Dr. Kapoor suspects most of the damage from getting hit by the car is purely external, and that I should heal with minimal scarring. Just to be safe, she admitted me into Cedars-Sinai for observation and a few tests that include X-rays.

The door to my private room swings open and in steps Violet with a handful of flowers and Andrew trailing behind her with at least a dozen balloons.

"Oh, my God, Sage. I thought Cole was joking when he said you were hit by a car." My best friend rushes to my bedside. "Where's Julie and Isaac? I bet they're freaking out."

I shift, wincing when my bandaged arm presses into the bed. "I sent them to get me something from Newman's Hillside Grill." I picked a place I knew would keep my parents away from me for at least an hour if not more. Mom wanted to stay, but I told her I just wanted to sleep. I lied. I'm sure they both knew it. But they took my phone with them and there's no way I'll make it past the nurse's station to leave even if I wanted to.

"Yikes, you must be mad at them," Violet says, pulling up a chair to sit next to me. Andrew stands by the window and gazes outside.

"You have no idea. I'm basically on house arrest. They took my phone. Promised to take away my computer, like getting hit by a car wasn't enough," I say.

"What happened anyway?" she asks, giving me her full attention.

I've already told the story a handful of times—to the cop that rode in the ambulance with me, and then to another two who came to see me with my parents after Dr. Kapoor made sure I wasn't critical. I told Cole and Beau before Cole left to take his dad to the airport when Mom said it was best if he waited to hang out with me until I was home tomorrow.

Hitting the button on the side rail, I raise the bed. "My parents went all crazy on me and Cole, basically trying to control our relationship, and it pissed me off so I ran out of the restaurant to call for a ride—"

"Seriously?"

"It's worse," I say. "Cole and Beau were there, and I just couldn't stand it."

"Ugh. I'd die." She's quiet for a moment. "Glad you didn't though."

I recount the rest of what happened, explaining about the creepy paparazzo and me not paying attention. Violet and Andrew both listen, Andrew shaking his head while Violet watches me with wide eyes.

"This is going to be all over the internet," Violet says.

"That's why you have to let me use your phone. I'm pretty sure if Cole posts something, my parents will do everything they can so that he can't see me anymore, but I can't just let things go. I need people to hear it from me," I say.

"I'm going to miss you when I'm banished," Violet says, handing me her phone. "But Julie and Isaac can't hate me forever."

Andrew laughs. "No one can, babe."

I smile at Andrew. I haven't really had the chance to hang out with him, but he seems like a nice guy, and Violet likes him a lot.

"So how are you going to get the word out? You have like no followers." Violet's right. I barely made an official page, and haven't even posted on it except for one of the good photos of me in the fashion show wearing the gray mini dress and pattern tights.

"Let me text Ariel," Andrew says. "She'll share it for you."

"You're a genius, babe," Violet says, hugging Andrew before kissing him. She pulls away and smiles at me. "Cole should be the least of your parents' worries."

I laugh. "Right? It's definitely you."

It only took twenty minutes to convince Mom to go home for the night when she laid down on the chair that folds into a bed around nine. And I'm glad that she did. Andrew was sweet enough to run out and get me a prepaid phone to use since mine is on lockdown, and he and Violet escaped ten minutes before my parents showed up with dinner.

Now, since the nurse just left, I browse what is probably the most ridiculous "nice to meet you, world" post in existence. I was hoping to post something more general, just a few things about me, maybe a few pictures, but I had to resort to telling my accident story for the billionth time. And I didn't leave anything out. Why lie? I can't be the only one who thinks my parents are out of control.

Brooke Haley: That is so crazy, Sage! I can relate to overprotective parents.

Zenna Bay: Ohmigosh, that creep should be punished!

Sabi Quintino: Sending healing thoughts your way!

Levi Reed: I love your beautiful face.

Henry Powers: Attention whore!

Bea Lovits: I can relate. Not the accident but the strict parents.

Marc Davidson: If you're reading this, will you marry me?

Daphne O'Hare: Don't let anyone get you down. You're beautiful. Cole's the lucky one.

For the first time in a while, I'm not on the verge of tears reading over what people have to say about me. Sure, not everyone is nice, but the majority of people who comment on my story are a lot friendlier.

A knock sounds on my door, and I quickly hide my phone under the blankets. The door swings open when I say it's okay to come in, and I half expect to see my mom, but Jen Novak stands in the doorway holding a vase of flowers.

"Hey, Sage," she says, coming into the room, clicking the door closed behind her. "How are you feeling? I was worried when Cole called me and told me about your accident."

"Cole called you?" I ask. Everything was so hectic that I had forgotten all about the dinner I was supposed to have with Jen.

"Yeah. The poor guy was so shook up." She sets the vase on the table with the other five vases of flowers and few bouquets of balloons. "I was going to come by earlier, but he also warned me that your parents have no idea about any of this. Is that right?"

I sigh, frowning. "I wanted to be sure before I told them. They keep telling me that until I'm eighteen and out of the house, that they don't want me anywhere near the industry or fame. Even fame by association freaks them out."

She strolls to my bed and sits down. "I see. You do know that since you're a minor, you'll need parental consent, right? I had assumed since they allowed you to participate in Lele's show that—"

"About that. They didn't know."

She doesn't react. "You'd be surprised how often things fall through the cracks. Since you didn't need a work permit, I could see how this happened."

"Am I going to get into trouble?"

She shakes her head. "With your parents, maybe. Lele won't pursue anything. She wants you, and I'm willing to do anything in my power to make that happen. My firm would like to represent you. We work with some of the best agents in the industry as well."

"But my parents." I stare at my hands with a frown. "I'll have to wait six months."

"I want to advise you against that. Opportunities like this are hard to come by and who knows what could happen in six months, you know. There are other ways to go about this if your parents refuse to sign. I can recommend another lawyer at my firm that will help you become emancipated. With the right contract, we could get the costs covered. It'll be easy since you'd be able to financially support yourself and because you're already so close to being an adult."

Emancipation? That's basically divorcing my parents. Could I go through with it? Maybe. Do I want to? Not really.

"This is a lot to think about," I say.

"How about I rework a few things in the proposed contract, follow up with Lele, and then we can have a sit-down with your parents once you're healed?"

"How much will this all cost?" I haven't even had the chance to deposit my check from the fashion show yet.

"I work on a contingency for a lot of new clients and have my fees negotiated into the contracts. As long as everything goes smoothly, you'll be all set for a strong start to your career."

I sit up straighter. "This is all so unbelievable. I never in my wildest dreams imagined this could be what I do with my life."

She smiles. "And I'm here to help."

Jen stays for a bit, going over a few things about what to expect and what to look forward to. With the help of her firm, I won't have to worry about any of the legal stuff or contracts, and she mentioned that an agency she works with will be contacting me soon. Lele isn't the only one interested in working with me.

Another knock sounds on the door, and Jen gets to her feet, gathering her designer bag from the floor. It opens without me saying anything, and I expect to be greeted by my nurse, but instead, Cole smiles at me.

"We'll talk more soon," Jen says. I give her my temporary number, and she leaves with a friendly goodbye to Cole.

The second the door closes, Cole crosses the room and stands next to my bed, peering down at me. He trails his fingers along the collar of my gown, carefully pulling it from my shoulder to see the blackened bruises that disappear into a bandage made from gauze. The worst of my injuries is on my hip where the car bumped into me. Had the woman been driving any faster and unable to stop, she'd have gone right over me.

Cole carefully sits on the bed, and I grimace as I scoot over to make room for him to lie next to me. He picks up my hand, pouting at the bandages taped to my palms where I skinned them on the asphalt. Beside my knee and part of my arm, they're the only other place to have gotten road rash. It could've been a lot worse.

"I couldn't wait until tomorrow to see you," he whispers. He leans over and kisses my temple. "If anyone asks, I'm family, okay?"

I giggle. "My nurse shouldn't be back in here for another few hours to give me medicine. Just don't kiss me in front of her, and we'll be fine."

"I can work with a few hours," he says, kissing me again, careful not to press against my bad arm.

"Good, because I could use something to get my mind off things," I say, snuggling against him. "Tomorrow should be interesting. I can already see my parents now."

"They're going to hate me," Cole says quietly.

I pout my lip. He might be right. My parents will assume that he was the reason that I put myself out there. They're going blame him for my interest in wanting to be a model. But Cole is the last person they should lash out at. This has never been about Cole. This has been about me and what I want, which is this. Being in love, having control over my life, treating life like it should be treated with enthusiasm and hope and knowing that everyone can be someone, no matter who you are, no matter if others don't see it.

"If anything, they'll be disappointed in me. But they'll have to get over it," I say. "This is the life I want."

"Even after today?" he asks.

I nod. "Yeah, because even with the bad—" I pause and kiss him. "The good makes it worth it."

chapter 20

Model Behavior

COLE SITS NEXT to me on my bed, clicking through at least twenty different shows on my TV to decide what to watch next. My official summer on lockdown started the moment I hobbled up the stairs to my room five days ago when I got out of the hospital.

Both Mom and Dad have taken off the entire week to make sense of this unwanted, according to them, situation. Dad even convinced Mom to unplug and step back from all electronics except what we could stream on TV and focus on how to move forward amid all the semi-craziness I stirred up in their lives. It's not like I was some A-list celebrity who got hit.

"God, I'm so bored," I say, stretching my arms over my head. The movement stings the scabs on my arm, but I've barely even left my bedroom in days. "I miss going out."

Cole sets the remote down. "Why don't I help you out to your balcony? The sun should set soon." We can't see the actual sun setting, but we can watch the city lights blink on the darker it gets.

I grin. "I can walk, you know."

"But I like carrying you."

I laugh as Cole hops from the bed and scoops me into his arms. I don't let him cradle me and wrap my legs around his waist so I can shower him with kisses instead. He strolls blindly in the direction of my balcony door, holding one arm around my back and the other out to make sure he doesn't crash me into one of the windows or the door.

Summer air warms my skin, the invisible sun sweltering over the endless city below us. The shade from my patio umbrella doesn't help cool the air much, but I don't care how hot it is out here, I'm sick of being in my room.

Cole sits down in one of the padded chairs with me on his lap, and I shift my legs to hang them off his knees sideways while I press into his side. His arm drapes over me, playing with my hair cascading down my back.

"Almost feels like I'm not a prisoner," I say, cupping his face to kiss him more deeply, desperately, so the world feels like it's all Cole, and I don't have to think about anything else except the way his lips feel against mine. How his mouth tastes like the vanilla French macarons he surprised me with this morning. How it doesn't seem so bad not being able to do whatever I want like I used to before unexpected fame put me in a rainbow bubble I'm not willing to pop.

"You know, your parents have to sleep sometime. We can sneak out," Cole says, smirking at me.

"Who are you and what have you done with my perfect, good guy, won't-do-anything-bad boyfriend?" I ask, laughing.

He holds his hand to his chest like I've offended him. But really, Cole should win an award for at least acting the part of the boyfriend every parent should want for their daughter. He's respected all my parents' wishes, has invested time hanging out with my dad every day he's come here and not just because Dad is letting him help with his latest mysterious art piece. He's even managed to get an invitation to stay in the guest room down-stairs so he wouldn't have to stay at home. Though, I'm pretty sure it's because my parents feel like keeping Cole in my same prison somehow makes a difference.

"He's just as bored as you are," Cole says, lacing his fingers with mine.

I fake a pout.

"Not that hanging out with you is boring..."

"Mmm-hmm."

"I mean—"

I tilt my head back, resting it on the back of the chair, and grin at the sky. "You're cute when you're—"

"Sage!" I hear Dad's voice before I see him striding through my bedroom. The way he says my name has me wanting to hide, but all I do is stare wide-eyed from Cole's arms as he rush-es onto the balcony, waving what looks like a stack of magazines. Dad drops the stack on the table in front of us, and I seriously consider trying to flip myself out of Cole's arms and over the railing just so I don't have to face Dad when he's angry.

"Cole," I whisper. "You should go."

Dad points at my boyfriend. "No, you stay."

Oh, crap.

"Isaac?" Mom asks from the door, drawing our attention away from my dad, who looks like he's going to ground me for the rest of my life. "What's going on?"

"Look at this, Jules! I was in line at the grocery store and looked at the magazine rack and couldn't believe it," he yells, picking up one of the tabloids. "Sage is on the cover."

"Isaac, calm down. We knew it was a possibility. I'm sure it'll blow over. Come inside and take a breath," Mom says.

Dad waves the magazine again. "Read the headline."

"Model behavior? Sage Meadows, Lele Rose's freshest face, hit by car after fleeing restaurant in Playa del Rey. Turn to page thirty-nine to find out why this party girl was on the run."

I cringe at the words. I've been extremely lucky until now. The accident basically saved me from having to tell my parents about the fashion show or the contract Lele has to offer me. I've been waiting on Jen to arrange a meeting with my parents, but she hasn't been able to reach either of them with the electronics ban.

"I don't understand," Mom says.

I use the arm rest to push to my feet. "I can explain."

"You better," Dad says. "Because according to this magazine, you are a model for Lele Rose, and we did not sign any parental consent forms. There are going to be a lot of people in trouble for this."

"Dad," I say. "It was a misunderstanding. They thought I was eighteen. It was just one show."

Mom flips to the article in the tabloid and pales. "Oh, sweetie. What were you thinking? Look at these photos." She holds out the magazine and sure enough, one of the ones with me in the sheer top with a black box over my chest is front and center in the collage of pictures of me.

"So what?" I say. "You can't see anything."

"Sage, do you hear yourself? We didn't raise you to flaunt yourself like that," Mom says.

I puff air through my lips. "Like what exactly? It's fashion. You're freaking out over nothing."

Mom closes the magazine and holds it under her arm. "But you're only seventeen. Our—your—privacy is important to us. This could follow you all your life. What if after college, you're passed up for jobs because of this? What if—"

"What if this is what I want to do with my life?" I ask, cutting her off.

"Really, Sage?" Dad asks. "A model? Is that how you want to be known?"

I frown. "And what's wrong with that? You're an artist, Dad. You're a photographer. You out of everyone should understand."

A scowl crosses his face, and he turns to Cole. "This is your doing."

Cole shifts in his seat. "Isaac, even if it was my idea, I couldn't have made this happen. Sage is beautiful and smart and amazing. She has this presence around her that people notice, and you can't ignore her when she walks into a room."

I smile at Cole even though Dad looks like he wants to drag him out by his ear. The two of them stare at each other, and Mom stands there quietly, wringing her hands together.

Dad takes a breath. "It's time for you to go, Cole."

"Dad," I say.

"Sage, I'm sorry. I like Cole, but this is too much right now. You got hurt because the paparazzi harassed you. You went against our wishes after you knew how we felt about the industry. I'm not saying you two have to break up, but I think things are moving too quickly, and you're too young to be this serious."

Tears rim my eyes. "I'm sorry, Dad. I am. Don't blame any of this on Cole. It's not his fault."

"Cole, I'll walk you out. Please, give us some space for a few days. Sage will call you," Dad says.

Cole stands, hurt sweeping across his face, and we stare at each other. Anger twists in my chest, coiling around my heart. Furious tears burn down my cheeks as Dad tries to motion for Cole to leave.

"Don't bother walking him out," I say. "Because I'm going with him."

"Sage, please. Just give your dad a day to cool off. We'll work all this out," Mom says.

I shake my head, taking Cole's hand. "No. You're both overreacting. You act like I'm ruining my life, but you can't see that I like where it's going. I even got offered a contract with Lele Rose."

"Not happening," Dad says.

I pull Cole to the door to my bedroom to go back inside. "Well, maybe you should talk to my lawyer about that."

"Lawyer?" Mom asks.

I don't respond. Instead, I slam my balcony door shut and tug Cole through my room. My parents don't chase after us. They remain on the balcony, probably in stunned silence, as I make my escape.

"You sure you want to leave? It might make things worse," Cole says.

I nod. "I can't be here right now."

He studies me for a minute. "Will you be okay?"

I shrug. "I have no idea."

chapter 21

The Night is Ours

NEITHER OF MY parents call or text Cole or Violet. It's been hours since I stormed out with Cole, and I'm shocked they haven't tried to chase me down. Guilt weighs on me just thinking about this afternoon and how disappointed they both looked when I basically told them that they aren't controlling my life.

The next headline that'll appear in the tabloids will probably read, *Upcoming model, Sage Meadows, breaks parents' hearts.* Because I know I hurt them. I know they probably won't trust me again, and that I ruined everything. I never wanted things to turn out like this, but I couldn't just turn away a great opportunity for my parents' sakes. They don't live in my skin. They don't know what it's like being me.

Just weeks ago, I thought I was no one—that I was never going to be someone. But I am someone. It might not be what they wanted, but I've never wanted anything more. Dad can't blame me. I've been his model more often than not for photo pieces. While I've never been permanently on display, he's instilled in me how beauty can be found in many forms, and I love the creativity and beauty of showing off people's creations—bringing it to life on the runway.

"You're going to end up with a funny looking tan if you don't come back and sit in the shade," Violet says from her place on a lounge chair within the covered back patio of Cole's beach front condo in Santa Monica. From here, the pier looks like a postcard with how clear the sky looks.

I sigh, digging my hands into the sand to get to my feet. I blow them off so I don't open any of the scabs on my palms. I'm still wearing my yoga pants and a tank top, but Violet's right about the tan lines. I don't need a lingering reminder of my bandages or the accident.

Taking a seat in a lounge, I glance from Violet, who sips on some fruity creation she probably spiked with alcohol from Beau's stash in the bar, to the busy beach in front of us. Surprisingly, Beau's condo isn't part of a private beach. It doesn't bother me any. Everyone's too busy enjoying the hot day.

Violet waves her drink in my face. "You look like you could use this."

I laugh before I push it away. I regret leaving my house without anything, including the pain medicine I've been taking. I'm really starting to hurt, and this is probably the universe punishing me for being me. "Maybe if you didn't put it in such an obvious glass. The last thing I need is to have some creepo snap a shot of me taking a sip. I'm in enough trouble. I'm still surprised no one has come to drag me away."

Violet's smile falters, and she takes another sip. "They'll get over it. They're crazy for even suggesting that you ditch Cole. If they didn't want you to be tempted into the glamorous life, they should've sent you to boarding school and stopped taking you to celebrity events."

"Right? I bet they're looking up schools now," I mutter.

"I love Julie and Isaac but come on!" Violet's voice rings through the air, and I catch sight of a few people peering in our direction from the beach blankets in the sand. "If they're worried then maybe they should think about how to keep you safe instead of being dream destroyers."

"I'd like to see you tell my parents that to their faces."

"Is that a dare? Because you know I—"

The sliding glass door opens just in time to cut Violet off. Cole greets us with a smile, and the scent of garlic wafts outside from within. He went alone to pick us up something to eat since the place only had stuff to drink, and no one felt like sitting down to eat at a restaurant.

Violet jumps to her feet. "God, I'm starving. I hope you have good taste in food."

Cole helps me to my feet and turns to Violet. "I braved the Promenade and got Three Sisters for us. People wanted to know where you were."

Violet's eyes widen. "Seriously?"

Cole chuckles. "No. It was an uneventful trip."

Glaring, Violet playfully slaps Cole's arm. "That was mean!"

"And you are obsessed."

"Never said I wasn't," Violet says, strolling inside in front of us.

"Hey, Sage? Cole?" a voice calls from behind me, stopping me in place.

I spin to face three girls around my age. Two of the girls wear swimsuits while one wears a sundress. They stand close together as they kick up sand, closing the distance to the back patio. Cole grabs my hand, motioning me to follow him inside, but I don't move.

"Can we get a picture with you?" the brunette asks, holding up her cell phone.

Cole's jaw twitches, and he looks at me to make the final decision even though I can tell he'd rather we just go inside.

I shrug with one arm. "Yeah, sure."

The three girls join us on the patio, and we all squeeze in for a picture together. All it shows is our faces, which is fine by me. I half expect the girls to ask us to hang out, but they quickly jog away and rejoin their group of friends near the water.

"You're sweet, you know?" Cole asks, kissing my temple, hurrying to get me inside.

"There was no way I was turning down my first fan photo opportunity." I'd rather have those girls post pictures of me, telling the world that I was nice instead of having them complain that I was stuck up or something. I get enough hate as it is. "It might be my last."

"It won't be," Violet says, already eating, standing at the counter of the bar of the open kitchen.

We have a surprisingly peaceful dinner where it doesn't feel like the world will explode at any second, and Violet even manages to refrain from checking her phone every two seconds.

When the sun disappears on the beach, I hover in the window and stare at the bonfires peppering the beach. From here, I can't see any lights apart from the sporadic fire pits, and the dark world out the window feels enormous and dark and empty, but not in a bad way.

Cole slides his hands around my waist and rests his chin on my shoulder, peering out the glass door from behind me. He trails his lips across my neck, sending a rush of warmth through me, and I consider sneaking upstairs as Violet watches TV.

"Okay, I'm bored." So much for sneaking. Violet rises from her spot on the couch and heads toward us. "Let's take a walk or something."

Cole shifts me so I spin with him. "Sage can't really wa—"

"I'm fine, really," I say, cutting Cole off. "A walk will be good for me. I haven't done much all week. Let's just stay off the sand."

"Then it's settled!" Violet squeals, slipping into her wedged sandals. She's the first to head to the front door which leads to a gated complex. Only certain condos have direct beach access, and we're one of them.

Cole helps tie my Converses despite my protests and offers his arm out to me. I take his hand instead. I'm sore, but I can walk on my own. The more I do it, the better I feel anyway. I'm more stiff than anything and as long as I don't bump my bruised hip or scabbed arm against anything, I'm fine.

Before we leave, I slip into one of Cole's hoodies to help hide the damage the pavement did to me. I'm already sweating when I step outside into the balmy summer night, but I'd rather be hot and covered than have people wondering about what's under the bandages. I can't help being vain.

Strolling through the small community, we reach the front entrance that leads to Ocean Avenue, heading in the direction of the pier. The ocean breeze cools the sweat prickling on my neck, and I twist my hair up into a bun, using the ponytail elastic from my wrist to keep it in place. Cole wears a baseball cap, looking different enough that someone would have to really know who he was to recognize him. There's nothing I can do about my lavender hair though. People who've followed me in the tabloids and online would notice.

Instead of walking on the pier, we head left and cross the street to Colorado Avenue. Strings of lights glow overhead, making the outskirts of the Santa Monica Place shopping area more magical than in the daytime. The tall palm trees are lit by the streetlamps, and in the distance I can hear the sound of the subway horn.

I train my eyes on the wavy patterned sidewalk as I walk. The last time, I only saw it from Cole's car, and the sidewalk is like an art piece in itself with how it gives the illusion of strolling down a curvy sidewalk with the waves of light brown and dark gray stones.

Stopping in place right in the middle of the sidewalk, I tug my phone from my pocket and hold it out to Violet. She frowns for a second, probably because I'm having her take a picture of me and Cole first instead of me and her, but her eyes light up when she holds my phone up, capturing the glowing twinkle lights above us amid the chaotic sidewalk of tourists and locals enjoying a night out.

Cole takes a shot of me and Violet sitting on crate-like wooden seats that line the sidewalk, and I take a minute and upload both pictures online, tagging them both for all the world to see. I don't care if it pisses my parents off. I want to show whoever follows me the beauty I see in this dazzling night. Making myself more real has helped a lot with the negativity. I'm no longer just a face on Cole's page to be judged and ridiculed because people don't think I'm deserving of his love. I'm real, and I'm not going anywhere.

We cross the street at Fourth Street and walk into the outdoor shopping mall through a department store. The three story mall is crazy busy, and Cole shifts to put his arm around my shoulders like the crowd will somehow steal me away from him. Violet saunters on my other side, and we head to a seating area in the middle of the mall.

I take a seat on one of the pod-like chairs while Violet and Cole stand next to me peering around. I glance at a jewelry store, one my mom bought me a necklace from for my sixteenth birthday, and imagine that she probably won't be buying me anything else for a while.

"Let's get some ice cream," Violet says, shifting on her feet to look around.

Cole bobs his head. "Sure, there's a creamery toward the north side of the mall." He offers his hand to me to help me to my feet, but I shake my head.

"Why don't you bring me something back? I'm going to sit here for a bit," I say.

"I'm not going alone," Violet says.

Cole frowns, looking between us. He's acting just as protective as my parents. This is our first real outing since the accident, but it's not like I'll be running into streets anytime soon. "We can wait."

"No, it's fine. Go with Violet. Surprise me with something, okay?" I lean back in my chair. Neither of them moves. Sighing, I say, "Seriously? I can see the place from here. I promise I won't even get up."

Violet relents first and tugs on Cole's arms. "I know that look she's giving us, and we better listen."

"You sure you'll be okay?" Cole asks.

I narrow my eyes without saying anything, and Cole lets Violet drag him away. Pulling out my phone, I check over the photos I posted not long ago. It never fails to amaze me how quickly people respond.

Anita Burrows: Aw man! I was just there today. I can't

believe I missed you.

Jon-Jon Hiddles: Who's the other chick? She's smoking hot.

Gwen Devine: Y'all are so beautiful. Well, not Cole. He's hot. So jealous!

Stevie Nguyen: When was this taken? I'd drive the hour to see my beautiful goddess in person.

Benji Lakes: Not your best look. Did you just roll out of bed?

Felix Chow: 3sum?

Kate Somers: Still think Cole should be with Ariel.

Hilary Clifford: OMG! I'd never go out like that.

Zerena McPhee: I think you look great, Sage!

A flash of light draws my attention away from my phone, and I watch as a paparazzo crosses through the center of the mall in my direction. Instead of getting up like I want to, I turn in my seat to face my back toward him. The Promenade across the way is more likely to get paparazzi attention since celebrities, and pretty much anyone, like to go there, but this guy probably saw my post and took a guess.

I've had several reporters from different gossip magazines reach out to me through my social media this week about the accident, but I haven't responded to anyone. I said all that I wanted to say on Friendconn and was hoping that would be that.

"Looking good, Sage," the guy says like he knows me, circling around the sitting area like a shark hunting for its next meal. "How you feeling since the accident?"

I ignore him completely and pull my hoodie up to cover half my face.

"Aw, come on now. You shouldn't hide your pretty face like that. People wanna see it." He snaps a few more pictures.

I get up this time. His behavior crawls under my skin and makes me want to run away. He got a few shots of me already, but to just stand there and take more is causing a scene and other shoppers are starting to notice.

"You don't even look like you're hurt," the guy says, strolling closer. "I bet it was all some press stunt. That's why there's been no word on the pap who was harassing you."

"Believe what you want," I say against my better judgment. I need to learn to steel myself.

"Why don't you show me the damage? I bet I could get you on the cover of Teen Heartthrob with an exclusive story. People would eat it up."

"No thanks," I say, heading in the direction Cole and Violet had left in.

He follows me, running ahead to snap another picture. I frown, spinning to go toward the nearest store. A group of people watch the guy trying to cut me off to get in my way again, and no one does anything. Just like in Playa del Rey, I've never felt so helpless. If I had my purse, I'd probably clobber him with it. But all I can do is try to move past him.

"Hey, leave the girl alone," a feminine voice calls out.

I flush from the warm night and embarrassment. The

crowd thickens, and I hear a few guys laugh loudly. I'm about to give up and just sit in the middle of the courtyard to wait for Cole to come back, because this is ridiculous. It's like the guy is baiting me on, trying to get a dramatic reaction out of me.

Sucking in a deep breath, I orient myself in the busy mall and attempt to stroll in the direction of the creamery again. The sound of the camera flash popping and the people blatantly gossiping about me forces me to nearly jog away as fast as I can, even with the pain in my hip.

A boy my age steps in front of me, laughing, when I nearly knock him over.

"Excuse me," I say, shoving past him.

Another person knocks into me, hitting right into my hip, and I cringe as pain leaves me breathless. Tears burn in my eyes, and I blink them away. There is no way in hell someone is going to capture me crying on camera.

"Break it up!" a masculine voice yells.

I've never been so relieved to see a security guard in my life. A woman motions toward me, and the security guard heads in my direction while another one goes toward the paparazzo who started this whole thing. He evades the security guard, raising his hands in defeat and disappears into the crowd. It doesn't stop the madness of the onlookers.

"Come with me, miss," a security guard says, motioning people out of the way. He's probably in his mid-twenties and looks like an aspiring actor who works out every day. A tattoo peeks out from his short sleeved shirt, and he leads me through the crowd toward a security office.

"Am I in trouble or something?" I ask. "I didn't do anything wrong. That guy wouldn't leave me alone."

My phone rings from my pocket, and I pull it out to see Cole's smiling face flash across my screen. I answer it before the security guard says anything to me.

"Hey," I say. "I'm in security."

"What? Are you okay?" Cole asks. "We came back for you but there was a huge crowd, and some people recognized me. I had to slip into Kelley's to get them to stop snapping pictures."

"Blame the paparazzo that wouldn't leave me alone," I say.

Cole's quiet for a moment. "Did he hurt you?"

I shake my head even though he can't see me. "I just want to get out of here."

"Ask her if she hurt him?" I hear Violet say over the line.

I laugh. "Tell Violet that he got lucky."

"I'm coming to get you. Why don't you get us a ride back to the condo?" The line erupts with outside noise, and I can't hear what he says before the line clicks off.

"Do you need an escort to finish your shopping?" The security guard asks, pulling my attention away from my phone.

I glance up and meet his annoyed expression. "So, I'm not in trouble?"

He shakes his head. "The paps love roaming these parts. They usually keep their distance and celebrities are used to it, so you must be sitting on a big story, huh?"

"Nothing you can't find on the internet," I say.

The glass door that leads back into the mall opens, and Violet struts in with Cole right behind her. She waves a small cup of ice cream into the air, a grin parting her matte brown lips. Her eyeshadow sparkles in the fluorescent lighting, and the highlighter on the apples of her cheeks gives her an ethereal look.

"I guess I shouldn't have posted the photos," I say, getting to my feet.

Cole holds out a cup of slightly melted coffee ice cream to me. Violet must've told him it was my favorite. I take it in my hands, half expecting him to chide me, but he doesn't. Instead, he kisses me softly on the lips.

"I'm just glad you're okay," he whispers, hugging me for a moment. "I swear, I'm not going to ever leave you alone in public."

I smirk. "As long as you don't suggest we hide in your house all the time."

"Would that be so bad?" His heart beats against mine, and it takes Violet fake gagging to get me to take a step back.

"It would be horrible. I need my BFF, and I need her to do fun things," she says.

My phone buzzes in my hand, and I frown when I look at it. "I don't know how much fun we'll get to have." I hold up my phone to her. "It's my mom. She wants to talk."

Me: I'm in Santa Monica right now.

Mom: I know. I saw it online.

Me: You looked me up?

Mom: You're my daughter, so yes.

Me: Can we talk later?

Mom: Are you safe?

Me: Yeah, we're heading back to Cole's.

Mom: Come home, please.

Me: So, you can yell at me some more?

Mom: Why don't you take tonight to cool off then? I'll get Dad out of the house tomorrow so we can talk without him if you want.

Me: Really?

Mom: Yes. I love you, Sage.

Me: TTYL. Love you, too.

I turn my gaze to Cole and Violet. "Something's changed with my mom."

"What do you mean?" Cole asks.

I shrug. "I don't know, but I guess I'll find out tomorrow."

"Isaac isn't claiming that Cole kidnapped you?" Violet asks. I know she's joking, but Cole's eyes widen for a second.

I lace my fingers through Cole's. "He wouldn't. Now, come on. The night is ours."

chapter 22

Not Always Glitz and Glamour

"DON'T LEAVE, OKAY?" Shifting in my seat, I turn to face Cole.

His fingers rest on his steering wheel for a second. He shuts off the engine, swiveling to face me head on. "Want me to come in?"

I consider saying yes but shake my head. "I'll text you when it's okay."

He reaches up and brushes strands of lavender hair from my cheek, gently cupping my face. Brushing his lips against mine, he kisses me sweetly, his lips so soft that he leaves me craving more when he pulls away.

I groan. "I don't want to leave you."

"It might not be so bad."

"It could be worse."

Flinging my door open, I climb from Cole's car and head to my front door. Mom stands in the foyer like she's been waiting for me. Without a word, she wraps her arms around me, squeezing me against her. It's been a while since she hugged me like this, and now I'm really starting to worry.

"You hungry, sweetie? I made some breakfast," she says, motioning me to head downstairs to the kitchen.

"Sure," I say. I'm not actually hungry since Cole picked up breakfast sandwiches that we ate on the back patio this morning, but Mom looks like she's on the verge of tears and anything could set her off. "Where's Dad, anyway?"

"He had a meeting this morning," she says. She heads to the stove and dishes out scrambled eggs mixed with vegetables onto two plates and sets them both on the bar where we usually eat instead of the table.

"What kind of meeting?" Nerves bunch in my stomach.

"With your lawyer," Mom says flatly.

I grimace. "Mom, I—" What do I even say? "I never meant to hurt you. Things just happened so suddenly, and I just..." My words trail off.

"We had no idea that you even wanted to be a model, Sage. It caught us by surprise. And after your accident, well, your father and I are scared. Fame is a lot to handle as an adult, and you're only seventeen."

"Almost eighteen," I add.

She gives a small laugh. "Which is why your father and I had a long talk yesterday."

"You talked about my future without me?"

She sets her fork down and turns to me. "No, we talked about what you wanted and how we can make this all work."

"What are you saying?" I ask. This isn't exactly the conversation I was expecting to have, especially without Dad here to throw his two-cents at me.

"I'm saying that we're going to look at things with an open mind. While you went about this all wrong, and it doesn't change the fact that you're grounded for lying and going behind our backs, Dad and I are willing to help you pursue your dreams, whatever they are."

"Really?" I bounce in my seat, not even fazed by the fact that I'm grounded. I knew that was coming already. What I didn't expect was that Mom is willing to let me do what I want with my life. "Oh, my God. You're the best."

She hugs me. "All I've ever wanted was for you to be happy and safe, and I can see how much this means to you."

"What about Cole? Is Dad going to freak out on him again?"

She shakes her head. "We weren't lying when we said we liked Cole. And we know that while this came about while you were together, we know it wasn't his doing. I'm sure it would've happened sooner or later. Now, we just need to adjust. I don't want you dealing with everything alone. I saw what happened at the mall yesterday, you know."

"Someone filmed it?" Of course they did. I'd have filmed it if I were them.

She nods. "You sure you're up for all this? It's not always glitz and glamour. It'll be hard to go out without being bothered. People aren't always nice either."

"Yeah, I'm sure. It's worth it to me."

"As long as you're sure."

"I am."

"Good. Now why don't you text Cole to come in? I know he's waiting in his car."

I laugh. "Thanks, Mom. For everything. I mean it."

I follow Mom into the swanky Anderson and Novak Associates building on Wilshire Boulevard in Beverly Hills. Jen Novak's name is etched into the frosted glass door to her office, which is down the hall from a small lobby with a friendly receptionist. Dad sits in a small sitting area across from Jen.

Dad stands up from his spot and crosses the room to hug me. He kisses the top of my head before motioning me to take one of the seats next to him. Jen offers her hand to Mom and then shakes mine, greeting me with a smile.

"I'm so happy to see you up and about, Sage," Jen says, crossing her legs at her knees. "Your Dad said you feel much better."

"I'm almost all healed. Just some bruising left," I say.

"That's good. I know Lele is anxious to get you into the studio soon," she says. "I've been going over your contract with your father, making some adjustments to send back to Lele."

My eyebrows furrow together. "What kinds of adjustments?"

"Your parents agreed to sign as long as it's in writing that Lele must work around your education, which isn't a huge deal. You'll be required to get an entertainer's work permit unless you pass the California High School Proficiency Exam since you won't be eighteen until January."

"I can graduate early and not have to deal with all that?" I ask, sitting up straighter. Going back to Sunset Prep seems crazy now.

Dad holds up his hand, cutting Jen off. "Actually, Sage, your mom and I have some rules you'll need to understand and agree to before we sign anything. The first being that you graduate from Sunset Prep. We want you to have some normalcy."

"But—"

"If it makes you feel any better, my niece's boyfriend's parents had the same conditions," Jen says.

"You mean Elijah Rousseau?" The only high school I can imagine Elijah attending is Slaughter Creek High. I knew that Nora went to Beverly Hills High School because of her blog but never paid attention to where Elijah went.

"That's right. He and Nora graduated from Beverly Hills High School last spring. I can put you in touch with them if you want. Nora's been through a lot this last year, and like you, she fell into the spotlight." Jen writes on a notepad in front of her and tears off a sheet where she wrote a phone number and hands it to me.

"Thanks," I say.

"You're welcome. Now, let's just go over a few of the details of your contract together, and we can get this all worked out."

I turn to my parents. "So, this is really happening?"

Dad nods. "Yup. Yesterday made me realize you are definitely my daughter, and there was no way I was going to be like my dad. If I had listened to my parents, I'd have been working at a job I hate. I don't want our relationship to turn out like the one I have with them." Grandpa hates that Dad is an artist. I can't even remember the last time I saw Grandpa and Grandma Meadows. They usually only send cards at Christmas.

I pout out my bottom lip. "I don't want that either. I'm sorry for how things have been."

"Things will be different from now on," Mom says.

I smile. "Good. I'm ready for it."

chapter 23

Strike a Pose

Mikayla Klein: Amazing! Congrats!

Billy Ky: Oh.

Maria Gonzalez: Hate her.

Cassie Raso: Luckiest girl EVER!

Noel Trippe: Won't be long for the nudes.

Izzy Alex: Sage and Cole forever!

Cole steals my phone from my hand, stopping me from reading any more comments on the press release I shared from Lele Rose's website introducing me as the newest face of her latest fashion line.

My first photo shoot happens next week right here in LA, which is for Lele's winter campaign. I thought I was excited about the fashion show, but nothing compares to the excitement I feel knowing this isn't a onetime thing.

"You're obsessing again. I think I'm going to hold onto it for the night," Cole says, holding my phone on his leg as he pulls to the curb outside a red brick building. A blue carpet lines the sidewalk with two ropes stopping the paparazzi and onlookers from getting in our way before we enter the night-club.

Bright camera lights dazzle my eyes, and a boy in a silver vest with a black bowtie opens my door to help me out. I knew Lele had something special planned for tonight, but I definitely wasn't expecting her to arrange a private gathering at one of the most popular celebrity hangouts in Hollywood. Famous is nestled on North Las Palmas Avenue near Hollywood Boulevard between Rock, a club known for live music, and a bar called Tipsy's.

"Sage, what's it like working for Lele Rose? It's been two years since she's had a new face for any of her lines," a woman with an A-line bob asks.

"Amazing. I love Lele's vision. It's such an honor to work with her." Mom helped prep me for any and all questions people might ask me at any given time. She said that being caught off guard is what leads to mistakes being made—or said in this case.

"What about Cole? How does he feel knowing that you're stealing the limelight from him?" a man with long, curly hair asks. He snaps a photo.

Cole slides his hand around my waist. "I love it, and I love her." He kisses my cheek, making me blush.

Pulling me forward, he guides me to the front entrance where a bouncer awaits with the door open. The voices of the onlookers and reporters mingle together in a cacophonous symphony loud enough to make me dizzy.

"Sage! Sage!" a woman yells. "What's it like knowing that you'd be a nobody without Cole? Isn't Lele his godmother?"

I freeze under her question. It's not the first time I've seen someone question why I was chosen, but it's the first time it's been said directly to my face.

"Sage wasn't—"

"Are you saying you have to be famous to be someone these days?" I ask, cutting Cole off. "Because I'm pretty sure I haven't changed since signing on with Lele, and I doubt she would choose me to represent her brand solely because she's Cole's godmother."

The woman gapes at me for a moment without a word.

"Sage, is it true you're teaming up with Ariel Marin on a song?" a man asks, stepping in front of the woman.

I shake my head. "Definitely not. That would be my incredibly talented boyfriend," I say, beaming Cole a smile. "They'll be performing it tonight. Maybe I'll post a clip."

That little tidbit sends the crowd into a frenzy, so much so that the bouncer waves us forward and into the club before things get out of control. I exhale a long breath, letting go of Cole's hand only to turn and hug him. I bury my face in his shoulder, forcing my oncoming nerves away.

"You did great out there," Cole says. His lips brush against my earlobe, and I shiver in his arms.

"It's getting easier," I say.

"Babe!" Violet calls, sauntering through the throng of dancing people in the small club open just for my party. "Finally! I've been here for thirty minutes. Everyone's been waiting." You'd think it was the end of the world that I made Cole take a detour so we could swing by Potato Pete's for some fries. I was too nervous to eat all day until the moment we pulled out of my driveway.

I raise an eyebrow. "You're being dramatic."

She laughs. "Well, I can't call it a party without my BFF."

I make my way around the packed dance floor with so many faces I recognize but haven't personally met. I know they're mostly here for Lele, but it's unbelievable that this is for me as well.

Colorful lights shift and move to the beat of the music pulsating through the hidden speakers around the room. Cole holds onto my hips, and I stop to sway to the music long enough for Violet to realize I'm not right behind her. A smile crosses my face when Delano slides up next to me, holding his phone out to take a picture with me and Cole. He hugs me, kisses my cheek, and asks for me to save a dance for him later.

Violet motions for me to follow her, and we make our way to a line of tables with black cloths draped over them.

"Caraway!" a familiar voice calls.

Old Man Felix waves from his seat next to Mom, Dad, and Ms. Meyer at the end. The only way my parents would agree to let me come tonight was if they were here, too. We made a compromise to let me ride with Cole since Mom and Dad prefer to be on the outside of things. I think Mom also sees this as a business endeavor. I swear she never stops working.

"Look at you, Thyme. I almost didn't recognize you with blond hair. Looks great, kid." Felix offers his fist out, and I bump mine against his. The lavender color was fading from my hair so I decided to change it to match my natural color for now. Who knows what it'll be for my first shoot for Lele?

"I'm so happy for you, Sage," Ms. Meyer says, standing up to hug me. "We'll miss you at LACMA." I'm sadder than I thought I'd be about not volunteering at the museum anymore, but with how much Cole loves the place, I'm sure we'll still visit often. Plus, it was the place we met, and I do still love the lights.

"Thanks so much, Ms. Meyer. You'll still see me around." It's pretty impossible to volunteer now with the constant harassment of paparazzi.

I excuse myself from the table, pulling Cole to where Violet stands with Andrew next to Ariel. A familiar friend slides up to me, and I swivel to smile at Summer. She looks stunning with her dark hair curling down her back, her smoky makeup and pale pink lips. I don't think I've ever seen her in a little black dress before, and it suits her.

"You look so pretty," I say, waving my finger from her face to her spiked heels. "I'm so glad you came."

"I wouldn't have missed it," Summer says. "I thought you might've forgotten about me."

I pout my bottom lip. "Never. Just because I'm not volunteering at LACMA anymore doesn't mean we won't see each other. We'll just do more fun things."

She laughs, hugging me. "We better." She turns to Cole. "Don't let her forget that I covered for her so you could hang out."

Cole chuckles. "I'll never forget that."

I introduce Summer to Ariel, and they hit it off right away. I spot Lele talking to a small group near the dance floor and make my way in her direction. Cole stays behind to talk with Andrew, and I smile and hug a few familiar models that I pass. Everything feels so surreal, I'm almost afraid I'll wake up at any second. I never knew my life could change so drastically over a few weeks, but I wouldn't change it.

"My doll," Lele says, wrapping me in a hug. "I hope you're having a great time."

I reciprocate her air kisses, letting her hold my hands. "It's amazing. Thank you."

"Of course, my dear." Lele introduces me to the group of people she's with, including the photographer I'll be working with for the ad campaign.

Shane interrupts, kissing my cheek, and then pulls Lele away. I watch as she heads in the direction of the small platform. My heart races when she greets the crowd and thanks everyone for coming to celebrate me as the new addition to her brand's family.

People cheer and cameras flash. The attention warms my

chest and neck, and I'm thankful for the dancing colorful lights that hide my blush. Lele introduces Ariel and Cole, calling them to the stage, and I make my way to the front. Violet slides her arm through mine, resting her head on my shoulder. I've never felt so lucky.

"This song is for Sage," Cole says, smiling at me.

He begins strumming a guitar, the bright lights shining on him and Ariel. It's like the world fades away, and all I can see is Cole. His blue eyes shift from Ariel's to mine, and he sings, "Loving you is like loving the lights. You light up my world. You shine in the night. With you around, I can clearly see, how perfect you are. How you belong with me."

Pulling out my phone, I record a few seconds of the performance. When I first met Cole, I wanted nothing more than for him to look at me like he looked at the art pieces at the museum. But I had it all wrong. Cole looks at art with appreciation. The look he gives me is a million times better. In this moment, with the way he holds my gaze, he tells the world how he feels about me, and I can feel his love with every bit of my soul. With everything I have to offer.

The song ends, and I rush to meet Cole. He embraces me, kissing me tenderly on the lips even though the whole room is looking at us. I don't care, though. Not with the way he sends a rush of love over me.

"You're perfect, you know," I say, pulling away to look into Cole's blue eyes.

He smirks. "And I love you, you know."

I kiss him again. "Like I said. Perfect."

At the end of the night, I make my rounds to say goodbye to those still remaining at Famous. Mom and Dad suggested we leave before the last call at the local clubs, and I agree for the sole reason that it'll give me and Cole some alone time before I have to be home.

"All ready?" Cole asks.

I nod, standing near the bouncer who holds the door open for me.

The crowd outside died down and is nearly non-existent, so I let Cole pull me out into the cool night air. The valet goes to retrieve our car, and I lean against Cole, resting my head against his shoulder.

A camera flash pops from the sidewalk. A lingering paparazzo snaps another picture of us, and Cole shifts me so that our backs face the guy. "Hey Sage, strike a pose, will you?"

I put my hand on my hip and let him take the picture.

"Have a nice night, you two?" the guy asks, strolling into the street to take another picture.

I force myself to smile. "It was great. Thanks."

"What are you doing now? The night's still young."

Neither of us responds to the paparazzo's question.

He takes another picture. "Come on, Sage. You look like a party girl. I bet you'll show Cole a good time."

I grimace. "Excuse me?"

"Nothing wrong with a little fun, if you know what I

mean."

"Hey, that's enough," Cole says. "Leave my girlfriend alone."

"She can tell me that herself," he says.

I squeeze Cole's hand. "What's wrong with you?" I ask the paparazzo. "You have no right to talk to me like that. I'm not some party girl or piece of meat or whatever it is you're insinuating. Get a life."

The valet pulls up in Cole's Porsche, and I rush to get inside. The paparazzo stands in front of the hood and snaps a picture of us in the front seat. I pull out my cell phone and start taking pictures right back of him. Cole honks his horn, and when the guy doesn't move, he reverses a bit and flips a U-turn to head toward Sunset instead of Hollywood Boulevard.

I lean my head back on the head rest. "That was a mostly fun night."

"I just wish you didn't have to deal with idiots like that," Cole says, resting his hand on my knee. "But you know what? The night's not over yet."

I smile. "You're right. Think we can make a quick stop?"

"I think I know just the place."

Twenty minutes later, Cole pulls next to the curb at a meter across from Urban Light. We get out and head toward the glowing beacon that now always reminds me of the first time I met Cole and how I crashed into him.

Standing under the lights, I look up at the glowing lamps. Cole hooks his fingers around my hips and pulls me in for a long, magical kiss in the same spot of our very first kiss. Traffic zooms by, even this late at night, and I spin around. In this spot, I questioned who I was. I thought I was no one, but it's only because I hadn't found the someone I wanted to be. But now, standing here with Cole, all I can think about is the endless possibilities of our futures. A future I can't wait to embrace.

I pull my phone from my clutch purse and let Cole hold it out to take a few pictures of us with the lamps behind us. With a few taps on my phone, I post it to my Friendconn page immediately with the caption, *Loving the Lights.*

Comments pop up immediately, but I don't read them. Instead, I put my phone away and kiss Cole again.

I don't care what the world thinks about me anymore. Because what the world thinks doesn't matter to me. What matters is what I think. The world can put me down and claim that I'm undeserving of Cole all they want. They can say that I'm undeserving of being the new face of Lele Rose. But no matter what they say, they can't change my truths, and the truth is that I'm happy being Sage Meadows. They can't change that. They can't change anything. Only I can. This is my life, and I'm going to live it how I want to, and no one can stop me.

epilogue

"CHIN UP A little more," Raven Hope says. "Perfect."

She snaps a few photos, the light umbrellas flashing brightly. Strutting forward, she brushes strands of my golden hair off my shoulder and adjusts the ribbon lacing up the long sleeves of my sweater as I lie on a chaise lounge in front of a wintery setting with a green screen in the fake windows to probably add snow later on.

"Raise your right shoulder just a little," she says. "And look at Paige." She motions to her assistant.

Paige smiles at me as I look at her, but I hold a serious expression.

Raven snaps a few more photos before she sets her camera down. She strolls to a small desk in her studio and messes with her computer for a minute. "Go ahead and take a break, Sage.

We have one more outfit and set change, and then we'll call it a day. You're doing great."

I swing my legs off the chaise lounge and kick off the too tall heels before standing up. I've been here for at least five hours. Lele's been in and out all day, letting Raven and her team take care of most things.

"I just love that top on you," Mom says, coming from her spot on a couch where she left her laptop. "Want some water, sweetie?"

I take the bottle of water from her and take a drink. "You don't have to stay here, you know."

"That's right, Julie," Violet says, standing from her chair near the window. She must've just pulled her attention away from her phone. "I'm here."

"And miss my daughter's first shoot? Yeah, right." Mom squeezes my shoulder, smiling at me. Once my parents got over the fact that this is what I wanted to do with my life, they've been so supportive. Mom even keeps up with my online persona, making sure I don't let people get me down. I wish I had talked to her sooner.

"Okay, I just don't want you to be bored." I stroll to where my phone sits with my bag on a table near a curtained window.

"There is nothing boring about this," Violet says, following me. "Well, except that I can't take pictures of you to share."

"After the ad launches, you can. I'll even let you post them first," I say.

Violet beams at me. "You're the best."

Smiling, I turn my attention to my phone. I expect Cole to text at any moment since he couldn't join us this morning because he'd scheduled studio time to work on his album with Gavin Simone, one of the music industry's most sought after producers.

Cole: Finished up at the studio early.

Cole: I'm dying to see you.

Cole: I'm waiting outside.

Along with his texts are a few pictures he had taken at Sound Wave Music Studios. They'll be launching his album next summer. He's already had even more recognition since I posted the small clip of him and Ariel singing, and she released *Loving the Lights* as a single featuring Cole just last week, which will be on her next album to release in the beginning of fall.

And surprisingly, Ariel and Cole singing a song that was inspired by me hasn't had much backlash on my part. It helps that Ariel recently started dating Delano Crews. People love them together and call them DelAriel. It's way better than SaCole in my opinion.

Handing my phone to Violet, I have her take a picture of me, and I send it to Cole.

Me: Better hurry if you want to see me in this.

A knock sounds on the metal door of the studio, and Paige opens it. I wave to her that Cole is with me, and she lets him pass. He crosses the room, his eyes trailing from my bare legs to the high-waisted, patterned mini-skirt and gray top with the sleeves laced up with ribbon, showing off one of my shoulders.

"You look beautiful," he says, kissing me softly on the lips despite my dark purple lipstick.

I smile against his mouth. "Thanks. It's been so much fun."

"I have a surprise for you," he says, pulling away to look me in the eyes.

My heart races, and I can't stop smiling. "Yeah?"

"You're going to be in the *Loving the Lights* video, that is, if you want to be," Cole says.

My eyes widen. "Really?"

He nods. "Really."

"That's so amazing!" I hug him once more, kissing him deeply, pressing so closely to him that I can feel his heart beating against mine.

"Sage, wardrobe is ready for you," Paige calls, drawing my attention away.

I pull Cole along with me, and he takes a seat next to my mom while a few of Lele's designers start getting me ready for the next set of photos.

A million thoughts whirl through my mind. First the fashion show, then this ad campaign, and now I'm going to star in a music video. My life isn't exactly what I imagined it to be, but it's so much better. It's full of glam and glitz and even a little dirt—just like LA—and completely mine for the making.

acknowledgments

THIS BOOK WOULD not have been possible without my amazing team, who offers invaluable help—from critiquing and editing to blurb slaying and being a sounding board to bounce ideas off of. A huge thanks to Sarah Collier, Katie Harder-Schauer, Jan Moran, and Nikki Godwin for everything you do for me. You're all the best!

Thanks to my husband, who has driven me around LA many times in the worst traffic, who let me drag him to the Los Angeles County Museum of Art and to the Santa Monica pier in a span of two days. Who has told me countless stories from his time living in LA to help inspire me, like the time he went to a club in the backyard cellar of a mansion in Holmby Hills. You're the best, Eric!

Thanks to Aly Spencer, who has shared many exciting stories with me surrounding her career as a model. Your life is quite inspiring.

Thanks to my friends and family—my parents, my siblings, my friends. You guys offer endless encouragement and love, and for that, I'm eternally grateful.

Lastly, thank you, my lovely readers. Thanks for taking a chance on my books and for your support. It makes sharing my stories with you such a joy. XOXO!

about ginna moran

GINNA MORAN IS the author of an array of both paranormal and contemporary young adult novels including the *Demon Within*, *Falling into Fame*, and *Spark of Life* series.

She started writing poetry as a teenager in a spiral notebook that she still has tucked away on her desk today. Her love of writing grew after she graduated high school and she completed her first unpublished manuscript at age eighteen.

When she realized her love of writing was her life's passion, she studied literature at Mira Costa College in Northern San Diego. Besides writing young adult novels, she was senior editor, content manager, and image coordinator for Crescent House Publishing Inc. for four years.

Aside from Ginna's professional life, she enjoys binge watching television shows, playing pretend with her daughter, and cuddling with her dogs. Some of her favorite things include chocolate, anything that glitters, cheesy jokes, and organizing her bookshelf.

Ginna loves to hear from her readers so visit her online at

www.GinnaMoran.com where you can find book extras, including quizzes, character bios, playlists, and more. You can join her group on Facebook or follow her page. You can also find her on Instagram, Twitter, and Snapchat @GinnaMoran. To stay up-to-date on new releases, sign up to her newsletter. You'll not only get a FREE ebook, but you'll be able to participate in monthly giveaways!

Ginna is currently hard at work on her next novel.

Other Young Adult Novels by Ginna Moran

PARANORMAL

Destined for Dreams Series

Demon Within Series

Finding Nate Series

Going Ghostly Series

Spark of Life Series

When Souls Collide Series

Demon Watcher Series

Call of the Ocean Series

CONTEMPORARY

Falling into Fame Series

Life After Lila